I kept my voic... ...ners wouldn't overhe... ...few minutes ago. Sh... ...ing upstairs in my B&...

Her pale eyebro...

"How did you already hear he was dead?" I asked.

"Police scanner app." She pointed to the phone. "But the site is within South Lick town limits, so not in our jurisdiction."

I knew the county sheriff handled homicides in unincorporated territory, as they had in June with the murders in neighboring Beanblossom.

"Jurisdiction," I said. "Does that mean they've already decided it was an unnatural death?"

"Starting to look like it." She started to say more but clamped her mouth shut, instead.

"How so?" I doubted she'd tell me, but it was worth a try.

"Not at liberty to divulge."

Yeah. As I'd thought. "Did Buck go on the call?"

Wanda shrugged. "No idea. Probably."

"Miss?" A diner waved from across the room. "I'm in a bit of a hurry?"

I held up my index finger in acknowledgment as I sighed. "Did you want to order?" I asked Wanda.

"Pancakes, bacon, and biscuits with gravy," she muttered at the phone. She looked up and added, "Please."

"You got it." I headed over to the customer who was in a hurry, and then to the cooking area and handed Danna the order slips. Another homicide in South Lick. Another unnatural death. I was starting to feel like I lived in Cabot Cove. But this wasn't Maine. It wasn't a television show. I wasn't Jessica Fletcher.

This was real life, right here in Indiana . . .

Books by Maddie Day

Country Store Mysteries
FLIPPED FOR MURDER
GRILLED FOR MURDER
WHEN THE GRITS HIT THE FAN
BISCUITS AND SLASHED BROWNS
DEATH OVER EASY
STRANGLED EGGS AND HAM

Cozy Capers Book Group Mysteries
MURDER ON CAPE COD

And writing as Edith Maxwell
A TINE TO LIVE, A TINE TO DIE
'TIL DIRT DO US PART
FARMED AND DANGEROUS
MURDER MOST FOWL
MULCH ADO ABOUT MURDER

Published by Kensington Publishing Corporation

Strangled Eggs And Ham

MADDIE DAY

KENSINGTON BOOKS
KENSINGTON PUBLISHING CORP.
www.kensingtonbooks.com

KENSINGTON BOOKS are published by

Kensington Publishing Corp.
119 West 40th Street
New York, NY 10018

All Kensington titles, imprints, and distributed lines are available at special quantity discounts for bulk purchases for sales promotion, premiums, fund-raising, educational, or institutional use.

Special book excerpts or customized printings can also be created to fit specific needs. For details, write or phone the office of the Kensington Sales Manager: Attn.: Sales Department. Kensington Publishing Corp., 119 West 40th Street, New York, NY 10018. Phone: 1-800-221-2647.

Kensington and the K logo Reg. U.S. Pat. & TM Off.

First Printing: July 2019
ISBN-13: 978-1-4967-1125-0
ISBN-10: 1-4967-1125-4

ISBN-13: 978-1-4967-1126-7 (eBook)
ISBN-10: 1-4967-1126-2 (eBook)

10 9 8 7 6 5 4 3 2 1

Printed in the United States of America

*For Ramona Defelice Long
and her seven AM Writing Champions.
Thank you, Ramona, for inspiring me
and the others in our group to get working
every morning and to be accountable to ourselves—
and also to each other.
And thank you even more for your friendship.*

Acknowledgments

My gratitude always to John Scognamiglio—the most responsive editor who ever lived—for your support of my stories, and to the great support team at Kensington Publishing. Thanks, too, to my agent, John Talbot, for your continuing enthusiasm and troubleshooting. The Wicked Cozy Authors, Jessie Crockett/Jessica Ellicott/Jessica Estevao, Sherry Harris, Julie Hennrikus/Julianne Holmes/Julia Henry, Liz Mugavero/Kate Conte, and Barbara Ross are friends, lifelines, inspiration, and therapy group all in one. Sherry Harris also read a draft of this book and once again saved Robbie from being too stupid to live. You're the best, Sherry.

Thanks to Kathy Boone Reel for the Southern Jam Cake recipe, and to Susan Oleksiw for clarifying Turner Rao's father's heritage. To my cousin Pell Fender for the long-ago Yogurt-Honey Fruit Salad Dressing recipe—whether he remembers it or not. And to Mrs. Schwartz, a woman I cleaned and babysat for when I was in college. I was eagerly broadening my food horizons at that time and loved her Cucumber-Dill Soup recipe. It's as good now as it was then.

As I've done twice a year for the last few years, I treated myself to a solo writing retreat at the West Falmouth Friends Quaker House, a Wi-Fi–free, modest cottage on Cape Cod. I had only four full days alone there, but I managed to create almost half of this manuscript's first draft. I am grateful for the quiet solitude, the beach nearby, and the Wi-Fi provided by the West Falmouth Public Library across the street, where I can catch up on personal and world events—and then leave them behind in favor of my imaginary worlds.

In this book, we learn that Robbie calls her phone Carmen—after the video game, *Where in the World Is Carmen Sandiego?* My sons played the game on one of our first personal computers, and Robbie played it in her youth, too.

Once again, a big huge thank you to Allan, John David, Barbara, Janet, and Hugh, and to so many friends and Friends. I love you, you know. I'm particularly grateful that Barbara—my older sister and one of my sources for Hoosier language and culture—survived a life-threatening heart incident with her health intact. We three sisters aren't ready to stop having fun together!

To my cozy fans, I thank you for adoring this series. You delight me with your e-mails and social media comments. Keep them coming! As always, a positive review of a book you liked goes a long way to help authors. I would be ever grateful to see your opinions on Amazon, Goodreads, Facebook, and elsewhere if you enjoyed my story (and please check out my other author persona, Edith Maxwell).

Chapter 1

I plopped down on the towel. Stroking through Lake Lemon's cool water had made me forget the controversy brewing in town, at least for a while.

Lou Perlman hit the towel next to mine, her tank suit agleam with water. "That was the best, Robbie. You can't beat an August swim." She stretched out on her back with her hands clasped behind her head. She closed her eyes, bliss etched on her face, her skin nut brown with the tan of a dedicated sun lover. We'd been hanging out as friends for about a year. I shared a love of bicycling with the Indiana University graduate student, and we supported each other as friends.

"Isn't it way hotter than usual this year?" I was already steaming from the sun and the humidity typical to southern Indiana.

"Definitely."

Riddle Point Beach was surprisingly empty this late afternoon. An older couple sat in collapsible chairs, reading, and one young mother played with a toddler at the water's edge, but otherwise we had the place to ourselves. I massaged my sore knee, a casualty of a spill I'd taken a few days ago on my bike. I scanned the perimeter of the lake and spied a great blue heron standing in a shallow marshy area to my right. Its long neck was hunched in, and the narrow, pointed beak waited patiently for an unsuspecting fish or frog. A movement to my left caught my attention.

"Speaking of hot," I said.

I watched as Gregory DeGraaf parked his bicycle next to Lou's and locked it to a bike stand at the edge of the parking lot. He slipped out of his bike shoes and socks, grabbed a towel out of a pannier slung over the back of the bike, and strolled toward us.

"Afternoon, Lou, Robbie."

Lou's eyes flew open.

"Mind if I join you?" The lawyer, a guest in one of my bed and breakfast rooms, was a dark charmer of forty. Black, curly hair, smile lines around his eyes, and a lean, trim build were an attractive combination, but it was his deep, resonant voice and the longest eyelashes I'd ever seen that clinched the deal. I knew Lou felt the same. I was already in a relationship. She wasn't.

She smiled up at him and patted the sand on her other side. "Hey, Gregory. Pull up a beach and sit down." She curled up to sit, wrapping her arms around her knees.

"I'm going to cool off first. Back in a flash." He dropped his towel and jogged into the water still wearing his biking togs. The bright yellow shirt clung to his torso, and the black stretch shorts showed off his muscled backside to great advantage.

"Mmm," Lou murmured. "Want."

I laughed. I had hosted a gathering of Lou's cycling club at my country store restaurant on Saturday, and they'd invited the Indianapolis Bike Club that Gregory and my other upstairs guests were with. Lou had clearly fallen for Gregory at first glance. And why not? He didn't wear a wedding band. They shared a love of biking. They were both intelligent—you had to be to earn a law degree, and Lou was nearing completion of her doctorate in sociology—and most important, there was a spark between them. The Indy group had left on Sunday night, with new guests filling one of my three rooms. Gregory had extended his stay.

He emerged from the lake shaking the water from his hair. He stripped off the shirt, twisting the water out of it as he joined us.

"That was the perfect end to a hilly ride." He smiled at Lou.

"Except you have to ride back." She answered his smile and raised one eyebrow.

"I can throw your bike in my van if you want," I offered. Because of my sore knee, I'd driven here instead of riding. I far preferred traveling by bicycle.

"Thanks, but I'll ride back. You can't get much better scenery—"

"Or a better workout," Lou finished. "No way to avoid hills in Brown County."

"I rode by a big sign for a new resort." He frowned. "Right at the South Lick town limits. What's going on with that?"

I groaned. "What isn't going on with that? Some real estate developer wants to build a huge luxury resort right on top of one of the loveliest hills in the county. They're going to have a spa, tennis courts, swimming, gourmet meals, the works, and they expect to draw paying guests from all over the country. Maybe the world. People around here are really steamed about it. That is, half the people are, and the other half want it to go through."

"What's the developer's name?" Gregory asked. "I might know him. I practice real estate and environmental law, as I think I mentioned."

"It's a she," I said. "Fiona Closs."

He thought, then shook his head slowly. "No, I guess I don't. Let me guess. The conflict is your basic NIMBY versus employment. Am I correct?"

"You are, Counselor," I said. "The Not-In-My-Back-Yard contingent are worried about traffic, about ruining the view, about cutting down trees, about all those strangers coming to stay at a resort far from town and possibly not shopping locally."

"Let me guess. The rest of the county wants jobs building the resort and providing services," Lou said. "That happened up north near Lafayette where I grew up. It turned out the service jobs weren't so great, and the construction didn't end up being locally sourced. Lots of bad feelings resulted."

"I can understand both sides," I offered. "I doubt I would lose breakfast customers to the resort, and this county has a lot of people who are pretty hard up. They could use the jobs. On the other hand, destroying a hilltop doesn't make much sense to me."

Gregory pushed his already drying hair back off his forehead. "Is the NIMBY group organized? Do they have a leader, a spokesperson?"

"It's my Aunt Adele, in fact," I said. "She's right in the thick of it. She says it makes her feel like she's doing something worthwhile again. She was apparently quite the protester back in the sixties."

"I can totally see that, Robbie," Lou said. "She's a toughie, your aunt."

"I'll say." Adele was the reason I, a California girl, was here in southern Indiana at all, instead of back in Santa Barbara where I'd grown up. After my mom died suddenly, my aunt had taken me to visit a country store full of antique cookware. We were surprised to learn the store was for sale. Adele encouraged me to buy it, and now I was the proud proprietor of Pans 'N Pancakes. It was a popular breakfast and lunch restaurant in a renovated country store, with vintage cooking implements for sale and three B&B rooms upstairs. I was living my dream, complete with an apartment behind the store, a hunky boyfriend, and a cat.

Gregory stared out at the water, having assumed the same seated position as Lou. "I'm on sabbatical right now," he began. He twisted to face us. "I have some pretty strong feelings about not ruining a beautiful place just so rich people can come and pretend to enjoy it. I'd like to meet your aunt, Robbie, if you'll introduce us. I can offer my legal services to the group on a pro bono basis."

"She'll appreciate that," I said. "I'd be happy to hook you two up. I'm sure they're going to need legal advice. She's already planning a protest that'll stop traffic on the main road to Nashville, and who knows what else."

Lou reached out a hand and squeezed Gregory's bare shoulder. "You're Mr. Awesome, you know that?"

His cheeks pinked. "Not at all. But I do like to support worthy causes." He pushed up to standing. "How about another swim, ladies?"

"You go," I said to Lou. "I'm going to lie here and do nothing."

He extended a hand to Lou and didn't let go of it. After I watched them run hand in hand splashing into the water, I lay back and closed my eyes. Good. Lou might have found herself a new man. Adele was going to get some needed help. And maybe that resort wouldn't get built, after all.

Chapter 2

My old van sputtered up a hill on the way home from the lake. One of these days I was going to have to get new wheels. The air conditioning hadn't worked for years, and the hot air blowing past me had zero cooling effect. The shocks were shot, magnifying every ridge and crack in the road into a teeth-jarring ride. A spring had started to ease its way through the driver's side seat cushion, forcing me to perch on my right cheek so my left one didn't get impaled. And every door and window rattled like I was in a 6.5 magnitude earthquake.

At the crest of the hill sat a gigantic sign emblazoned with CLOSS CREEK RESORT above an artist's rendering of the new project. *Closs Creek?* I'd missed that on my way to the lake. The developer must have decided to rename South Lick Creek after herself. She had a lot of nerve. That maneuver was not going to go over well with the long-time residents of South Lick, the delightful town I'd called home for a couple of years. I slowed and turned left onto the dirt road leading into the building site. It was time to check this place out.

After a few minutes, I bumped past a dilapidated

house on the right with a beat-up green truck parked to the side. Tidy flower beds in the flush of summer bloom contrasted with the peeling paint and sagging roof on the house. A woman sprawled on a lawn chair in the dappled shade of a big black walnut tree in front of the house. She lifted a hand in greeting, her other hand holding a cigarette. I waved back. It was what one did around here.

Around a bend, the road widened and ended at a chain stretching between two posts. To each side the posts led to more posts, with a single strand of barbed wire stretched between them. A red PRIVATE PROPERTY, NO TRESPASSING sign hung from the chain. Naked tree stumps created a clearing in the woods, and the torn-up ground was evidence of heavy machinery having been at work. A new-looking but dusty white SUV was parked beyond the barrier next to a double-cab, black pickup truck. A tall woman in construction-work clothes leaned against the truck, arms folded on her chest, talking to someone in the SUV.

I pulled to the side and idled the van. So the project was going ahead? As far as I knew, the resort hadn't gotten final approval. There wouldn't be much point in Adele and the others protesting if the resort had already been green-lighted. Or maybe this was private property the developer had acquired, and she'd decided to get started without town permission. Except I didn't think you could do that.

I had my hand on the gearshift to turn around and leave when the SUV's driver's side door opened. A woman in a sleeveless dress slid out and picked her way toward me. The other woman followed. I turned off the engine and got out to meet them.

"Can I help you?" the one in the dress asked from the other side of the chain. She was slim and about four inches taller than me, putting her at five-foot-seven. Her tanned and muscular arms and calves were shown off by the black-and-white patterned sheath dress. It was the kind of outfit women normally wore heels with, but a pair of practical black canvas sneakers were on her feet instead. Dark hair framed her face, and her wide mouth was painted a deep red.

"My name's Robbie Jordan." I extended my hand above the barrier. I also wore a sundress, but mine was a swingy loose number that I could easily throw on over a bathing suit. I knew my long, curly hair was a mess from my swim, and I felt distinctly underdressed. Which was a ridiculous reaction to have at a building site. "I own a business in town and wanted to take a look at what's happening up here."

"Fiona Closs. This is my project." She shook my hand with a firm, dry, meaty grip. Her nails were trimmed short and painted the same color as her lipstick. She gestured to the clearing with a grand swoop of her arm. "And this is one of my employees, Micaela Stiverton."

"Nice to meet you both." So this was the developer-in-chief and her minion.

"Call me Mike." Micaela smiled from a face dusted with freckles. "Everybody does." Her curly red hair was a sensible two inches long all over, and her clothes were a no-nonsense Indiana Colts T-shirt tucked into khaki cargo pants. Dusty work boots completed the ensemble.

I liked the open expression on her face, but I

didn't think she'd ever come into my store, and I wondered if she was local or not. Fiona Closs had not suggested I use her first name.

"Mike it is. So, Ms. Closs, it looks like you got the final approvals to go ahead with your resort." I sniffed. Fiona wore some kind of scent. It reminded me of incense. Sandalwood, maybe?

"Nearly. It's simply a formality from here on out." Closs lifted her chin ever so slightly.

Really? I knew from my restaurant and B&B renovations that South Lick officials were extra careful to cross every T and dot every I in the permitting process.

"I know a number of people in the county are eager to be employed locally," I said. "There isn't any industry here to speak of. When will you be hiring on more people?"

Closs blinked, cocking her head to the right. "Do you run an employment agency?" Her dark eyebrows naturally dipped down and toward the center, giving her an intent look, which reminded me of some film actress. I couldn't put my finger on who.

I laughed. "No. I own a country store restaurant and bed and breakfast. My place is kind of the town water cooler. Word spreads fast in a place like South Lick, and I've heard folks mention wanting to work up here." That, and mutterings about blocking the resort entirely, but I didn't need to get into that with Fiona Closs.

"I see."

"Excuse me," Mike said. "I've got to get going to pick up my kids." She gave me a wry grin. "I'm single mom to twin four-year-old boys. They're fun, but they're no angels."

"It was nice to meet you, Mike," I said, meaning it. So she must live somewhere in the county.

"Likewise." She climbed into her truck.

Closs unhooked one end of the chain and threw it to the side, and we both stood back as Mike drove off.

Closs continued. "You can tell your customers we're not quite ready to hire on anyone new."

"I'll do that. My restaurant is called Pans 'N Pancakes, and I'm open for breakfast and lunch. You should stop in some time." I smiled.

Her gaze cut to a crunching noise behind me. I turned to see Gregory and Lou braking their bikes to a stop.

"Great minds think alike, Robbie," a pink-cheeked Lou called. She walked her bike up next to me, followed by Gregory. "We wanted to stop by and see what's going on." Her skin glistened from the effort of riding up hills on a hot afternoon.

I glanced back at a frowning Closs and introduced everyone.

Gregory pulled off his fingerless biking glove and extended his hand. "Pleased to meet you, Ms. Closs." He was remarkably free from sweat, despite the climate and the steep hill he'd just ridden up.

Closs shook his hand but didn't smile. "Likewise."

"Gregory is a guest in my B&B," I added.

"DeGraaf," Closs said, gazing at his face. "I've heard your name before. You're some kind of environmental lawyer, correct?"

"That's not all the work I do, but, yes, I have won several high-profile environmental protection cases."

Closs looked like she'd eaten a rotten egg. "I know of your reputation."

Lou peered at Closs. "Do you work out at the Hard Knocks Gym in Bloomington?"

Closs nodded slowly. "I do. Why do you ask?"

"I joined last week. I thought you looked familiar. You're a weightlifter, right?"

Closs sighed as if she didn't want to talk about it. "Yes." She cleared her throat. "I'm afraid I was about to leave, and I don't have time to chat at the moment. I'm sure Ms. Jordan can fill you in on our progress up here. If you'll excuse me?"

Lou and Gregory walked their bikes over behind my van. Closs turned her vehicle around and drove toward us. She slowed after she passed through the posts.

"I'll get it," Gregory said, waving her on. He hooked the chain across the entrance.

Closs waved her thanks and sped around the bend.

"She lifts weights?" I asked. No wonder her arms and legs were so buff.

"She does." Lou stared down the road. "And not like you or I would. She must compete or something. She's hugely strong, and she has like no body fat. You should see her abs." She shook her head.

"Does anybody else think she was trying to get rid of us?" Gregory asked.

"Kind of." Lou wrinkled her nose. "So what did she tell you, Robbie?"

"She seemed to think the final permits are a done deal. But she also said she's not ready to start hiring locally."

"Somebody's been working here." Gregory gestured to the clearing.

"I know." I nodded. "The rest is a mystery." A pileated woodpecker echoed that thought with its machine gun *rat-a-tat-tat* from the trees beyond the scarred hilltop. I couldn't see it, but no other woodpecker made such a loud sound.

Chapter 3

I chatted with Lou and Gregory for a few more minutes, then headed down the road after my friends decided to hang out at the site for a bit. My stomach was growling, so my cat's would be, too. I needed to get home to do breakfast prep for tomorrow, anyway.

When I approached the run-down house, though, the woman in the front yard beckoned, so I parked on the verge and watched her stroll toward me. She was big-boned and hefty but moved her weight with grace, as if she'd formerly been a dancer or a skater. She wore a loose flowered top over navy blue shorts. On her feet were a worn pair of moccasins.

"Howdy, there," she said. "Name's Yolene. Yolene Wiley." She was so tall she had to stoop to see in the van's window. She laid large hands on the window opening.

"I'm Robbie Jordan. Nice to meet you, Ms. Wiley." I'd never seen her in my restaurant, but that didn't mean anything. She was right on the town limit here, and from the looks of her house and vehicle, she might not have enough extra money to make a practice of eating out.

She snorted. "I'm no Ms., hon. Just call me Yolene."

Up close, I saw that something had taken a toll on a previously lovely face. Her blue eyes were clear, her cheekbones delicate but covered by deeply weathered skin, and her smile a pleasant one marred by more than one missing back tooth. I thought she was probably younger than she looked. Silver strands mixed into her ear-length, dark hair.

"Y'all having a party over to the resort?" she asked.

"No. I wanted to look at the progress of the new place, and my friends out on a bike ride did, too. Have you met Fiona Closs, the developer?"

"'Course I have."

"What do you think of a resort going in so close to where you live?"

"I'm selling her part of the land, ain't I?"

"Really?" *Interesting.*

"You better believe it." She bobbed her head down and back up in emphasis. "My daddy left me quite a patch, but I can't barely make the property tax and the bills. Happy to sell off the wood lot and a bit more, besides, so's I can pay off my debts. All's I need is my house, here, and a little bit of land to grow my flowers." She smiled with pride as she twisted to gaze at her colorful beds.

"Your flowers are lovely, Yolene. But you're not worried about the increased traffic, and a bunch of rich strangers passing through? I know some people in town are."

"Nah." She brushed away the concern, then coughed the deep throaty rattle of a chronic smoker.

"Won't bother me none. I'm kinda like a Teflon Buddha, you know. Stuff rolls off me. Don't matter one way or t'other."

I smiled at the image of a Teflon Buddha. A friend who practiced daily meditation had told me something similar. She'd said that while sitting and trying to empty her mind, she'd developed a non-stick coating. When thoughts rolled in, she let them roll off or float away.

"And as you can see, we got plenty of trees hereabouts," she went on. "Cuttin' a few down don't matter none. Them environment nuts are just that— nutty."

I wasn't so sure about that, but I wasn't going to argue the point.

"Plus, you know what Fiona promised?" she asked. "Her company's gonna pave my road. The town? They never cared enough to do it. So I'm in for a quality of life improvement, and I'm right happy about it."

The quality might suffer when the paved road became full of speeding luxury cars. "I'm glad. Sorry, but I need to be going. I hope you'll stop by my country store restaurant someday soon. It's called Pans 'N Pancakes."

She peered at me. "Is that Jo Schultz's old place?"

"Yes. I bought it from her and made it into a breakfast and lunch place."

"And Jo's okay with that?"

"She seemed relieved to unload the building. I live in the apartment in the back, and I rent out the upstairs rooms to tourists and travelers."

"Well, shut my mouth and call me a clam." Yolene shook her head in wonder.

"It's become pretty popular. I kept all of Jo's antique cookware, and I've acquired a bunch more, too. She still lives in town, not too far away."

"I guess maybe I will stop on by your store, then, after my ship comes in."

Lou and Gregory rode toward us, Lou raising a hand in greeting.

"Who are them folks?" Yolene asked before they braked.

"A couple of friends. I like to ride, too, but I have a bum knee at the moment."

"Sorry to hear that."

The cyclists pulled to a stop next to Yolene. Lou clicked out of her pedal and put a foot on the ground. Gregory balanced upright, pedaling a half turn backward and forward to keep from falling to the side. It was a hard trick to maintain.

"Lou, Gregory, this is Yolene Wiley," I said, leaning my head out the window.

Gregory clicked out of his pedal, too, and swung his leg over the bike's crossbar. The three exchanged greetings and shook hands.

"Ma'am, I'll bet you're not too happy about the building project going on around the bend there," Gregory said with a smooth smile. "I've just joined the anti-resort coalition, offering legal representation at no cost. I'd be pleased to advise you on same."

Yolene stared at him. "You gotta be pulling my leg. I ain't been so happy about something in fifty dog years. This here's my big chance."

Lou and Gregory exchanged a glance.

"Ah," Gregory said. "I wish you all the best, then, ma'am. We'll be on our way."

Lou shot me a pair of raised eyebrows from behind

Yolene. "It was nice to meet you, Yolene. Talk to you later, Robbie." She and Gregory rolled away toward town.

"Anti-resort coalition?" Yolene said, fists on her hips. "What in the blue devil was he going on about? This project is good for the town and good for me."

I just smiled. I was so not getting in the middle of this.

She squinted down the road even after the cyclists had disappeared. "Why, I don't know that boy from Adam's off ox. He ain't from South Lick, that's for certain." She turned to me. "Is he?"

"I don't believe so, no. I'd better be going. Have a great rest of your day, Yolene."

"You head on home, now. Nice to meet you, Robbie. I don't get many visitors up here." Yolene brightened. "Guess that's about to change."

I said good-bye and drove off. Yes, that might be about to change, Yolene. Big time.

Chapter 4

I had my hands deep in flour and butter when someone knocked at the store's front door a few minutes past seven that evening. I was tempted to ignore the visitor. The sign was clearly turned to the side that read CLOSED. But curiosity won over. I dusted off the biscuit mix and grabbed a dishtowel. When I peered out through the heavy glass in the door, I smiled.

"Come on in, Adele," I said after unbolting the door. My aunt was welcome any time of the day or night.

"Hey, darlin'," she said, kissing my cheek. "Sorry to catch you all floured up."

"Not a problem. You want tea? Coffee?" When she didn't respond, I added, "Bourbon?"

"Now you're talking. I know where it's kept. Get yourself back to those biscuits or what all." She grabbed a mug and headed to my private stash of Four Roses in a cabinet over near my desk. "Pour you some?"

"Why not?"

Adele splashed some of my favorite Kentucky liquor into a coffee mug for herself, then did the same for me. She perched on a chair near where I'd resumed cutting butter into flour.

"What's happening?" I asked. I sipped the bourbon, savoring the flavor and the warm burn as it went down. "You didn't stop by to watch me do breakfast prep."

"No sirree, I did not. I've been working real hard on a project, and I was bustin' at the seams to tell somebody."

"Where's Samuel?" The two senior citizens had a sweet romance going on, of which I entirely approved.

"The old darlin' went up to Chicago to see his nephew."

The theme song from the decades-old Carmen Sandiego video game played on my cell from the table where I'd left it. "Shoot. Can you see if that's Abe?" I'd been expecting my boyfriend to call.

Adele picked up the phone I affectionately called Carmen. "Yep. Says Abraham O'Neill."

"Swipe to the right and tell him I'm deep in flour, will you, please?"

She told him, listened, and laughed, then poked at the phone and set it down. "He says he misses you. Where the heck is he?"

"The electric company sent him to a training in Cincinnati. He won't be back until next week." The butter in my mixture was now as small as peas, so I made a well in the middle and started cracking eggs into it. "Spill about the project, already."

"You probably know that ridiculous Closs Creek Resort still has to go before the planning board. And we're doing some planning of our own, me and my cell."

"I know you are. But . . . your cell? What, you and your phone are a committee of two?"

"No, cell like a protest movement cell." She laughed, and her long dangling earrings tinkled with the movement. "That part's a joke. By cell I mean the group of us opposed to the building project. We got a half dozen who all feel the same. Even Vera, my friend from Indy. She's coming down tomorrow. Oh, and Martin."

"Who's Martin?" I stirred the eggs with a fork, gradually incorporating them into the flour, then measured milk and added that.

"The Mennonite fellow, Martin Dettweiler? I thought you told me you met him a few months ago."

"I did." I'd encountered the gentleman when I'd paused on a bike ride to ponder the words on the front of the Mennonite church in neighboring Beanblossom. STRANGERS EXPECTED was inscribed in big black letters on the white building. Martin had been raking leaves at the church that day, and we'd had a nice chat, which resulted in my buying jars of his honey to sell in my store. "I don't think of Mennonites as being political."

"Maybe they aren't, but he's all het up about this new thing."

"By the way, one of my B&B guests is Gregory DeGraaf, a lawyer in Indy. He told me he's on sabbatical, and he wants to offer his legal services to your group."

"Well, now, isn't that nice?" She glanced toward the ceiling. "Is he here now? I can loop him into our plans."

"I'm not sure if he's back." I had an outdoor egress

that my B&B guests could use to come and go without having to walk through the store. "Lou and I ran into Gregory at the lake this afternoon. The two of them ended up riding together. I can give you his cell number when I'm done here." I gestured to my flour-covered hands.

"That'd be fine."

"What do you and your group have planned, then?" I asked, even though I kind of knew.

"We're going to march out to the state route tomorrow or the next day and stop traffic. We'll carry big signs and make an impact, get in the news, that kind of thing." Her cheeks glowed.

"Is that safe? Won't you be arrested?" I turned the dough out onto the floured counter and lightly kneaded it until it came together.

"All the better if we are. Make more of a splash. Robbie, it's called nonviolent, passive resistance. We did a lot of it back in the day. Phil's joining us, too, and maybe his girlfriend, Noreen. Gotta show these young folks how it's done."

Phil was a friend of mine, and Samuel's grandson. "I don't know, Adele. It sounds kind of dangerous."

She brushed aside my concern. "It's not. Don't you worry about a little thing."

"I was going to call you if you hadn't stopped by. I went by the Closs Creek site on my way home today, and I met the developer."

Adele gaped. "Well, slap my head and call me silly. Did you, now?"

"Yep." I encased the disk of dough in plastic wrap. "And they're already cutting down trees."

"What?" she screeched. "They can't do that."

"Closs seems to think the final approvals are a formality. She's buying land from a neighbor, too. A Yolene Wiley."

"Jumping june bugs. Yolene? Of all people! I've a mind to drive up there right now and knock some sense into that girl."

"Wait a sec, Adele. It's the land her father left her. She seems to be hurting for money. Shouldn't she be able to sell it to whomever she wants?"

"Robbie, do I have to go through all the reasons again why this development is a bad, stupid, pea-brained idea?" She swigged her drink.

I was about to tell her she didn't have to. Instead she launched into the list, ticking the reasons off on her fingers.

"It'll jam up the roads. Bring a bunch of riffraff into town. Destroy one of the prettiest hilltops in the county. Threaten the Greasy Hollow Swamp—what they call wetlands nowadays. It's just plain wrong." She stood and paced to the door and back. "There's gotta be some dirt I can dig up on Fiona Closs. You're the detective, Roberta. Help me figure out how to stop her."

"I'm not a detective, and you know that." The fact that I'd happened to do some digging after several murders in the past year didn't mean I was suddenly a licensed private investigator. "I like puzzles, but this situation needn't be one. If the planning board disapproves the project, that'll be that, right?"

Adele faced me, fists on her waist. "So you're not going to help me? A little old lady who's done so much for you?" Her tone was plaintive, but a smile played at the edges of her mouth.

"Hey, Jordans don't guilt trip, right?" I lowered my head and gave her the look my mom used to give me. "And you're hardly a helpless old lady." On the contrary, my aunt was one of the most competent women I knew.

She chortled. "I'm pulling your leg, sugar. That said, I mean to stop this Fiona if it's the last thing I do."

I shivered. If this conflict led to another murder, it had better not be Adele's. "Promise me you'll be careful?"

"Girl Scout's honor." She held up three fingers.

Except her other hand was behind her back, and I was willing to bet my month's profit she was crossing her fingers back there.

Chapter 5

By seven thirty the next morning, Pans 'N Pancakes was hopping. We'd only been open for thirty minutes, but every table in the restaurant was full. Our royal blue cloth napkins and matching staff aprons contrasted nicely with the barn-board walls, and the white-painted, stamped-tin ceiling brightened the space. The air smelled delectably of grilled bacon and sausage, of maple syrup and apple butter, of fresh-baked biscuits and just-flipped pancakes. Three men in work clothes milled hungrily among the shelves of vintage cookware, waiting for a table to become available so they could wolf down breakfast and get to the job.

At a ding from the Ready bell next to the grill, I hurried over and loaded up a round tray with two orders of my signature Whole-Wheat Banana-Walnut Pancakes, one Kitchen Sink Omelet, and a basic two eggs sunny-side up with ham and white toast. That is, I wanted to hurry over, but my knee was acting up big time this morning, so I semi-hobbled over, instead.

"Thanks, Danna," I said to Danna Beedle, one of my two able, young assistants. Today she'd tied her flaxen dreadlocks in a big knot on top of her head using a pink polka-dot ribbon, and she wore pink overall shorts over a blue Pans 'N Pancakes T-shirt, blue high-top tennies, and a store apron. The girl had style, no two ways about it.

"No prob, boss." She checked a ticket, poured out two disks of beaten egg, and laid six pieces of bacon and two sausages next to them. Using a flipper/scraper in each hand, she pushed around a pile of sautéing peppers and onions and turned a couple of pancakes.

I headed over to deliver the plates, glancing at the door when the cow bell on the front door jangled. A couple strolled in and caught my eye. *Huh*. It was Lonnie Dinnsen, a security guard at the music park in the next town, with the construction worker I'd met yesterday at the site, Micaela somebody. No, she'd asked to be called Mike. Lonnie wore the yellow polo shirt of the park staff, and she was in a clean version of the work clothes she'd worn yesterday. Which probably meant more site work was planned for today.

"Hey, folks," I called to them. "It's gonna be a few minutes." I wondered if Lonnie and Mike were a couple or simply friends.

Lonnie waved his acknowledgment. He found a piece of wall to lean against and pulled out his phone, while Mike sauntered off in the direction of the cookware. The big, burly guard had saved my bacon at the start of the summer, when a murderer had been up to no good at the Brown County Bluegrass Festival. Lonnie had become a regular in the restaurant since. That's what I was all about— building a happy customer base, one diner at a time.

The next ten minutes zipped by. I delivered food, topped up coffees, and took the orders of the most recently seated, then delivered more breakfasts. Our special today, in a nod to the temperatures, was a fruit smoothie featuring ripe local cantaloupe and strawberries, vanilla yogurt, and a dash of cinnamon. And it was a popular one. I was glad I'd cut up the fruit last night, so now all we had to do was whiz up a smoothie in the blender when somebody ordered one.

The workmen got their table. After four diners rose to leave, I cleared the table quickly and made my way toward Lonnie.

"You and Mike had better grab that table now before anyone else comes in." I smiled at him and pointed at the four-top.

"I heard that." Mike reappeared from around the end of the shelves. "Good. I'm super hungry." She grinned and patted her tight abs, but her smile slid away as she sniffed. "Is that cigarette smoke? It's against the law to allow smoking in a restaurant."

"Of course, it is." I sniffed, too. "Somebody must have been smoking outside. You know how the smell sticks to people's clothing."

"Cigarettes are vile." She grimaced as a shudder rippled through her. "I hate them."

"You're not alone in that," I said.

Lonnie looked up from his phone with a frown. "Say, Robbie, do you know anything about these so-called protesters?" He wore his thin, pale blond hair about an inch long, and now he rubbed his hand over his head, making it stick up all over. "The ones who don't want that new development going in?"

Gah. "Not much, really." I didn't really want to rat out my aunt or Phil. "Come on over to the table and tell me what you've heard."

"Local news says they're planning to close down the highway. That's a very bad idea. Could turn a lot of folks against them." He lowered himself into a chair and laid the phone on the table next to him, as if he couldn't wait to get back to it. Mike sat, as well.

Adele had said they were going to stage the demonstration today or tomorrow, but I didn't know what time. "I heard that, too. Does the article say when?"

"It's vague on the specifics."

Gregory clattered down the interior stairs from the B&B rooms upstairs and strolled toward me. When the restaurant was open, I left the door to the second floor unlocked, and then locked it after I closed for the day. Today, Gregory wasn't in biking togs. His long-sleeved dress shirt, pressed linen pants, and a brightly colored silk necktie screamed "lawyer" to me.

"Good morning, Robbie," he said. He smelled like he'd used the hotel-sized apple shampoo I stocked. He was freshly shaven, and his black curls were still damp.

"I hope you slept comfortably," I said, taking a step away from Lonnie and Mike's table.

"Absolutely." He glanced around the room. "All the tables are full, and I'm ravenous. How long before a table opens up, do you think?" He tapped his fingers on the cover of the digital tablet he held in the other hand. A working breakfast or catching up on the world via the Internet?

I always let my B&B guests know that breakfast was first-come-first-served in the restaurant, even for them, and at peak times they might have to wait to be served. One guest had inquired about getting breakfast in her room, and I'd had to say that wasn't in the plan, at least not yet. For room service to happen, I would almost have to hire yet another employee. Right now, I could pay my bills and the costs associated with employing Danna and Turner Rao, my other employee, but I wasn't pocketing too much beyond that. Plus, I'd have to deal with cleaning up spilled food in the guest rooms, and I didn't want to attract mice or cockroaches on my newly renovated second floor.

I surveyed the current diners. "Fifteen, twenty minutes I'd say," I replied. "Sorry about that."

Lonnie looked up. "You can join us, if you'd like." He pointed to the chair opposite his.

"That's awfully nice," I said. "Lonnie and Mike, this is Gregory DeGraaf."

Lonnie lowered his hand to the table in a slow deliberate move. His eyes narrowed for a brief moment as he gazed at Gregory.

What was that about? It was almost like he recognized the name. "He's staying upstairs," I went on. "Gregory, Lonnie Dinnsen and Mike . . . I'm sorry, I forgot your last name."

"Stiverton."

They both shook hands with Gregory before he pulled out a chair and sat.

"I appreciate the offer, folks," Gregory said. "What do you all do?"

"I work construction," Mike said. "Heavy equipment, mostly."

"And I run security at the music park next town over," Lonnie said, "but it's seasonal, so I have a few other irons in the fire, too. You?"

"I practice law in Indianapolis. I'm on sabbatical for a few months, though, and I took on a new project yesterday, in fact."

"What's that?" Lonnie asked.

I lurked, listening, order pad in hand.

"I'm providing legal services for the group trying to stop the new resort going up. It's an excellent cause."

Lonnie's nostrils flared. "Is that so?" His deep voice was terse, as if he was barely holding back a strong emotion. "What about the good cause of employment for locals who otherwise would be unemployed? We have carpenters and electricians who need jobs."

Mike raised her hand. "And I'm one of them. Single mom of twins. I need the work."

"Masons and painters are looking for employment, too," Lonnie continued. "And we have people in the county who are desperate to snag the service jobs after the resort opens. I know a lady can't wait to sell her land, so she can get out of poverty. What about those folks, Mr. DeGraaf, not to mention the tax revenues that South Lick would gain?" His deep blue eyes were intent on Gregory's face.

Uh-oh. Bad combo of table mates.

"Conversely, what about the wetlands that would be destroyed, Mr. Dinnsen?" Gregory kept his voice level, almost conversational, but not mocking. "That picturesque hilltop, painted by artists for the last century and a half, the hilltop that would be razed, paved, and built on? The lowered quality of life for county residents with the increased traffic, the influx of out-of-towners?" He folded his hands on the table and leaned forward. "What do you folks say to that?"

I could picture Gregory talking with a client or a district attorney about a law case. He sounded ultimately reasonable. Me, I had to admit I was still leaning toward Lonnie's camp, one he clearly shared with Mike. His arguments seemed more persuasive than Adele's or Gregory's. Yolene had appeared to really need the money from a land sale. I'd be willing to bet Lonnie himself was looking forward to a steadier gig if he could get hired to run security at the new resort. And single-mom Mike clearly wanted the building job. Developer Fiona Closs? She'd probably survive fine if this resort didn't go through. She'd simply find land elsewhere. Unless she'd personally invested in the South Lick property and stood to lose her funds if the permits were denied.

"What do you think about the illegal action the group is planning, Counselor?" Lonnie asked.

"I wouldn't worry," Gregory said. "We're in ongoing discussions about that."

That must have happened quickly. Last night at seven, Adele hadn't known about Gregory's offer, although I'd given her his number before she left.

"You must know the consequences of stopping traffic on a major state route," Lonnie said. "The demonstrators should all be jailed and kept there, as far as I'm concerned."

Gregory gave a small smile. "We're in discussions, as I said."

Mike shook her head without speaking. The Ready bell dinged again. A customer with an empty plate was waving her hand. The workmen looked like they were ready to order.

I took a deep breath, stood tall, and said, smiling, "Coffee, Mike? Gentlemen?"

"I'd love some, please," Gregory said, but his gaze went back and forth between Lonnie and Mike. "Shall we agree to disagree?"

Lonnie blinked. "I suppose so."

Mike shrugged.

To my eyes, Lonnie looked as if he'd much rather get into a heated argument with NIMBY Legal Services. For the sake of peace in the restaurant, I was glad he didn't.

"Tell me about the bluegrass festival," Gregory went on, sitting back in his chair for all the world like he was chatting with an old friend. "I've heard about it for years but never made it down here."

"I'll get those coffees," I said, as Lonnie's expression lightened, and he began to talk about last June's event. Dodged that bullet, for sure.

Chapter 6

By eight thirty we were even busier. Sure, it was still vacation season for many, though the Brown County public schools had been in session for ten days already. But today was a Thursday, not even a normal busy weekend. The Indiana University students in the next county were back in class already, too. Maybe the parents were taking a few days off after moving their charges into the IU dorms. That's what my guests in the other occupied B&B room were doing. Busy was good for the bottom line, and Turner, my second helper, had come in promptly at eight to take up the slack.

Lonnie and Mike had finished their breakfast without coming to blows with Gregory and had left around eight o'clock. From the door, Lonnie had turned and given Gregory one parting look, a dark expression on his face. Gregory had stayed, but he shifted to a chair in my waiting area after he'd eaten, so he wouldn't hog a table, as he explained. He sat immersed in the tablet on his lap, typing on the keyboard that was part of the cover.

Danna, Turner, and I were doing our careful choreography of cooking, serving, busing, and cleaning when the cow bell jangled once again. Phil stood in the open door, his arms filled with pans of brownies. He had a job at IU, but he loved baking and filled the position of my dessert chef on the side.

Phil pushed through the door, and I did a double take. Directly behind him filed in Adele and her friend Vera, with Abe's brother Don bringing up the rear. Phil headed toward me, while the others peeled off and made for Gregory. This was looking a lot like a meeting of the South Lick Anti-Resort Coalition. I stifled a giggle at the thought of the acronym, imagining Adele introducing herself to someone. "Hi, I'm with SLARC."

Phil deposited the pans on the counter. "These should hold you for a couple days, Robbie."

"Thanks." I pointed with my chin to the waiting area and the newcomers clustered around Gregory. "Is that what I think it is?"

"The *ad hoc* protest committee? It sure is, except Noreen couldn't join us." Phil's startling blue eyes twinkled in his dark face. "I better get over there."

"Phil." I touched his arm. "Be careful, okay? People are starting to get hot under the collar about both sides of this project. I don't want anyone to get hurt."

He slung his arm around my shoulders and squeezed. "Of course, we'll be careful. It's simply a harmless exercise in civil disobedience."

Harmless? Possibly. But such exercises could turn deadly, too.

"Miss?" a diner called out from across the room. Another waved, gave me a stern look, and pointed at her coffee cup, empty, no doubt. Danna was flipping food like mad. Turner zoomed around busing and wiping down one table after another.

"Take care of Adele and Vera, too," I urged Phil. "They seem tough but they're senior citizens, after all."

"I will. Grandpa would have my hide if I didn't. Now go work." He sauntered over to the group.

The doorbell jangled yet again to admit Martin Dettweiler, the gentle Mennonite I'd met earlier in the year, as always in a white collarless shirt with suspenders holding up dark pants. I waved a greeting, which he returned. He removed his flat-brimmed hat and pulled up a chair with the others.

Half an hour later, the rush had eased up and the demonstration planners still huddled in a small circle of chairs, leaning in and speaking in low tones.

"What's your aunt doing with Phil and the others?" Turner asked. He shut the door to the full dishwasher and pressed Start.

"They're planning a protest against the new resort going up out near Greasy Hollow."

"Interesting. My dad thinks the project is a good idea, that it'll bring fresh blood to the county."

I shuddered. It had better not.

Turner noticed and added quickly, "His words, not mine. He means new tourists, new customers for our maple products, that kind of thing." Turner was the son of an Indian scientist and a local Hoosier woman. The family owned and operated a maple farm, producing syrup to die for. So to speak.

"I agree. I think the resort would bring new tourists. What does your mom think?" If I had to guess, I'd say she'd be against it.

"She doesn't like the idea. I'm actually surprised she's not over there with the rest of them, helping make plans."

Danna returned from the restroom. "Plan what?"

I repeated my explanation to her.

She rolled her eyes. "My mom is way excited about that resort deal. She's thinking tax revenues, obviously."

"She's the mayor of South Lick. Of course, she is," I said. I thought of Lonnie's impassioned list of reasons the resort should go forward. "I actually think the people in support of the project have some pretty good arguments on their side."

Turner shrugged. "I'm not getting involved. That food chemistry class I signed up for has tons of reading, and it's keeping me busy when I'm not here."

"So we're going to start serving fancy-pantsy dishes here once you finish the course?" Danna asked in a teasing tone. "Molecular foams or whatever the rage is?"

"That's up to Robbie," Turner said. "But I kind of doubt it."

"We'll talk," I added. "What we have now is working pretty darn well. I'd hate to fix what's not broken."

"I had an idea for a lunch special," Danna said. "We have lots of cucumbers, and you ordered buttermilk for something, right?"

I nodded.

"I can make a great cold cucumber soup and some savory biscuits to go with. I know you have dill out in your herb garden. Okay? It's too warm for hot soup."

"Sounds perfect," I said.

I glanced over to see my other B&B guests approach. They were a petite, trim couple somewhere around fifty. Wayne was maybe five-foot-six, with silver streaking his dark hair at the temples. His wife Emily was my height but probably twenty pounds lighter, and looked like she might have had one parent from an Asian country. I greeted them.

"Sit anywhere that's open," I said. "Can I get you coffee?"

"Please, for both of us," she said with a smile.

I carried the coffee pot over to the two-top they'd chosen. "What do you have planned for today?" They both wore khaki cargo shorts and hiking boots.

"We're going to hike in the state park," the man said.

"And do some birding, too," his wife added.

"That sounds perfect. Give us a wave when you've decided what you'd like for breakfast."

Wayne nodded, focusing on the menu. I made my way back to the grill.

"Hey, guys, while it's kind of quiet, I'm going to get off my knee for a little bit, okay?" I made a little gesture toward the couple. "Those are my other upstairs guests. You might have met them yesterday. You know the drill—take their order but mark it B&B."

"Sounds good. Go elevate your knee." Danna grabbed a rag and set out for several uncleared tables while Turner checked a ticket and poured out six disks of pancake batter.

I sat in my desk chair and wheeled it over to the protest group. I kissed Adele on the cheek and greeted Vera.

"I don't get a kiss, too?" Vera asked in her surprisingly deep voice, one which carried. Her words sounded as if she was deeply offended, but her smiling eyes betrayed her.

"Of course, you do." I leaned out of my chair to kiss her cheek, the color of brown sugar and as soft as new flannel.

"That's better," Vera said.

"How are you, Mr. Dettweiler?" I asked him.

"Very good, thanks be to our blessed Lord." He smiled, his chinstrap beard outlining his jaw. He was otherwise clean shaven.

"Okay if I listen in for a few?" I asked as I sat. I maneuvered a wooden box over to put my foot up on. I should have been icing my knee, but I didn't have time for that until after we closed this afternoon.

Adele and Gregory exchanged a glance. Gregory cleared his throat.

What was that about?

"Of course, you may," Gregory began. "We are meeting on your private property." His eyebrows went up. "That said, you might not want to become overly informed of our actions."

Geez. Were they going to do more than simply stop traffic? "What do you mean?" I asked.

"He means if we get busted for doing something against the law and you knew about it, you could be held responsible, too." Adele smiled like she'd won the lottery.

I looked from Adele to Gregory, then checked the expressions on the others' faces. Not a one of them showed even a trace of worry at the "against the law" part of what Adele had just said.

"Gregory, I thought you were providing legal assistance." I folded my arms.

"I am indeed offering counsel and will be happy to provide representation pro bono should that become necessary."

"And you're going to sit there and let them do something illegal?" I couldn't believe it.

"Robbie," Don began in a soft voice. "There comes a time when citizens must stand up for what they believe is right. As did Jesus before us. Did he not overturn the tables of the usurers?"

Wonderful. Now Bible stories were getting dragged into this.

The female B&B guest approached the group tentatively. "Is that you, Vera?" she asked.

They knew each other? Vera lived north of Indianapolis, and my guests were from that area, too, so it was possible.

Vera glanced up, and then stood. "Why, Emily Babson. What brings you here?"

"Wayne and I dropped Lizzie at IU and thought we'd take a little Brown County vacation. We're staying upstairs, in fact. What about you?"

Vera clapped Adele on the back. "This here is Adele Jordan. She and I were childhood friends and rediscovered each other only last year. I'm down here for a visit." To Adele, Vera added, "Emily and I quilt together in the Stitch and Bitch group."

Small world. And a great name for a quilting club. The moniker alone made me want to take up the hobby.

Adele held up a hand. "Howdy, there, Emily."

"Pleased to meet you, Adele."

"Where is this mysterious Wayne?" Vera asked. "You talk about him while we quilt, but I've never met him."

"He's over there eating." She pointed at Wayne, who was staring at his phone instead of eating.

Vera glanced at Wayne and seemed to freeze. Her gaze traveled slowly back to Emily, and she mustered a smile, but it was a faint one.

It seemed as if Vera had recognized Wayne but

didn't like what she saw. *Huh?* I would ask her about him later, if I remembered.

"Good morning, Gregory," Emily said. "Did you get your ride in yesterday?"

"I did, and a swim, too."

The two must have met in the hallway upstairs. Each room had a private bath, but the three rooms shared the hallway and the exit to the outside.

I stood. "I better get back to work. You all stay safe, okay? Promise?"

Vera nodded. "You can bet your sweet bippy we will."

I didn't want to bet anything. I just didn't want them to get into trouble.

Chapter 7

The restaurant buzzed all through lunch as the air filled with the familiar smells of beef and turkey patties grilling. The vent fan was on overdrive trying to cool the place. I left the front door open, propped a big box fan in one of the side windows, and switched on the fans that hung from the stamped-tin ceiling.

Diner after diner stopped me to ask what was going on with the resort project.

"Do you know when they're hiring?" an older woman asked after I'd delivered her cucumber soup and biscuits. "My daughter needs a job something fierce."

"I really have no idea."

"I hear tell a bunch of folks from away are gonna chain themselves to trees up there," the woman's friend said. "Is that right, Robbie?" She patted her forehead with a cloth handkerchief.

"I don't think so. At least, I haven't heard of such a plan, ma'am. Enjoy your lunch, now." I made my escape before the next outlandish claim. That is, I hoped it was outlandish. I'd hate to see Adele, or any of the rest of them, chaining themselves to a tree. True, Martin Dettweiler was technically from "away," since he lived in Beanblossom, but since it was the town adjacent to South Lick, he wasn't from very far away.

Danna dinged the Ready bell, so I headed toward her.

"These are for Mom." Danna pointed to two plates.

I loaded them up and made my way to Danna's mom—Corrine Beedle, mayor of South Lick—where she sat at a small table. Corrine stared at her phone so intently she didn't seem to see me approach.

"Afternoon, Corrine. Here's your lunch." I set down a loaded cheeseburger, cucumber soup, biscuits, and a dish of coleslaw. Corrine was nearly six feet tall, more when she wore her signature heels, and never seemed to gain weight despite her hefty appetite.

She glanced up and gave me a toothy, red-lined smile. "Thanks, hon. This sure looks good. Can you set a while?" She pointed to the chair opposite.

I surveyed the room. No tables that needed bused, as Adele would say, and if there were, Turner could handle them. No patrons who looked like they needed attention. No coffee that needed topping up, that I could tell, anyway. And my knee could use the break.

I sat. "Sure, for a minute. Thanks."

She had already taken a healthy bite of burger and was buttering her first biscuit. She swallowed. "Town's kind of hopping today, wouldn't you say?"

I nodded. Danna had said Corrine was on the side of the resort project, but she was everyone's mayor, too.

"I'm trying to figure how to best wrangle the current situation," Corrine said. "I'm sure you're not a speck surprised to hear I've been in favor of the resort all along."

"Danna did mention something along those lines."

"But I also have to think hard about those opposed to the project. Like your aunt, for one."

"I'm glad you're looking at both sides, and I don't envy you the job."

"I hope they don't do nothing foolish, that group of hers."

Ack. Should I tell her about the traffic-stopping plans? Nah. She'd hear about it soon enough, and at least they weren't planning to chain themselves to trees. Not that I'd heard of, at any rate. "I'm curious about why the developer has already started clearing trees up there. I thought she still had to have one more sign-off before she could start."

"As a matter of fact, she does. The planning board gets the last say."

"Who's on the board?"

"Mostly folks you don't know, Robbie. I will tell you that I'm not at all happy Closs jumped the gun, so to speak."

"Are you going to do anything about it?"

"The trees are already cut. Nobody can undo that." She lifted a shoulder and dropped it. "Anywho, I sent Buck up there this morning to tell 'em to cease and desist further work. That Closs needs scolded."

Buck Bird, the lanky police lieutenant, was a regular here at Pans 'N Pancakes, and I realized with a start he hadn't been in this morning. Maybe delivering the cease-and-desist order hadn't gone well.

Corrine upended the coffee mug we were serving

the cold soup in. "That there soup is so good it deserves to jump the line at St. Peter's pearly gates."

"Danna invented it."

Her eyes roved to her daughter working the grill. A proud smile crept over Corrine's face. "She's something, isn't she?"

"She certainly is."

Corrine had wanted talented Danna to go to college after high school. Instead, Danna had insisted on working for me when I'd opened almost a year ago, and she was doing what she loved best.

"She dropped a mention recently about going to either the culinary institute or a college where she could study food science," I said. "I would hate to lose her, but there's only so much she can learn and perfect with a breakfast and lunch menu."

"She said that to me, too. But she was talking about a year or two from now."

Whew. So not this fall. I hadn't dared ask Danna about a timeline for furthering her education.

"I still think she oughta get her college degree." Corrine tapped her fork on her plate. "But there never has been any rushing that girl. She'll do it when she's good and ready and not a New York minute sooner."

I glanced at the door when the screen door thwacked shut. Buck ambled toward us, hat in hand. I pushed up to standing. "Looks like you've got company."

"Speak of the devil," Corrine said when he reached the table. "Was your ears burning, Buck? We was just talking about you."

"Mornin', Corrine, Robbie," he said. "Madam Mayor here is exactly the lady I was looking for. Mind if I join you?"

"Chair's got your name on it." Corrine pointed to the seat opposite hers.

"Missed you this morning," I said.

"Yeah, I know. And now I'm so hungry my belly thinks my throat's been cut."

I winced at the phrase.

"Sorry, that wasn't particularly tasteful, then, was it? How about, I'm so hungry I could swallow a horse whole. Better?"

"Yes, much," I said.

He folded his long body onto the chair, laying his hat on an empty chair. "Boy, howdy. That didn't go so swell, up there to the site." He shook his head with a baleful look.

I knew I should take his lunch order and let them talk, but I was dying to know what he meant by "not so swell." Over the last year, Buck had gotten used to sharing certain bits of information with me, which my puzzle mind welcomed.

"Fiona didn't take your order lying down, I take it?" Corrine tapped her plate again.

"She surely did not. Whooee, that lady's got herself a temper."

"Was Mike Stiverton up there, too?" I asked. "She drives the heavy equipment."

"Indeed, she was," Buck replied. "I didn't get any lip from her, but she looked real sad when I said she had to turn off the machine and go home. And then Yolene waylaid me on my way out and wanted to know what the fuss was." His stomach gurgled, loud. "Robbie, any chance of lunch?"

I laughed. "That's what I'm here for, isn't it? And why you came in?"

He nodded. "Yup."

"The usual then?" I asked.

He nodded. "But hang on a chicken-pickin' minute. Do you happen to know what all Adele is getting up to now? I heared some rumors."

Corrine's expression perked up, too.

I wished I didn't have to tell him, but a direct question from an officer of the law? It pretty much required a direct and truthful answer. "I think she and a group opposed to the resort are planning a march sometime soon."

"A march from where to where?" Corrine asked.

"Adele said it was going to be out to the state route. To stop traffic and raise awareness."

"Aw, geez," Buck said. "Why do they want to up and do something fool-brained like that?"

"And when is 'sometime soon'?" Corrine asked.

I thought. "Last night she said it would be tomorrow or the next day. Which means today or tomorrow."

"I best give her a call," Buck said. "After I eat, that is."

I left to put in Buck's order. When I glanced back, Corrine was showing Buck something on her phone, and they both looked worried. *Great.* I'd never hear the end of it from Adele if I got her in trouble.

Chapter 8

By three thirty, the restaurant was closed and cleaned, and I'd locked the door after Danna and Turner left. I hoisted the bin of dirty store laundry—cloth napkins, aprons, dishtowels, rags—and carried it to the washing machine in my apartment. The store income wasn't quite at the level where I could hire a laundry service, even though a truck coming to take away soiled linens and deliver clean folded ones would be an awfully nice addition to my life.

While the front-loader machine churned away in the wide back hall I'd converted into a laundry and mud room, I threw together a cheese sandwich. I sat at the round kitchen table with the sandwich and a beer and stroked the grains of the beautiful wood with my finger. The table was one of the pieces of furniture my mom had made for me. It both warmed my heart and made it pinch with sadness to have these reminders of her artisan talents everywhere in my life. There would never be any new tables made by Mom.

A blessed breeze wafted the smell of freshly cut grass through the open window, followed by the drone of a small airplane. Birdy whapped in through the flap on the cat door, racing to his dishes on the floor. He licked up and crunched the last few morsels of food.

"Hang on, little man." I scooped out a helping from the can where I stored his dry food. I held his head to the side, so he wouldn't knock it all over the floor before I poured it in. "Where have you been all day?"

He ignored me and munched away. My store was at the edge of town, and woods came up to the back of the property. I kept Birdy inside at night but let him roam where he wanted during the day. My reward was sometimes a dead mouse or vole on the patio, but so far, he hadn't brought them into the house, and he didn't seem quick enough to catch the songbirds and sparrows that frequented the area.

But my thoughts were on the conflict brewing in town, which could also affect our southern Hoosier wildlife. A conflict Gregory had jumped into as if it were Lake Lemon. Tax revenues were pitted against leaving wilderness intact. Creating jobs for people were being touted instead of saving the birds and critters. Lining Closs's pockets would be the result—or so I assumed—instead of saving the view for artists and tourists. Was there any way the issues could be resolved peaceably and satisfy both camps? I wasn't sure of an avenue that led that way. I thought about the look Lonnie had given Gregory after I introduced him. Some kind of history there, but Lonnie hadn't recognized his face, so maybe he'd read about Gregory. Gregory hadn't seemed to know Lonnie, either.

I hauled Carmen out of my back pocket and tapped Lou's number. After we exchanged greetings, I asked, "Lou, I know you're only getting to know

Gregory DeGraaf. But one of the supporters of the building site, Lonnie Dinnsen, gave Gregory a funny look in the store this morning. Has he mentioned Lonnie at all?"

"No, I don't think so. We just had lunch, in fact." She was clearly smiling as she talked.

"That's cool."

"He was telling me about his difficult ex-wife."

"Ouch. Difficult how?"

"Kind of a backstabber. She's an architect with a good job, but he said she tried to really soak him during the divorce a couple of years ago."

"Not successfully, I hope."

"Robbie, he is a lawyer. No, he made sure the deal was fair to both of them. But it sounds like she's nuts, as well."

We chatted a little more before ringing off. I popped in the last bite of sandwich. What else could I learn about the various players in the conflict? Googling Fiona Closs got me a Scottish solicitor. Where was the Indiana real estate developer? Was Fiona not her real name, or maybe Closs wasn't? I got better results when I searched for Closs Creek Resort. Fiona Closs McGill was listed as the contact person. So maybe McGill was her married name. I couldn't remember if I'd seen her wearing a wedding ring or not. I tapped in Fiona McGill and my eyes widened. Lou hadn't been kidding about the weightlifting. Fiona was the champion in her size class, apparently. Her event seemed to be the bench press, whatever that meant, and her personal best weight was a number I would have thought impossible for such a slender woman to lift. She must use the full name to keep her competitive identity separate from her day job.

But my mission wasn't to learn about female weight-lifting. What else could I find out about Fiona whatever-her-last-name-was and her business practices? Like her banking, the secrets in her closet, her debts, or details about her family. What did her husband do? Did she have kids, an ailing mother, a brother in prison? The possibilities were infinite. I poked around some more. Huh. It looked like she supported the local no-kill pet shelter, which showed she had a soft spot for animals, always a plus in my book. And that she'd sold a house in Evansville, down in the bottom left corner of the state, two years ago. That was all I could find, at least for now.

Chapter 9

"I miss you too, sugar," I said to Abe at eight o'clock that night as the sun disappeared, the air finally cooling from the heat of the day. I sat in a lawn chair on the small patio behind my apartment, a little glass of bourbon on ice at my side and a completed crossword puzzle on a clipboard on the table next to me.

"I'm sorry I'm calling so late. It was a long day of training, and then we all went out to dinner."

"It's fine. I'm all finished with breakfast prep." My one-bedroom abode had been added on at the back of the store a century ago. I glanced up to see lights on in all the B&B rooms upstairs. In June, I'd rented one of the rooms up there to a person who'd ended up being arrested for murder. It hadn't been pretty. I'd made some changes since then, including mounting a camera above the outside egress, so I could track who came and went, and when.

"Is it a good course?" I asked, pulling myself back to the present. I'd put my foot up on an inverted milk crate and now adjusted the ice pack draped over my knee. Crickets buzzed everywhere, and fireflies lit the trees beyond the barn like it was Christmas.

"*Mezzo mezzo.*" He laughed, a sound that always made me tingle. "Did I say that right?" He'd picked up a few words of Italian when my father and his wife had visited from Pisa in late spring.

"Sounds good to me."

"The course material is useful, but they brought in a new teacher today, and he's pretty ineffective," he went on. "I doubt he's ever been in a cherry picker in his life."

I tried to parse that and failed. "What does picking cherries have to do with fixing electric lines?"

Now Abe really laughed. When he got hold of himself, he said, "Sweetheart, a cherry picker is the vehicle with the long arm and the bucket I sit in when I'm up in the air working on the lines. You've seen them on the streets, I'm sure."

"Aha. I know what you mean." Birdy jumped onto my lap, nestling in for a summer snooze.

"How's business and all?" Abe asked.

"Actually, we seem to have some trouble stirring."

"Trouble? At the restaurant?"

"Not at the restaurant, but I'm sure you've heard about the proposal for a resort up on the hill."

"The one above Greasy Hollow."

"Exactly." I explained about Gregory joining Adele's group and outlined my conversations with Fiona, Yolene, Mike, and Lonnie. "For example, Mike could really use the construction job because she's a single mother of twins."

"Wait. Mike is a she?"

"Yes," I said. "Her name is Micaela, but she asked to be called Mike. Maybe it's easier being in construction to use a male-sounding name."

"Maybe. I might have run into her once on a job site. Tall, with curly, red hair?"

"That's her. Can you imagine being a single mom to twin boys?"

"That's gotta be hard." He laughed. "It's hard enough being a single dad to one boy, and he doesn't even live with me most of the time."

Abe was a great father to Sean, and spent a lot of time with him, even though the young teen primarily lived with his mom, Abe's ex-wife.

"Anyway, feelings are starting to run high," I went on. "I'm afraid somebody's going to get hurt."

Abe whistled. "You could be right. I hope you aren't, though. Did the demonstrators already do their thing?"

"No, I think it's now planned for tomorrow." I stroked Birdy's soft fur with my free hand, smoothing his long, black coat over and over. "I wish there was some way I could stop it, but Adele is determined. I think she's remembering her own student-protest days back in the sixties, and she's excited to get involved again. If the locals who want the project to go forward decide to organize a counter-demonstration, things could get ugly."

"Surely they'll have to pull a parade permit or whatever."

"I would think so. Adele's hoping to get arrested and get splashy news coverage because of it." I drained the last of my drink.

"Septuagenarian hauled off for civil disobedience?" Abe asked.

"Exactly." I yawned. "Sorry. I better hit the sack."

"Sweet dreams. I wish I was there with you."

"Me, too." We said good-bye and disconnected. I wasn't sure how I got so lucky to finally land a truly good man who cared about me. My history with men hadn't been great, what with my short-lived marriage and last year a romance that turned sour. But my luck seemed to have changed. Abe O'Neill was a keeper, no doubt about it.

Chapter 10

Seven thirty seemed awfully late for an August dawn. I supposed it was because South Lick was so close to the western edge of the Eastern time zone. Danna was already busy at the grill when I unlocked the door and flipped the sign to OPEN at seven o'clock on Friday morning. The sun was still in hiding, and not behind a cloud, either. I stepped out onto the wide porch. The clean predawn air brushed cool on my bare legs. Venus shone like a celestial beacon in the gradually lightening sky, and would for another twenty minutes before she made her way to bed.

For once, no hungry customers waited at the door. I stood still for a moment, breathing in the clean quiet of the morning. I was blessed to have found this new Midwestern life a few years ago. I didn't have my mom or California, but I had an aunt who loved me, a newly discovered father, a successful business and property, and the best boyfriend around. I had my health—with a much-improved knee today—as well as my wits, happy employees, loyal friends, and a healthy body. I even had an adorable foundling cat.

From within, came the sound of a pan crashing and Danna swearing. Happy employee Number One

didn't sound too happy. I turned to go in and help
when my phone buzzed in the back pocket of my
short jeans skirt, which, with a store T-shirt, tennies,
and apron formed my summer uniform today. I pulled
out the phone. *Lou?* What was she doing calling at
seven in the morning?

I connected. "Lou, what's up?"

"Robbie, it happened again." Her voice was a
hoarse whisper, ending in a choked sob.

"What happened? Talk to me." My gut chilled as I
waited for her to explain.

"I was supposed to meet Gregory for an early bike
ride, while it's still cool out. We decided to meet at
that new resort site."

Why there?

"I was a little late," Lou went on. "I stopped to call
him, but he didn't answer."

A siren started up in town. I trotted down the front
steps and peered down the road.

The words tumbled out of her. "Riding up that last
hill is a killer. I kept going so I wouldn't keep him
waiting."

I glimpsed blue and red flashing lights cross my
road and continue. Straight toward Greasy Hollow.
This was bad. Very bad.

"When I got to the top, at first I didn't see him. But
his bike was leaning against a tree."

"Was anybody else around?" I asked.

"No. Then I . . ." Her voice trailed off into a mewl-
ing weep, a wail, a sob.

"Lou, tell me what happened."

Another wail, then a trembling set of inhales, like
she was trying to get hold of herself.

"He's dead!"

Chapter 11

The sirens grew louder again. But this time the sound came from Lou's phone.

Gregory DeGraaf was dead at the job site. Found by Lou, who had already come across one body last winter. I grieved for Gregory, a handsome, fit cyclist and lawyer donating his time to a cause he believed in.

"Did you call 9-1-1?" I asked.

"Yeah," she whispered, her sobs subsiding.

"I am so sorry, Lou. He probably had an undiagnosed heart condition." That happened all the time, didn't it? An apparently healthy person—often a man—dropped dead during exercise, and the autopsy discovered a congenital bad heart valve or a weak artery wall or whatever. I was terribly sorry Gregory was dead, but it was most likely a normal event. I really, really didn't want it to be a violent death. Because wasn't six murders in a year enough for one county?

"No." Her whisper was urgent. The sirens in the background strobed. I heard a car door slam amid them.

"What do you mean, 'no'? How do you know?" I

asked as two cars and a pickup truck pulled up and parked in front of me.

Men's voices sounded through the phone. Here, hungry diners climbed out of their cars. "Robbie," Danna called from the restaurant.

"I have to go," Lou said and ended the call.

I stared at the phone, my head spinning. I had a very bad feeling about what she'd meant by "No." But a spinning head was not in my immediate future. I took a deep, calming breath.

"Good morning. Come on in," I said to the first couple up the steps. I held the screen door open and followed them into the store. Having been outside for a few minutes made the inside smell that much more delicious, with the sizzle of bacon and the fresh-baked aroma of biscuits filling my nostrils. Still, the smells clashed with my knowledge of Gregory's premature death.

"Sit anywhere you'd like," I told the couple, then hurried over to the cooking area. "Are you all right?" I asked Danna.

"Yeah. Except first I dropped a pan onto the grill, and then I dropped the bleeping pancake batter." She pointed to a damp spot on the floor. Splashes of whole-wheat flecked batter still clung to the cabinet door. "I have to make up more real quick."

"Don't worry. No real harm done." We used a plastic juice pitcher to pour the batter onto the griddle. The top must not have been on securely. Too bad, but not fatal. Not like a man dying. We had plenty of ingredients, and pancake batter was easy and fast to put together. I grabbed both high-test and decaf coffee pots and headed for the rapidly filling tables.

I poured and greeted and took orders. At the fourth

table, I was surprised to find Buck's cousin Wanda. I hadn't seen her come in. She wasn't wearing her county sheriff's deputy uniform this morning, and she sat with her phone in her hand, scowling at it.

"Hey, Wanda. Coffee, right?"

She glanced up. "Um, sure. Yeah, thanks, Robbie." She stared at the phone again.

I poured and hesitated. "Is something wrong?"

"Maybe. You ride your bike a lot. Ever run into a guy named—"

"Gregory DeGraaf?"

She scrunched up her face. "How did you know what I was going to say?"

I kept my voice as soft as I could, so the other diners wouldn't overhear. "I talked to my friend Lou a few minutes ago. She found his body. He was staying upstairs in my B&B."

Her pale eyebrows went north.

"How did you already hear he was dead?" I asked.

"Police scanner app." She pointed to the phone. "But the site is within South Lick town limits, so not in our jurisdiction."

I knew the county sheriff handled homicides in unincorporated territory, as they had in June with the murders in neighboring Beanblossom.

"Jurisdiction," I said. "Does that mean they've already decided it was an unnatural death?"

"Starting to look like it." She started to say more but clamped her mouth shut, instead.

"How so?" I doubted she'd tell me, but it was worth a try.

"Not at liberty to divulge."

Yeah. As I'd thought. "Did Buck go on the call?"

Wanda shrugged. "No idea. Probably."

"Miss?" A diner waved from across the room. "I'm in a bit of a hurry?"

I held up my index finger in acknowledgment as I sighed. "Did you want to order?" I asked Wanda.

"Pancakes, bacon, and biscuits with gravy," she muttered at the phone. She looked up and added, "Please."

"You got it." I headed over to the customer who was in a hurry, and then to the cooking area and handed Danna the order slips. Another homicide in South Lick. Another unnatural death. I was starting to feel like I lived in Cabot Cove. But this wasn't Maine. It wasn't a television show. I wasn't Jessica Fletcher.

This was real life, right here in Indiana.

Chapter 12

News spread so fast in South Lick, that by nine o'clock the restaurant was more than full, and Gregory's death was the topic *du jour*. Turner, bless his heart, had come in a few minutes early. It was all he and Danna and I could do to keep up with the rush. Two couples perused the cookware while a half dozen others milled about near the door, waiting for tables and looking hungry. Seven of the members of the men's Bible breakfast group sat at my biggest table, which was reserved for them every Friday morning at this time. Samuel was the missing eighth, but he was still in Chicago. Emily and Wayne ate and perused the newspaper at a table. Adele and Vera had arrived in time to grab a table, too.

Wayne hailed me. "You sure make a great breakfast, Robbie." He'd demolished a hearty helping of pancakes and had only one sausage to go. Emily had opted for a veggie omelet and wheat toast.

"Thanks so much."

"I read there's a molecule in maple syrup that fights inflammation," Wayne said. "So I felt obliged to double the syrup on my pancakes." He grinned.

I laughed. "I read about that, too. It's called quebecol. They do make great syrup in Quebec."

Wayne's expression turned somber. "We keep hearing people talking about a man who died this morning. Was it someone from here in South Lick?"

I stared at him. Did I have to tell him the victim was their floormate? Yes, I did. He'd learn the news soon enough. "It was actually Gregory DeGraaf. The man who was staying across the hall from you upstairs."

Emily drew in a sharp breath. "Really?"

I nodded.

"That's so sad. Did a car hit him while he was out riding?" she asked. "I know he was big into bicycling."

"I'm afraid I don't know how he died. It's very sad, indeed. If you'll excuse me?"

Adele was waving from across the room, so I headed her way.

"I heard the news on my scanner," Adele said. "That poor, poor man." Adele loved her police scanner. Even after she'd left the post of mayor, she'd refused to give it back.

Vera shook her head with a sad look. "What's the world coming to?"

"How's your friend Lou doing?" Adele asked.

"I don't know. She called me, but then had to hang up. And I've been too busy to take the time to call her back." I resolved to try the minute I caught my breath. "I hope she drops in this morning once they're done talking with her."

"She found poor Chuck in the ice last winter, didn't she?" Adele asked.

"We both did." I had spied the dead man first while

Lou and I were out snowshoeing on Crooked Lake, but I'd seen a homicide victim before then. Lou never had.

Turner dinged the Ready bell, and Danna was busy busing, so I excused myself once again and headed for the cooking area. A minute later, I carried a Kitchen Sink Omelet with home fries and an order of Whole-Wheat Banana-Walnut Pancakes to Lonnie Dinnsen and Mike Stiverton. They'd snagged the last free table ten minutes ago.

"Enjoy your breakfasts," I said as I set down their meals. "More coffee?"

"No, thanks," Mike said with a wrinkled forehead.

"I'd like more coffee when you get a chance, Robbie," Lonnie said. He glanced up at me. "Terrible news, isn't it?"

I nodded. "Tragic."

"I'm sad for the dude, don't get me wrong. But this is going to throw a huge wrench in the project," Mike muttered. "First we had that cease-and-desist order. Now the police say we can't go anywhere near the site until further notice. And who knows when that'll be."

Adele and Vera's table was the next one over. I shifted my gaze to my aunt, who had clearly over-heard Mike, because she wore a satisfied smile.

Mike continued. "Some dude in a suit and a Colts cap told me he was going to need to interview me, and that anyone associated with the resort should stay away until future notice. But if I don't work, I don't get paid." She picked up her coffee mug, but her hand shook so much a little bit sloshed onto her pancakes, leaving a dark puddle in the middle. She swore under her breath.

The dude in the suit and ball cap had to be Oscar Thompson, the odd, but competent state police detective who had worked on a murder case earlier in the year. If he was on the case, they had to be pretty sure it was a homicide. "Let me bring you a new order of pancakes." I reached out for her plate.

She stopped me with her hand. "No. I spilled the coffee. I'll eat it. You have enough to do this morning."

"Just pretend it's java-flavored syrup," Lonnie suggested.

Mike snorted. The cow bell on the door jangled, and a moment later Fiona Closs hurried up to their table, bringing a rush of fresh air with her. She pulled out a chair so fast it almost fell over. Her hair, not the perfectly curved bob she'd worn on Wednesday, was now windblown and curling at odd angles.

"What an effing mess," she blurted, looking from Mike to Lonnie and back. "That lawyer had the nerve to go and die at the work site. Now we're going to be delayed indefinitely."

Whoa. Not a drop of sympathy for Gregory in that statement. She made it sound like he died there on purpose. An image of Nicole Kidman popped into my head. That was who Closs's eyebrows reminded me of.

I cleared my throat. "Good morning, Ms. Closs. Can I start you with some coffee?"

She nodded. As I turned to go, Adele crooked a finger and beckoned me over.

"Just a sec, Adele. I have to get the coffee pot." I returned in a minute and filled Lonnie's and the developer's cups. Lonnie thanked me. Fiona Closs didn't.

"Did you want to order breakfast?" I asked the

developer. "Our specials are on the board there." I gestured to the blackboard, which today featured the applesauce muffins I'd baked before we opened, as well as fresh fruit salad in a honey-yogurt dressing.

She gave an annoyed little shake of her head. "Two poached eggs, the fruit salad, and four sausages."

I jotted down the weightlifter's breakfast and moved over to Adele and Vera.

Adele waggled her eyebrows in a surprisingly good imitation of Groucho Marx. "It appears we've gotten a temporary reprieve," she said. She pointed to Fiona but held up her other hand to block the gesture from sight.

Vera raised her eyebrows. "Somebody said the man was murdered."

I cringed inwardly, because Vera's words came out loud and clear in that deep, booming voice of hers. I'd rather not have my diners hearing talk about murder, despite the underbuzz of gossip being about exactly that. I must not have shown my reaction, because Adele nodded.

"Can that even be true?" Vera looked up at me.

"Sadly, it could be true." I kept my voice as soft as I could. "I haven't heard that it is, though."

In front of me, heads turned toward the two women, and I could almost feel them turning behind me, too, including those of Fiona Closs and friends.

"Sorry," I began in a bright voice, "I have coffees to refill." Anything to change the subject.

Chapter 13

"Lou, I'm so sorry I didn't call you back. The restaurant has been totally mobbed," I said into my cell at around ten that morning.

I stood in a quiet corner of the store away from the hubbub of the restaurant tables, but it was a lot quieter now, with fewer than half of them occupied. I didn't want even a single eavesdropper. Buck had come in to search Gregory's room. I'd hurried up and let him into the room half an hour ago, and he was still up there. We hadn't had a chance to really talk, but I'd told him I knew about Gregory's death, and that Oscar was on the case.

"It's all right." Lou's voice shook. "I didn't really have time to talk until now, anyway. They kept me up at the resort site for a while, and then I had to go to the police station to give them my statement. It took all this time."

"Do you want to come over and hang? A number of people are still here, but it's not crazy busy like it was before. I'll feed you."

Because she exercised so much, Lou had an appetite and a capacity for food much like Corrine's or Buck's, even though she wasn't really tall like them.

"Thanks, but I'm going to take a Lyft home and chill alone. If I can get one that'll take my bike." She sniffed. "Sorry."

"No apologizing." Lou was a scholar and an athlete, and normally she gave off an uber-competent air. But she had feelings like anybody else. "I know you liked him, and I know how tough it is to find a body. Are you okay to talk a little now?"

"Sure."

"Is it true that the police think he was murdered?" I asked softly. "That's what everybody seems to think."

"Then everybody is right. Robbie, I saw finger marks in the skin of his neck." Her voice broke. "He didn't deserve to die."

Strangled. "Of course not. Poor Gregory. And poor you, my friend."

She sniffed again. "You know that lady you were talking to the day we went to the lake? The one who lives near the resort site?"

"Her name is Yolene Wiley. What about her?"

"It was kind of creepy. She kept hanging around this morning, even after Buck told her to go home. I saw her peeking around a tree about ten minutes later. It gave me the shivers. Who wants to stalk a murder victim?"

"She told me she has a financial stake in the resort. Maybe she was simply curious about what happened."

"Or maybe she killed Gregory, so the project can go forward. She really creeped me out."

Except Gregory hadn't been the gating factor on the project. The planning board was, as far as I knew. Why would Gregory be the target of violence? It was like somebody had panicked. What if the killer was now going to target each of the other protesters?

Protesters who had Adele as their leader. I shivered involuntarily even as I realized that was quite a leap in logic.

I really needed to find out who was on the planning board and talk to one of them, see what the deal was. If the resort was close to approval, Adele's group wouldn't be at risk.

"Go home and rest, Lou. And give me a call if you want to get together later, okay?"

She thanked me and disconnected. Me, I blew out a breath and headed outside. If ever I'd needed to inhale some fresh air, it was now. But once I reached the front porch, I almost wished I'd stayed inside. The heat must have risen thirty degrees in the past two hours, and the humidity had kept pace. Who needed skin moisturizer when you had ninety-five percent moisture saturation in the air itself?

I headed back into my business. I cleared Danna for her break and told Turner he could go next. I bused a half dozen tables, scraped the grill, and mixed up a quadruple batch of muffins, since we were almost out. I'd just slid the muffin pans into the oven when Buck came clattering down the interior stairs from the B&B rooms. He didn't quite disappear behind the cookware shelves between him and me, because his head stuck up above. He caught my eye and waved, then emerged, hat in hand.

"Any chance of a late breakfast, Robbie?" he asked.

"Of course. It's only ten o'clock, Buck. You know we serve breakfast all day until we close."

"Whew. I'm running on fumes, here."

That I doubted, but I wouldn't say so to him.

He dusted off his hands. "Oscar made us promise to be extra thorough up there in the deceased's room."

"Did you find anything of interest?"

"Maybe." Buck shrugged. "Not that I can divulge. You know how it is."

"Yes, I do." Except that, on occasion Buck had shared information with me in the hope of getting my opinion on it. "You can go ahead and sit anywhere you want."

He checked the Specials board. "Still got some of them there muffins?"

"We will as soon as the timer goes off, which is in"—I leaned down to check—"five minutes."

"I'll take a couple of those, then, with extra butter. Plus three eggs, strangled . . ." His voice trailed off, and he crunched his head down into his shoulders. "Dang it all, I am so sorry, Robbie. I had no call to go and say that, what with the current situation."

"It's okay. My mom and I used to say strangled eggs for scrambled, too. I knew what you meant."

"Me and the wife always said that to our kids, too. They loved it. But saying strangled eggs don't happen to be appropriate today."

It wouldn't hurt to confirm what Lou had told me. "So, Gregory was strangled?"

He glanced around and lowered his voice to a murmur. "He was. With somebody's bare hands. Or maybe gloved hands. But you could see the finger impressions as clear as day."

"Wow. That seems like a crime of passion, doesn't it? I mean, if you planned a murder, wouldn't you go for a method that left less up to chance? Or required less direct contact with the victim?"

"Could be. You'd have to ask Oscar that."

Or not. I doubted the detective would be very

forthcoming with me on any topic. "We've never really talked about your children, Buck."

He beamed. "I know. I don't mention them much. We like to keep their lives private. Especially considering the line of work I'm in. Wouldn't want no disgruntled ex-con coming after them."

Yikes. "Good point."

"Anywho, the wife and I got married and started our family real young, so the kids are all growed up and launched now. I'm real proud of both of them."

He and his wife must have started young. He didn't look anything beyond his forties, although I supposed he could be nearing the far edge of the decade.

"You'll have to show me pictures some time when you're not hunting down a killer." I needed to get back to work. "So, three strangled eggs, two muffins, and a couple biscuits with gravy?"

"Yup. That'd be fine. And a coffee when you can."

I started to go, but he stopped me.

"And Robbie? Don't go around telling nobody about the means of death, all right? We got to keep it on the down low. And I know you can keep a secret."

"Girl Scout's honor, Buck." Somebody clearly forgot to caution Lou.

Chapter 14

Business had already picked up again by eleven thirty. More diners had asked about Gregory's death and about him staying upstairs. I did my best to keep a level, calm tone, and to counter with, no, I wasn't worried, and yes, the authorities were investigating every detail.

The dude in the black suit and a red Colts cap, Indiana State Police Detective Oscar Thompson in the flesh, clomped into my store. Wearing exactly the same clothes he'd worn during the case last spring, right down to the cowboy boots with their noisy tread. I was taking a shift cooking and had a dozen meat patties on the grill when Oscar beckoned me over. I shook my head and made a gesture for him to come toward me.

"Wondered if I could have a few moments of your time, Ms. Jordan." He focused on a spot beyond my right ear.

"How are you, Detective Thompson?" Just because he dispensed with the niceties of conversation didn't mean I had to.

He cleared his throat. "I am well, thank you. How are you?"

A robot could have put more feeling into it. I answered, anyway. "Pretty well, thanks. I can talk, but it'll have to be here at the stove. As you can see, you came at one of our busy times."

He pressed his thin lips together, but he didn't leave. He set a digital tablet on the far end of the counter, keeping well back from the sizzling beef. "You have heard, of course, about the death of Mr. Gregory DeGraaf."

"Yes." I flipped half the burgers and laid a slice of cheddar on two of them.

"I understand he was staying in one of your rental rooms. When did he arrive?"

"He and the rest of his bicycling group came last Friday. The rest of them left on Sunday night, but Gregory had reserved the room through this Sunday."

"Did he have any visitors to his room during the duration of his stay?"

"I don't know."

Oscar gazed at me over the top of his rimless glasses. "How is it possible that you don't track who comes and goes upstairs in your own building?"

"Detective," I said, doing my best to keep my tone level and patient as I turned the three ready patties onto their toasted buns and added a scoop of coleslaw to three little dishes, placing one on each plate. "I have an outdoor egress for my guests. They come and go as they please. I do have a camera over the door, but I haven't looked at the footage." I flipped the other patties before they burned and slapped the Ready bell for Turner to deliver the completed orders.

"Do you have guests in the other rooms?" Oscar continued his questioning.

"In one of the rooms. A couple named Emily and Wayne Babson."

"Were they acquainted with Mr. DeGraaf prior?"

"I don't think so, but you'd have to ask them."

"Are they here at this time?"

"No, they went hiking at the state park, I think." Or had that been yesterday? I hadn't seen them since after breakfast.

"I'll need their names and contact information."

"Sure."

Danna stuck two more orders on the wheel. She raised one eyebrow and curved her mouth in a wry smile. I gave a little shrug in return.

"Who might you be?" Oscar asked Danna.

That's right. She'd been away during the case Oscar had run last March. I jumped in. "Detective Thompson, this is my employee, Danna Beedle. Danna, State Police Detective Oscar Thompson."

Danna held out her hand, but dropped it when the detective kept his hand at his side. He never shook hands. I didn't know if he was a germophobe or what his issue was. She cast me a quizzical glance. I smiled and shook my head. She grabbed the coffee pots and turned away.

Turner hurried over and added pickle spears to the ready plates, scooped out a fruit salad for one order, and loaded up the plates.

"Yo, Detective," he said. He'd met Oscar last spring.

"Mr. Rao." Oscar gave a dip of his head in acknowledgment.

"Thanks, Turn," I called after him. To Thompson,

I added, "I'm happy to give you access to the video system if you need it."

"I'll need it, yes. Now, I believe Gregory DeGraaf was planning a political action with your aunt, Adele Jordan, and several others. Is that correct?"

I checked the next-up order slip and groaned. Two of the three patties I had on the grill were supposed to be salmon burgers—today's lunch special—not beef. I slid the beef patties onto a plate and set it aside, starting over with salmon. If my pescatarian customers didn't want their fish contaminated by a bit of meat residue, they were plum out of luck. I kept a strict don't ask, don't tell policy when it came to the grill.

I wrenched my attention back to the interview. "All I know is that the group had a meeting here, um, yesterday morning, I think it was."

He rounded his lips to ask, "Who," but I beat him to the punch.

"My Aunt Adele and her friend Vera Skinner, Martin Dettweiler of Beanblossom, Don O'Neill, and Phil MacDonald were in the group."

"Not Louise Perlman?"

"No." I frowned. "But why does it matter who the demonstrators were? Shouldn't you be looking at who opposed them?"

The detective ignored my question. "What did you think of the group and their action?"

"Who cares?" I heard my voice rising into the impatient range. "I wasn't going to march out and stop traffic, if that's what you want to know. I wasn't really for or against their position." If anything, I was against it, but he didn't need to know that.

The doorbell jangled, ushering in more than a half dozen diners. Danna hurried over with yet one more order ticket, which she slapped onto the carousel. Her look this time was less amused and a lot more impatient. The lunch rush was on.

"Have you made the acquaintance of a Ms. . . ." Oscar scrunched up his nose and peered through his glasses at the tablet. "Fiona Closs?"

"Yes, I happened to meet her up at the resort site on Wednesday afternoon." Now this was a more reasonable line of questioning.

"What were you doing there?"

I gave him a level stare. I knew he had to ask, but did he think I was involved with the protesters? "I was curious about the site. I drove by on my way home from a swim. I was surprised to see Fiona Closs and one of her employees there, and that trees had already been cut. Fiona introduced herself, and the three of us had a friendly chat. That's all, Detective."

"Did you get the name of the employee?"

"Micaela Stiverton." I sniffed. And swore silently. Now I'd burned the salmon patties. I flipped them, but they were too far gone, so I scooped them onto the same plate as the errant beef burgers. My staff and I were going to have a great lunch—if slightly charred—when we squeezed in time to eat.

"Excuse me, Detective, but I don't have time to talk right now. If you have more questions, we'll have to do it later." I turned my back on him and focused on my livelihood.

Chapter 15

It wasn't until two forty that Danna, Turner, and I finally sat down to those wasted burgers, now reheated and not bad at all. Both my employees knew it was fine to cook something from scratch for themselves, but we were always so bushed, we often settled for precooked and lightly reheated. Turner scraped off the burnt layer and dove into the salmon, while Danna and I demolished cheeseburgers, and we all finished off the fruit salad.

"That dressing is perfect with the fruit," Turner said.

Danna nodded, her mouth full of exactly that.

I dabbed my mouth with my napkin. "I imagine you both know by now that Mr. DeGraaf was killed this morning, and I'm sure you couldn't help but notice all the buzz today."

"Not to mention Detective Thompson bugging you," Danna said.

"Yes, that, too," I said.

"That's one odd dude," she added.

"Definitely," Turner said.

"He is a little strange, but he's a good detective." I looked from Danna to Turner and back. "I wanted to be sure we talked about the death if either of you wants to."

Turner studied his plate, pushing a last bite of pickle on a full circuit before he spoke. "It makes me, you know, nervous, having someone else killed."

He'd been my employee only since late winter. I'd been peripherally involved in three murders before I'd hired Turner, and Gregory's was the fourth since. And Turner was probably remembering his father being a suspect back in the spring after a man was found murdered on his family's maple farm.

Danna nodded slowly. She sipped from her glass of milk before responding. "It does seem like a lot, Turn. But I don't think it does us much good to be nervous. As my mom says—and it drives me nuts when she does—it is what it is." She traced a path in the condensation on her glass. "Mr. DeGraaf died. For this particular crime, Detective Thompson wants to find out why it happened and who did it. We should welcome that, right, Robbie?"

"Of course," I said. "I don't think you need to be nervous, Turner. Thompson, along with Buck and the other officers, they're the ones with the training. They know how to look for evidence and how to process it. How to interview everybody even remotely involved and make logical connections where people like us don't have the expertise." Despite my puzzle mind itching to look for exactly those connections. "The police are also trained in how to deal with dangerous people should they have the need."

Danna tossed her head. "Somehow that detective wouldn't make me feel real snuggly safe if it came to an outright physical battle. Does he look like he could even defend himself?"

Turner gazed at her. "You might be surprised. There are plenty of skinny geeks out there who are secret ninjas."

"Ninjas?" Danna scoffed.

"Down, girl." Turner made the tamping "slow down" gesture. "I mean it. For example, I don't look particularly buff, right?"

He was slender, flexible, energetic, but no. If queried, I wouldn't guess he was an extra-strong twenty-two-year-old. I was glad he'd asked Danna, not me.

"Ya gotta admit it, dude," she said with a grin.

"Did you know I have a third-degree black belt in tae kwon do?" A slow smile spread across Turner's face at the sight of Danna's dropped jaw. "That's what I thought. You're a tough, tall, volleyball-champion woman. But some of us on the geek squad have our chops, too."

"I love it," I said.

Danna held out a fist to bump Turner's. "Rock it, man."

"You should let us know next time you're in a tournament or whatever," I told him. "Really."

"I will."

"But back to the case," I said. "Gregory has been around here for a week now. Did either of you ever see him acting unusual, or hear him arguing with anybody?"

Danna thought, but shook her head. "I don't think so."

"Nope. That would kind of be too easy, wouldn't it?" Turner asked. "You know, suspect seen arguing in public with victim, arrest suspect, get him to confess. Right?"

"Exactly," I said. "In my experience, these investigations are never so neat and tidy."

"It's not a TV show," Danna agreed. She popped in her last bite and rose to take her plate to the sink. "So, do you have any plans for specials tomorrow, Robbie?"

"Hmm." I swallowed my bite before I spoke. "It's a Saturday, and I bet we'll be slammed again. What's easy and mouthwatering at the same time?"

"Turner, what's a typical Indian breakfast like?" Danna asked. "It's hot there, right? And tomorrow is supposed to be the hottest day of the week here."

He laughed. "Breakfast isn't that different from other meals, actually. Lentil crepes, *rawa upma*, spiced potatoes. *Rawa upma* is like couscous but with cashews and chili peppers. Probably too spicy for around here." He narrowed his eyes, as if staring back to his father's hometown. "I could adapt my *dadiji's* spiced roasted potatoes for the Hoosier palate. A bit of cumin, a bit of mustard, a bit of cilantro, and leave out the hot peppers entirely." He came back to earth. "What do you think, Robbie?"

"Sounds fabulous. Who is your daddy-gee?" I tried to imitate how he had said the word.

He laughed. "My grandmother. My father's mother."

"I think we should try it," I said.

"Great," Turner replied. "I'll need garlic, fresh ginger, mint, and lime."

"I don't think we have ginger or lime," Danna said.

"I'll pick some up at the market when I leave. It's

too late to order them for breakfast." Turner pulled out his phone and made a note.

"Those potatoes sound yummy," I said. "We might get a healthy helping of academic folks coming over from Bloomington to start their semester on a fun culinary note, and they tend to be a little more tolerant of international cuisine." I checked the calendar on my phone. "It's getting close to Labor Day, so we'll be closed because it's a Monday. For lunch tomorrow, we could do hot dogs with all kinds of toppings—chili, relish, cheese, you name it." I checked the clock. "As long as I submit the order in time."

"Robbie, you look wiped." Danna stood. "Let me do the order. I did it once when you were out, remember? I can handle it."

I smiled at her like she was my fairy goddaughter. "It's all yours, girlfriend. My tablet remembers the password. Have at it."

"Can we use canned chili for the dogs?" She headed over to my desk where I kept the digital tablet.

"I think so. We don't have time to make it from scratch. And really, it's going on top of hot dogs. Not exactly fine dining."

"And what about Sunday specials?" Danna asked.

I sank my head into my hand. "I'm kind of wishing we never started this habit of offering specials. If we don't have one on the board now, people ask what the special of the day is."

Turner worked his phone. "Sunday is August twenty-fourth. And that happens to be National Kiss and Make Up Day."

Danna snorted. "That's a lot of help." She'd already

grabbed the tablet and was thumbing items into my ordering software.

"Wait, wait." Turner held up his hand. "It's also National Secondhand Wardrobe Day."

I perked up and nodded. "Danna nails that one every day of the year, and stylin' it, too."

"Whiskey Sour Day?" Turner said, wrinkling his nose.

"Nope," I said. "That's not going to fly."

"Ooh, here's one. National Banana Split Day."

Danna, her hand on the walk-in cooler handle, spun. "Yes!" She fist-pumped the air. "Total no-brainer. Banana, three kinds of ice cream, chocolate syrup, whipped cream in a can."

"Don't forget the cherry on top," I added.

"And a cherry on top."

"Aah, wait." Turner looked up, dejected. "Banana splits were for August twenty-fifth, not the twenty-fourth."

"Forget it," I said, batting away his concerns. "We can still do banana splits for lunch. Our customers don't have to know why we picked them, right?"

Turner brightened. "Of course not. But we totally should do one of these National Day of deals some-time soon. Because, like, who can say no to a National Day of whatever?" He swiped his phone again and brightened at what he saw. "And we might as well start Sunday with National Waffle Day. That's on the twenty-fourth, for sure."

"Do we have a waffle maker?" Danna asked.

"We've never offered them before, but, yeah, do I ever have a waffle iron." I strode over to the cookware shelves and hoisted a heavy square appliance. It wasn't one of the pieces I offered for sale. Instead it formed part of my beloved collection. I lugged it over to the counter near the stove. The round black electrical cord was of fabric with a white stripe woven in. The plug was round and did not include a ground. I lifted the lid, then sneezed from the dust. Inside was black from use, but the tiny posts in four grids on the base and in the lid made it obvious that this machine made four square waffles at a time. "Voila. Waffles."

Chapter 16

I was beat by the time my employees left. All those customers, all that talking, with a measure of worry and grief overlaying almost every minute. And a serious discussion with Danna and Turner thrown in, too. I tossed my apron in the store laundry bin and flopped into a chair.

I knew what I needed was a long, exhausting bike ride. But, while my knee was a lot better today, I didn't want to test its healing by taking it out on a Brown County hill circuit. Ascents and descents were unavoidable no matter which route I picked. Oddly enough, every single hill had both an upslope and a down. If I couldn't ride, what I longed to do was recline on my couch with a puzzle, a glass of wine, and my cat, and take a nice afternoon nap. Normally I'd spend Friday nights with Abe, but with him away on business, that plan was down the drain. And I had this itch to figure out one or two more things on the conundrum that was Gregory's murder.

I wanted to check out Gregory's room, but I could do that later. I had no idea if Buck had taken all Gregory's personal belongings or if they were still up

there. And if they were, what I was supposed to do
with them.

One thing I knew I could do was check out the
members of the planning board. I dusted myself off,
figuratively, took a long drink of cold water, grabbed
my keys and bag, and headed out the front door. I
locked it, made sure I'd locked it, and checked it one
more time, just in case. Lucky for me, South Lick
Town Hall was only a couple of blocks away.

Today's weather was worsening by the hour. The
air was so saturated with water, it was like walking in
a steam bath. Sometimes this weather resulted in a
massive thunderstorm that cleared the air. I hoped
we'd get Mother Nature's light and sound show
soon, so I could breathe and move easily again.
Meanwhile, I made it up the wide granite steps of
the town hall without drowning and pulled open the
heavy antique door.

On the left was the door labeled TOWN CLERK. On
the right, FINANCE. Straight ahead, at the end of the
hall, was the big open space used for city council
meetings, big public forums, and voting. Where was
I going to find the planning board? You'd have
thought I could have stayed home and searched for
the members online, but South Lick had the world's
worst Web site. It was as useless as the proverbial fish
with a bicycle. Not only was it not up to date with the
decade, it wasn't even *au courant* with this century.

I spied a set of stairs on the right, beyond the
FINANCE door. A stylized hand pointed up on the di-
agonal above a sign reading MAYOR AND EVERYTHING
ELSE. *Bingo.* I trudged up in search of the "Else." I
found the mayor's door open, with her administrative
assistant working at the desk in front. I didn't see a

door labeled planning board, so I popped my head in and asked Corrine's admin.

"They don't have their own office," the woman replied. "But you can usually find Barb down to the Shamrock. She's the board's chairwoman."

"Barb Bergen at Shamrock Hardware? The cashier?" I had no idea she was on the planning board.

"The very same."

I thanked her and trotted down the stairs. Within five minutes, I was waiting in the checkout line at Abe's brother's hardware store, the only one in town. Bloomington had a big-box hardware store, but I was glad we didn't have a big-box store anywhere near here. Don O'Neill's Shamrock Hardware had everything you would ever need and then some. And the air conditioning was an extra blessing today.

Barb, unfailingly friendly to all, handed the person in front of the register his change, then beamed at me. "Howdy, there, Robbie. What can I help you find?" Her short cap of salt-and-pepper hair was as trim as her figure, and her makeup was applied as perfectly as always.

I checked behind me, but no one was waiting. "Good afternoon, Barb. I heard you're the big cheese of the planning board."

"I'm no big cheese, but I sure am the chair. Been on the board for years, and they finally saw fit to let me run the group." She leaned closer to me. "One of the fellas didn't think a lady could do the job." She gave a distinctly unladylike snort. "As if."

"I'm sure you're better than the rest of them put together. If you don't mind, I have a question about the permits for the Closs Creek Resort up on the hill."

The smile slid off Barb's face and was replaced by

a steely look. "That's been a real challenging process, I don't mind telling you. The lady who runs it, Fiona Closs? She's a tough nut."

"Will she get the final go-ahead, do you think?"

"I am not absolutely certain she will. Especially seeing as she's gone ahead and started removing trees, bless her heart. Why, we had to send Buck up there to make her stop. And now, what with the homicide and all?" She shook her head. "But even in the absence of those particulars, we're still waiting for a couple few of the other agencies to clear it."

"What other agencies?"

"State environmental, highway department, that kind of thing." She glanced over my shoulder. "Miss Dawson, it'll just be a minute, okay?"

I glanced behind me to see an elderly woman holding a box of light bulbs. She was followed by a man holding an extension cord and a box of screws, with other customers in line behind him. I doubted I'd get any more time alone with Barb for a while.

"You're busy. I'll let you go." I waved my thanks and headed for home, not much wiser despite what she'd told me.

Chapter 17

I walked slowly back to my store, floating in the deep end of my thoughts. What else could I do to make sense of this week? Lou had said Yolene was stalking the crime scene early this morning. Had she been the one to strangle Gregory? She was big enough, for sure. Actually, it occurred to me that all of the resort supporters I'd met were tall and strong enough to do the deed. Mike, with her construction-able hands. Lonnie with his sheer size. Even weightlifter Fiona. And how had the killer known Gregory would bike up to the resort this morning? Had he or she been watching him here at the B&B and followed him up the hill? It chilled me to think of someone spying on my home and business, on my customers and guests.

I wished I hadn't been too busy to spend more time with Oscar Thompson earlier. I didn't think I'd had a chance to tell him about Lonnie supporting the resort project. Finding out what Lonnie's real relationship had been with Gregory had to be important, too, if he'd had one. That dark look he'd given Gregory made me think so. I grabbed my phone to text Oscar but cursed when I couldn't find his number. Hadn't I saved it from the last case?

The detective and his team would surely learn about Yolene's land sale, and whoever was on the scene this morning would have reported her not leaving when they'd asked her to. I'd mentioned to the detective that Mike worked for Fiona, so the homicide team would be talking with her, and obviously with Fiona, as well.

All these thoughts were making me antsy. I gathered the store laundry and started a load of wash. I had never been a sit-back-and-let-things-happen kind of person. I needed to be active. That, and proactive. It was one reason biking was such a perfect outlet for my energy. I could mount up, point the bike, and go, exercising as hard as I was able. I never got antsy when I was riding regularly. So what else could I do right now? Sure, I needed to do breakfast prep for tomorrow, but by now I could almost do that in my sleep.

I snapped my fingers. I didn't know how to find any of the pro-resort gang except Yolene. I could drive up there and ask her some questions. I hadn't been able to talk with her in depth at all on Wednesday. Unlike the last time I'd encountered Thompson on a case, he hadn't warned me to butt out. Under what guise could I go talk to Yolene, though? Ask her about her beloved flowers?

Unfortunately, I'd been around enough murderers, that by now I knew better than to go alone, in case she had a hidden violent side. But who could I invite to be my sidekick? Abe was out of town. And speaking of Abe, I sent him a quick text. I'd rather have another long phone conversation with him.

Texting about murder didn't seem appropriate, so I kept my message short.

Thinking about you, loving you, missing you.

He texted right back.

Right back atcha. Sorry so busy. Will call when I can, might not be for a couple days.

Back to my hunt for a fellow sleuth. I couldn't ask Lou. She had to still be shell-shocked from this morning. Danna and Turner had worked hard enough for one day. Corrine, as mayor, had a stake in the conflict. My chef friend, Christina, would be getting ready to cook an evening's worth of gourmet dinners. I didn't want to involve Adele or Vera, plus they both were a little old to be effective bodyguards. Phil? *Phil.*

I perched in the lawn chairs on my back porch and stabbed Phil's number.

"Hey, Phil. What are you up to?"

"Yo, Robbie," he answered. "Heading out in a few to pick up my one true love and take her out to dinner."

Rats. He'd been dating Noreen for about six months now. "Okay."

"Did you need something? I brought brownies yesterday."

"No, it's all right. I'm going to make a sheet cake tonight for a dessert special." When Danna had put in the order earlier, we'd realized any bananas we could get on short notice would be too green to use in banana splits, so I'd offered to make a spice cake instead.

"Robbie? Why did you call? I know it wasn't just to say howdy."

I laughed. "Actually, I was thinking of going up to talk with Yolene Wiley, and I wanted some company. You know, the woman who wants to sell most of her land to Fiona Closs and her resort?"

"Got it. Sorry, no can do. Don't go alone, though. Promise?"

"Cross my heart and hope not to die."

It was Phil's turn to laugh. "Seriously, what were you hoping to learn from her?"

"I don't quite know. Lou said Yolene was lurking around the crime scene this morning, even after Buck told her to go home. I wanted to chat with her and see what I could learn, but I still haven't come up with a plausible ruse for why I would visit her in the first place."

"Call somebody else?"

"I can't think of anyone." Which was kind of sad, really. Normally I was perfectly happy with my small group of friends and family. I hadn't grown up here, so I didn't have an extended circle of acquaintances. "No worries, I'll stay home, do prep, and bake. You and Noreen have fun."

We said our good-byes and that was that. My phone rang again almost immediately.

I greeted Adele. "What's up?"

"I got me an entire cake frosted and nobody but Vera here to help me eat it. Samuel loves it, but it's his loss, since he's out of town."

I laughed. "Sounds like a national tragedy to me. What kind of cake is it?"

"Southern Jam. Want to stop on by for a slice and some conversation?"

I grimaced, glad we weren't having a video chat. I'd had that cake at a local restaurant once, and it was so sweet it made my teeth hurt to think about it. But I didn't want to hurt my aunt's feelings.

"I'd love to. As soon as the wash finishes, I'll throw it in the dryer and come over. Does that work?" I'd still have time to get back and do the breakfast prep for tomorrow.

"Don't you know you're never supposed to leave the house while the dryer's running?"

"Actually, I didn't. Okay, then I won't wait."

"All righty. I'm sure excited about our plans for tomorrow. This thing is really shaping up." The excitement in her voice came through loud and clear. "Makes me feel like I'm doing something worthwhile again. Making my voice count, exactly like we did back in the day."

"I'm glad. But—"

She cut me off. "No buts about it, Roberta. And I won't be talked out of my civil disobedience, neither."

Chapter 18

Adele pushed a slab of dark moist cake and a fork across the picnic table toward me. Caramel-colored icing covered the top and sides and peeked out between the layers. "Enjoy." She sliced another for Vera, who sat next to her, and one for herself.

On my way here, I'd made it to the bank before five o'clock to deposit the considerable till from the last couple of days. I'd wanted to do a search on Gregory, too, but I ran out of time. Now Adele, Vera, and I sat in the welcome shade of an old sugar maple behind Adele's cottage. Adele's white mouser lay on my right foot, purring like a well-tuned motorcycle, and her border collie dozed near the tree trunk. The sheep Adele raised for wool and meat ambled around the rocky fields stretching out in front of us.

I took a small bite of cake. It was definitely sweet, but Adele was a good enough baker that the rich texture and buttery mouthfeel made up for the sugar. And the spices somehow offset the sweetness. This cake was way different from the one I'd tasted previously.

"What spices are in here?" I savored another small bite, pushing it around in my mouth so I could fully taste it. "Cinnamon and cloves?"

"You're good. And nutmeg. I just can't help myself when the urge to bake strikes, even in weather like this." Adele sipped her iced tea. "Like it?"

"Mmm." I didn't even try to talk around my next mouthful. I was so making this for a dessert special. Maybe even tonight.

Vera swallowed hers. "It's near perfect, Addie. Like a spice cake with jam in it."

She was the only person I'd ever heard call Adele by a nickname. On the other hand, the two were childhood friends, so it made sense.

"There's cocoa in it, too. My granny used to make it," Adele said.

I swallowed. "My mom used to talk about her. I wish I would have known her."

"She was one heck of a dame." Adele set her arms on the table and her chin in one palm, with a fond, distant look in her eyes. "Granny lived in a town north of Boston and delivered babies. Hundreds of 'em, I s'pose."

"She was a doctor?" Vera asked.

How didn't I know that?

Adele laughed. "No, hon, she was a midwife. Even when her hair was snowy white, she'd still get called to births, and off she'd go on her bicycle."

"Amazing. I never knew she was a midwife." I thought back to what Mom had told me about her grandmother as I savored another bite of cake. Had she told me that detail? I wasn't sure. Maybe I hadn't been interested in family history back then, or in midwifery, for that matter. I'd never had childbirth in my sights until very recently. Finding a solid love with a good man could do a lot to change your view of babies and family life.

"Wait." I frowned. "If your grandmother lived north of Boston, why was she making Southern Jam Cake?"

"One of her mothers—you know, one of her birthing ladies—moved north from New Orleans, she told me. This lady had baked Granny a cake in partial payment for her midwifing services. Folks bartered more in those days. Granny liked the cake so much she asked for the recipe."

"I'm glad she did," I said. "How do you think it would do as a sheet cake? I could make it for the restaurant some time, but it's a lot easier to serve squares of cake than double-decker slices."

Vera chimed in. "Shouldn't be a problem."

"Will you give me the recipe, Adele?" I asked.

"'Course, I will."

A bell tinkled from one of the sheep. Sloopy, the border collie, perked up his head from where it rested on his front paws.

"You lie on down, Sloopy. Everything's fine," Adele instructed.

"Adele, tell me again how you came from Massachusetts, where your grandma lived, to southern Indiana." I forked in a bite of cake.

Adele gave me one of her signature looks down over the bridge of her nose. "Why in heck you're interested in family history all of a whipdoodle? You never was before."

I smiled. "I don't know. I'm twenty-eight. Life is good, mostly. I'm just curious. And I can't ask Mom."

Vera reached over to pat my hand.

"I know you can't, hon," Adele said. "Somewheres in my belongings I have Mama's diary. I'll dig it out one of these days, and we'll make a study of it. How about that?"

"Perfect." My gaze landed on a crow-sized, upright bird on the trunk of a dead tree at the edge of the field. I spied a black body, a white stripe rising up the neck before it crossed the head to a long, pointed beak, and a bright red cap ending in a point at the back of the head. I pointed at the regal woodpecker and whispered, "Pileated."

Sure enough, a moment later came the bird's loud, distinctive hammering.

"Don't that sound always conjure up Woody Woodpecker to you?" Vera asked.

I laughed, picturing the vintage cartoons my mom had loved to play for me. "Absolutely."

"Yup, it sure does." My aunt rapped the wooden table in a rhythm slower than the pileated's. "Listen Robbie, I'm not going to tell you any details, but we have a real good demonstration planned. I think we're going to change public opinion on that resort going in."

"And you're in, too, Vera?"

"Why not? If Addie thinks it's a good cause, I'm joining up."

"You two better be careful." I glanced at Vera. "Vera, you gave Wayne Babson a funny look this morning. You told Emily you hadn't met him, but it seemed like you recognized him."

Vera folded her hands and rested her chin on them, elbows on the table. "That's right, I did. I saw that man with another woman a few months ago." She squinted into the distance and blinked. "Yes, it was at that indoor market in Indy. What they call the City Market. Kind of like a farmers' market indoors, except everything's real expensive."

"In that big brick building that's always been a market?" Adele asked.

"Yes, exactly. Not far from Monument Circle. That Wayne fellow was holding hands with a lady, and it wasn't Emily."

"How did you remember him?" I asked.

"I was with my girlfriend standing in line to get into the beer restaurant upstairs, and it was real crowded. Those two were in front of me being all lovey-dovey." She rolled her eyes. "I wanted to tell 'em to get a room."

"I wonder if Emily knows," Adele said. "She seems like a real nice girl."

A girl of fifty. I hoped the affair had been short-lived. Maybe Emily did know, and she and Wayne had patched things up by now.

"He kept saying her name over and over," Vera went on. "It was a pretty, French-sounding name, like Genevieve, except he said it different, with an extra syllable or something."

Adele's expression turned somber.

"What are you thinking about?" I folded my arms on the table, watching her.

She reached down to stroke Sloopy. "I happened to overhear one uneasy set of words earlier."

"Uneasy? How?"

She straightened herself on the bench. "Counselor DeGraaf was talking to someone in Nashville yesterday, I swear, may God rest his soul."

"What do you mean, you swear?" I asked.

Adele held up a hand. "Hear me out, now, Robbie. Vera and I was eating lunch at that new restaurant at the edge of the main drag. We was sitting in a booth, minding our own business and eating, when this disputation starts in the next booth, the one behind Vera. Well, I never." She pursed her lips and shook her head.

"What did you hear?" I asked.

"That's the thing," Adele answered. "It was kind of noisy in there. I could make out Gregory's voice, but the other person was talking too soft. I recognized Gregory's voice right away."

I was dying to prod her to tell me what she actually heard, but there was no rushing one of Adele's stories. "Did you hear it, too, Vera?" I asked.

Vera flipped her palms up. "I suppose I did, but I wasn't paying attention."

"Anywho," Adele finally continued, "it sounded like somebody was threatening him. He said something like the person's threats didn't scare him, that he would do what was right no matter what."

"So, you don't know what the threats were about?" I asked.

"I thought I picked up the words 'the hill,' but I can't say for sure."

"The resort is on a hill," I said.

"If he was threatened, it could have come from anybody involved in one of his cases," Vera pointed out. "He's a lawyer, after all."

"Did you see him in the booth?" I asked.

"No," Adele said. "It was one of them places with real tall dividers between the booths. I got all involved telling Vera stories from when I was mayor here in town. During those years she and I were out of touch, doncha know? When I got up to go use the restroom, I peeked into the booth, but he was gone. Funny thing was, it looked like only one person had eaten there."

"He could have been talking on his phone." I popped

the last piece of cake into my mouth. It wasn't too sweet, after all. In fact, I wanted to use my finger to wipe up the crumbs on the plate, but I restrained myself. Just.

Adele smacked the table with her hand. "I never once thought of that, Roberta. That would explain why I didn't hear the other side of the conversation. I bet he was talking to the murderer." Her eyes went wide.

"Maybe those threats were from the person who killed the lawyer." Vera raised her eyebrows.

"I daresay you're right," Adele said.

If the threat had been about the resort, word had spread fast about Gregory offering his legal services to the protesters. If I'd learned one thing about South Lick, it was that news spread like the proverbial wildfire. Both good news and bad.

Chapter 19

A couple of hours later, I finished mixing up the dry ingredients for pancakes and was about to start the biscuits. Birdy dozed on my desk chair in his best Sphinx pose, but he cocked an ear now and then to check on the world. I'd opened all the windows in the store and in my apartment because of a brisk and welcome breeze blowing through an hour before sunset, and I'd switched on a few lights over the cook space. By seven o'clock, the sun had drifted below the trees to the west of my building, and clouds had raced in. Then the world exploded.

At least that was what it seemed like. First a mighty clap sounded, like a giant whacking her hands together a half inch from my ear. At the same time, daylight disappeared from the sky. Next, a crack of lightning split the air, followed by pattering drops that soon turned to a deluge worthy of Noah and his twosomes. The electric lights inside dimmed, brightened, faltered, and went out. The increasing wind dashed rain straight through my west-facing windows.

"Yowsa," I yelled as I raced to the leaking windows and slammed them shut. It wasn't too dark to see, so I rushed into my apartment, thankful I'd left the connecting door open, and did the same. The front windows in the store were protected by the wide porch roof, and the eastern and northern windows didn't seem to be admitting even a drop of rain. I left them open for the air.

I thought of my carefully renovated and redecorated B&B rooms upstairs. Were my other guests in the building? Grabbing my best flashlight and the master key from the cabinet near my desk, I raced up the steps. The hall glowed pale red from the required EXIT sign. Maybe Emily and Wayne were still out. Gregory had been staying in the only west-facing room, the Rose Room, which I had decorated in gentle shades of dark pinks and ivory. Yellow crime scene tape stretched across the doorway. I hesitated about a millisecond, then tore one end of tape from the jamb, unlocked the door, and pushed it wide open. I froze.

It looked like an explosion had blown up the room—and not a storm-related one. What was this, National Explode Robbie's Life Day? Every door and drawer was open. Black dust coated my neatly painted off-white windowsills. It covered the wood on the antique four-poster bed. Was this how Buck and his colleague searched a room? I knew the black was fingerprint powder. At least the western windows were shut tight, or I'd have had to clean black ink off their sills. Apparently, the authorities had no obligation to restore property to its original—that is, clean—state. Or . . . it occurred to me that encountering the police tape blocking the door meant they weren't done with the room yet.

The second egress door opened in the hall behind me, and I whirled. Emily and Wayne hurried in, rain dripping from their hats. They stopped short when they saw me. Emily's hand flew to her mouth, her gaze on the police tape.

"What's going on, Robbie?" Wayne asked. "What's that yellow tape doing here?" He squinted, tilting his head to the side to read it. "Police line do not cross?"

"I'm afraid Gregory DeGraaf's death is being considered a homicide. The police searched his room. I came up to make sure rain wasn't coming in the windows."

"So, it was true what we heard," Emily whispered. "Gregory was murdered."

"It looks like it," I said.

She glanced around her with wide eyes as if the killer might be lurking in the shadows. "He was such a nice man."

Wayne frowned at me. "But you took down the tape, anyway."

"Yes. I do own the place, after all." That sounded rude. I'd been on edge all day, but I didn't need to snap at my guests. "Anyway, as I said, I had to make sure the windows were shut."

"He wasn't killed here, was he?" Emily asked.

"No, not at all. But the police needed to check his belongings here and search for clues to the murderer's identity."

"Are the authorities in Brown County competent to investigate a homicide?" Wayne asked.

"Yes, I believe so." I cleared my throat. "I have to apologize to both of you. As you can see, we lost power. It happened a few minutes ago. I'm really sorry."

"You don't need to apologize," Emily said. "There's nothing you can do about it. We were out in that storm. It's a big one."

"Don't you have a generator?" Wayne asked.

"I don't, but there is a battery-powered lantern in your room, and I can grab one from the unoccupied room, too." I'd decided to invest in a battery-powered camp lantern for each room exactly in case we had a night like this. I didn't want to risk having candles lit upstairs.

"I would think any establishment serving the public would need an emergency power source," Wayne said, still frowning.

I smiled without responding, working on my "the-customer-is-always-right" routine. And he was right. If power didn't come back on by the morning, I wouldn't be able to open. I'd lose both supplies and customers.

"I got a message from a detective, said he wants to talk with us," Wayne said.

"Yes, I gave him your cell number. I'm sure he only wants to know if you saw anything suspicious in connection with Gregory. Did you see anyone else up here with him? Or hear any unusual noises?"

"No."

Emily shuddered. "I'm glad we didn't."

"I arranged a time for us to meet with the detective tomorrow. Good night." Wayne turned away and unlocked the door to their room down the hall.

"Once again, my apologies for the power situation," I said to Emily. "The county has a good department. I'm sure the electricity will be back on by the morning." I unlocked the vacant room and handed her the extra lantern.

"Thanks, Robbie. Have you . . ." she hesitated, then went on. "Have you ever had a guest who was killed before?"

"Absolutely not."

She gazed down at the floor where their raincoats had dripped. "Goodness. Let me get a towel and clean that up."

"I'll do it, Emily, but thanks."

When their door clicked shut after her, I drew the rag mop out of the hall cleaning closet and wiped the floor dry. I went back into Gregory's room and closed the door behind me. I stood in the middle of the room as the rain beat against the windows. I had to assume that the police had checked all the obvious places—the contents of the drawers, the closet, the bathroom cabinets, and so on. What if I could find something here they had missed? Maybe, just maybe, I could unearth a clue to Gregory's murderer. Or the reason he'd been killed, which I still didn't understand.

I didn't want to touch the lantern in here, in case it had evidence of some kind on it. I used the strong beam of my flashlight to examine a vertical section of the room, from where my feet met the floor across to the wall and up the wall to the ceiling. If I saw anything I wanted to look at more closely, I would make a mental note of it. I rotated my feet a few inches to the right and checked another section. And another, and another.

Starting to feel a bit foolish, I kept going. Three-quarters of the way around, my now-honed innkeeper's eye and my extra-strong LED beam saw what Buck and pal had missed. From behind the bedside table peeked a half-inch corner of white paper. My hand was halfway to it when I stopped myself. "Don't touch evidence" had been drilled into me by now. I didn't want to rise the ire of either Thompson or any other law enforcement official, no matter how much I was dying to see what was written on that white scrap. For all I knew, it was Gregory's grocery list that he'd removed from his pants pocket, which had subsequently slipped behind the bedside table. But maybe it was a note from Lonnie. Maybe it was scribblings about the resort project. Maybe . . .

From downstairs came the unmistakable full-throated ring of the store phone. Almost nobody called me on that but Adele and Abe, partly because no one else knew the number. I kept the phone for nostalgia's sake. It was also listed on the Pans 'N Pancakes Web site—which got nearly zero traffic.

I abandoned the paper, closed the door behind me, and dashed downstairs with my flashlight. Of course, by the time I got to the phone, it had stopped ringing. *Curses.* No caller ID on this old girl, either. The phone had modern innards housed in an antique, wall-mounted phone box. The receiver connected to the box by a curly black cable, and an honest-to-God working dial adorned the front. I checked my cell phone, but whoever had phoned hadn't also called me via normal channels. The unexplained call set up a little back current of worry, which I tried to ignore.

I heaved a maxi-sigh. I hadn't accomplished a thing this evening except mix up pancake stuff and close some windows. The rain was still coming down hard outside. If Buck was here, he'd say it was raining so hard the frogs were lined up on the banks wearing raincoats. It was time to get my work done, pioneer-style. At least I had a natural gas line. Before I got started, I headed back upstairs, locked Gregory's door, and replaced the tape. I should probably call in the piece of paper. Oscar wouldn't be happy I'd been in the room, but maybe it could help him out in the end.

After the power had gone out last winter, I'd gone over to Shamrock Hardware and invested in battery-powered lanterns for down here as well as upstairs, plus a half dozen fat, unscented candles. I hauled the lanterns and the candles out now and arrayed them around the cook space. The sky was still dark, and the rain pelted down as hard as it had before, but the dope-slap cracks of lightning and rumbles of thunder had moved on. By now it would have been nearly dark out, even without the storm clouds. Who knew when the power would be back, especially with the county's best lineman out of town. I probably should power down my phone to conserve battery power, but I didn't want to miss a call from Abe. The next thing I ought to invest in was one of those slim rechargeable battery packs for digital devices. And a generator.

I planned to make up the biscuit dough, then bake the jam cake, because I could light the old oven with a match if need be. If we didn't have power by the time I was finished, I'd go to bed with a lantern and a clear conscience. The butter for the cake warmed on the counter. As I reached for the flour, I heard a scratching noise. I stood as still as a wax statue, except for my racing heart, which tried to burst through my chest wall. I thought the noise came from the front door. I'd had people try to break into my store more than once, a couple of times successfully. I tried to listen, despite the now steady thrum of rain.

Crouching to get out of view of the windows on the porch, I crab walked into a pool of darkness, out of the light cast by the candles and lanterns. My throat was so thick with worry, I could hardly swallow. I cupped my hands to my ears for amplification and listened. More scratching, scrabbling, but it was too loud for a mouse. I rotated my head away from the door and the noise increased. I turned back, and it decreased. So, the noise was . . .

I collapsed on the floor, laughter bubbling up and out in mini hysterics. The sound came from the cabinet where I'd grabbed the master key. Where Birdy, per his nature, had spied an open door and gone to do his own investigation. Where the door, by design, had swung shut after him and latched.

No malevolent intruders in my corner of South Lick tonight. Only a frustrated little tuxedo cat.

Chapter 20

After I'd let Birdy out and prepped the biscuit dough, I paused before I tried to accomplish anything else in the kitchen. I needed to let Oscar know about the corner of paper I'd spied upstairs. Sure, it was Friday night, but it was only eight o'clock. Search as I might, I couldn't find either his number in my phone or his card in my desk from last spring. Rats. I didn't want to call the state police barracks in Bloomington. I gave up and speed dialed Buck.

"Bird," he answered more tersely than I'd ever heard him, but his voice also sounded hollow.

"Buck, it's me, Robbie."

"I'm kind of tied up here. What is it?"

All righty, then. "I wanted to call Oscar, but I couldn't find his number."

Buck read me Oscar's number, and I jotted it down.

"Thanks. Anyway, I went up into Gregory's room to make sure the windows weren't open during the storm a little while ago."

"You observed the police tape across the door, I assume? The tape that clearly states 'Do Not Cross'?"

"Of course. Should I have let my brand-new woodwork and paint be ruined because you guys didn't finish in there?" I heard voices and noises that sounded like furniture moving in the background. *Oh.* The hollow sound was because Buck was on speaker phone. He probably had at least Oscar, if not others, in the room with him. He'd had to react as he did.

I cleared my throat. "Anyway, I happened to see something the team seems to have missed. The corner of a piece of white paper is sticking out from behind the bedside table on the right side of the bed as you face it. I did not touch the paper. I am duly reporting it. All right?"

"Thank you, Ms. Jordan. Was there anything else?"

"No, that's it. Wait, yes, there is. When will I have the room returned to my control? It'll be cleaned and restored to its previous state, I assume." If he could get all formal on me, I could sure dish it right back at him. And if Oscar heard me, so much the better.

"I will inform you of that date as soon as possible. Thank you for being a keen-eyed and responsible citizen."

"You're wel—" I stopped speaking because he had disconnected. Another giggle burbled up. As a keen-eyed and responsible citizen, I wished I'd had the chance to give him the Star Trek salute and utter the words, "Live long and prosper."

In lieu of that, I got going on that cake. I was only half old school when it came to recipes. Lots of my standbys I kept in a cloud-based file I could access on my tablet. But a handwritten recipe from Adele like the Southern Jam Cake one she'd given me earlier? I hauled out my recipe binder and turned the plastic sleeves behind the CAKES tab until I found where I'd filed it.

I already had the white flour and butter out on the counter. I took the flashlight with me into the walk-in cooler, closing the door behind me, and loaded eggs and buttermilk, as well as a big jar of seedless black-berry jam, into an empty milk crate. I hurried out and made sure it was well closed again. I didn't think the quick loss of cool would affect what was inside. It was a well-insulated room with a heavy weather-stripped door.

Before I started assembling, I opened the oven door and lit a match. Turning the temperature knob to Low, I carefully held the match down to the small lighting hole, just like my great-grandmother must have done, unless maybe she'd baked in a wood-fired oven. It worked like a charm. The burner whooshed into flame. I adjusted the knob to 350 degrees and closed the door to preheat. Thank heavens for simple analog devices, and for the stove refurbisher I'd found, who was willing to take on this old six-burner treasure that had come with the store when I bought it. The stove was now a gem of cast iron, steel, and chrome.

When I cooked solo, like now, I often listened to Italian operas, a musical taste my mom had instilled in me many years before I learned my father was Ital-ian. Tonight, since I didn't have electricity, I whistled the arias from those operas instead of playing a CD or using up phone battery by streaming music.

I buttered and floured my two biggest rectangular baking dishes. I'd mixed the dry ingredients, dou-bling the recipe, and was beating sugar into the softened butter with a big hand whisk, as women had done for centuries before electricity came along. The sound of footsteps followed by banging on the front door startled me. This time it definitely wasn't from Birdy being locked in anywhere. The racket and my resultant fear made my heart rate zoom back up to an entirely unhealthy pace. The whisk in my hand kept pace with my heart. At the same time my phone trilled from my pocket. *Huh?*

I grabbed the phone. I let out a relieved breath. *Buck.* I connected.

"You wanna open the door, or what?" he asked.

What happened to, "May I come in, please?" I shook my head, restored the phone to my pocket, and unbolted the door.

Buck faced me, thin hair plastered to his head, with a bonus visitor of Oscar close behind. The latter still wore his Colts cap, although his glasses were spattered with drops. The rain falling beyond the porch's reach had slowed to a light shower, and the storm had cooled the temperature outside by at least twenty degrees. The air was a delicious dive into a cool pond.

"Good evening, gentlemen. That was fast." Even though the police station was only a few blocks away, I truly hadn't expected either of them to drop everything and hustle over here. "Do you want to come in?"

"No, Robbie," Buck said. "We thought we'd stand out here in the blowing rain and make polite conversation."

Was Buck on drugs? He'd never been snide or sarcastic with me for as long as I'd known him. Or was his attitude due to Oscar's lurking influence? Either way, I didn't like it. I mentally rolled my eyes, but stood back and gestured for the two to enter.

"Thank you, Ms. Jordan," Oscar said. "We'd like to see the slip of paper you discovered, if you don't mind."

"I don't mind," I said, turning back to my batter.

Buck cleared his throat. "Uh, excuse me, Robbie. We hadn't lost power at the station. Didn't know you had. You didn't say nothing about it."

"I didn't mention it because it wasn't what I called about."

"Think maybe we could borrow that there flashlight for a couple few minutes?" Buck asked, entreaty in his voice.

Weren't cops supposed to be sort of like Boy Scouts? Always prepared? Not these two, apparently. I let out a breath and turned to face them. The whisk somehow came with my hand. It spattered pellets of sweetened butter over both Buck's and Oscar's dark pants.

"Oops, sorry. There's a cloth under the counter there if you want it." I gestured with my elbow. "Yeah, take the flashlight." I grabbed the key out of my pocket and handed it to him. I pointed up. "As I told Buck fewer than three minutes ago, it's behind the bedside table on the right side of the bed as you face it. Help yourselves." I turned my back on them again, washed my hands, and picked up the abandoned whisk.

Buck grabbed the cloth and dusted off his pants. Oscar declined, but picked up the keys and the flashlight before the two trouped upstairs. Me, I kept beating the butter and sugar until the mixture was creamy. I whisked in the eggs, one at a time, then peered at the recipe in the warm candlelight. When did the jam go in? *Aha*. The recipe said to fold that in after I added the dry ingredients and the buttermilk.

As I worked, I mused on the scrap of note, or whatever it was. Had Gregory torn it out of a notebook to remind himself of a date, an obligation, an idea? Or maybe it had been a threatening note someone conveyed to him, meant for Gregory's eyes only. On the other hand, it could be simply an errant receipt from a store.

Oscar clomped down the stairs in those boots, with Buck close behind. Buck held a clear plastic bag labeled EVIDENCE, with a piece of paper in it. He set the flashlight on the counter away from the food.

"You got it." I stated the obvious. "Can I see?"

Buck checked with Oscar, who gave the slightest nod of his head. Buck extended it into the light, so I leaned over and peered. My eyes widened at reading the words written in block capitals: BUTT OUT NOW OR YOU WILL REGRET IT.

"So it was a threat," I said. "No signature, no envelope?"

"Not that we could find," Buck answered. "We'll take and bring it to the county evidence lab. They might could find somethin' to identify the author."

"Thank you for reporting it promptly," Oscar said.

"So," I paused, thinking. "Someone could have slipped it to him. Or"—I searched their faces—"gotten into his room and left it." My mouth pulled down. I did not want to think about a murderer tiptoeing around my B&B rooms.

"But you got you some better security last year, didn't you?" Buck asked. "Nobody could just sneak up there, could they?"

I shook my head slowly. "Not during business hours. If somebody slipped away from eating or shopping and headed up the inside stairs, the door isn't locked from this side. Of course, the outside door is locked."

"The door might not have closed properly. Alternatively, one of your guests could have left the note," Oscar chimed in. "Or let someone in."

"I kind of doubt it," I said. "I guess it's possible. The only guests here are Emily and Wayne Babson. They said you were going to talk with them."

Oscar nodded. "Now, you had mentioned your video surveillance system. I'd like a look at that now, if possible."

"Hang on a sec while I get this into the oven."

Oscar tapped the pointy toe of his cowboy boot. I ignored his impatience. I folded in the jam, spread the batter in the prepared pans, and slid them into the oven. I washed my hands and set a timer.

"It's over here." I led the way to my desk and powered up the laptop. I could have showed him on my phone, but it was a lot easier to see on a bigger screen. I found the app. Good thing I'd downloaded the video to my hard drive. "What time of day do you want to look at?" I twisted in the chair to gaze at Oscar.

"Any time yesterday when you weren't aware of DeGraaf's whereabouts."

I tapped the desk with my index finger. "He was in the restaurant in the morning until about ten, eleven, I think. I don't think I saw him again. I noticed a light on in his room last night at about eight, but I don't know if he was in there or not." I typed in the range of time but cringed at what popped up. "Darn."

"Darn what?" Buck asked, craning his neck to peer over my shoulder.

"I got the low-end version of the software, and it only saves twenty-four hours of video. You need major storage to save more than that. I didn't think to save the footage from yesterday morning."

"And?" Oscar asked, arms folded.

"And it's eight thirty now. So, the same time last night is the furthest back I can go."

He rolled his eyes. "And what might you be waiting for?"

I didn't say anything, but pushed Play, then sped it up a little so we wouldn't be here all night. The footage showed Gregory climbing the outdoor stairs and putting a key in the lock at nine thirty. So, he had left a light on in the room for himself. I sped through the next seven hours then slowed the playback. "Doesn't look like he went out overnight, at least."

Oscar grunted. The three of us watched closely, finally seeing Gregory jog down the stairs in the predawn darkness at five thirty.

I pointed at the screen. "Looks like he got an early start on his ride." His last ride, ever. I shook my head at the sadness of it, the unnecessary violence, the waste of a human life.

"Thank you, Ms. Jordan. Good night." Oscar headed for the door.

"See you in the mornin'," Buck drawled, back to his usual relaxed self. "I can't wait to try some of that, whatever you're cooking up."

"Southern Jam Cake."

"Are you serious?"

"Yep."

"Gol darn it, I think I've died and gone to heaven

in a chariot," Buck said in wonder. "That's one of my favorites, Robbie. My mama used to bake it most every week. How's come you never made it before?"

I opened my mouth to answer when Oscar spoke curtly from the open door.

"Bird?"

Buck picked up his normal ambling pace and off they went, leaving me here to wait for the cakes and muse about the writer of the threatening note.

Chapter 21

The two large sheet cakes were almost done twenty minutes later. I peeked to see them rising and starting to turn a golden brown. *Yum.* Time would be a little tight to frost them with the caramel icing tonight, since the cakes had to cool first. I could always apply the icing during tomorrow's midmorning lull.

I was in the middle of quartering a bag of small red potatoes to ready them for Turner's breakfast special. I'd lit the burner under a big pot of water to parboil the spuds when I heard another knock on the store's front door. Another visitor? It was nearly nine o'clock, a little late for a casual drop by. At least this time, whoever it was wasn't banging on the door, so I didn't automatically worry. I did, however, come at the door from the side again. I peered out a window onto the porch to see who my visitor was before I showed myself.

Mike Stiverton stood on the other side, a lit flashlight in her hand and a worried expression on her face.

Was it safe to let her in? Emily and Wayne were upstairs. They'd hear if I needed help. Plus, I liked what I'd seen of Mike. If she was a killer, she was an awful nice one. I unbolted the door and opened it. "Good evening. I'm closed, in case you couldn't tell." I kept my tone light.

"I know, of course. I wondered if I could talk with you for a few minutes." She wore outdoorsy sandals, clean jeans—size tall—and a light green T-shirt with a grinning child's stick-figure face and the words SOUTH LICK PRESCHOOL on the front. The green matched her eyes almost perfectly. "I tried calling the store's number a little while ago, but no one answered."

That explained the call. "Sure, come in. As you can see, the power's out." I stepped back.

She followed me in. "We don't have power, either. My kids think it's fun, like camping. They're home with a, um, friend, telling ghost stories."

"That sounds like fun for kids." Was the friend Lonnie? "If you don't mind, I'm going to keep working. Doing breakfast prep for tomorrow."

"Of course." She sniffed as she set her flashlight down. "What smells like heaven?"

"Southern Jam Cake for tomorrow. It's nearly done."

"My grandma used to make that." Mike watched me in silence for a moment. "You strike me as a sensible lady, and you're not part of the protest group. What I wanted to ask you, was if you'd be willing to ask your aunt to back off from her opposition to the resort."

I knew exactly how that would go over with Adele. Like a cast iron skillet full of lead. I laughed inwardly at how I was gradually acquiring a Hoosier's colorful turn of phrase.

Mike put her hands together and rubbed the back of one with the other, over and over. "See, I really need the work. I'm the sole provider for my boys."

"That's gotta be tough. How old are they again?"

"They're twins, and they're four. There isn't any other heavy construction going on in the county, and Greasy Hollow is so close to home. Otherwise, I have a really long commute to get to job sites."

I glanced at her sideways. She seemed like a nice person. But I didn't know her at all.

"I'll be honest," I began. "I doubt Adele is going to change her mind. She feels really strongly about not letting the resort go forward."

Mike's nostrils flared as she pressed her lips together. She stuck her hands in her back pockets.

"I'm happy to tell her your concerns, don't misunderstand me." I finished cutting the potatoes and cleaned the knife. I kept it in my hand, in case I needed it. "I wonder if Gregory's death will make any difference to the project. Would people want to come to a resort where a man was murdered?"

She shook her head in a fast, hard movement. "They don't have to know."

But they would. A Google search would tell them, or word of mouth. Either way, it wasn't really my problem.

"I promise I'll talk to Adele tomorrow," I said. "All right?"

"I appreciate that. I truly do. Thanks for hearing me out."

"Of course." I walked her to the door and bolted it after her.

The lid of the pot on the stove began bumping from the steam trying to escape. I took off the lid and dumped in the spuds, then turned down the heat. If only I could so easily turn down the heat on the South Lick pot that was close to boiling over.

Chapter 22

The electricity had blessedly returned at dark-something o'clock. Danna and I were able to get ready to open the next morning without needing to light candles. The cooler hummed along with the small fridge below the counter and the drinks cooler near the door.

Turner joined Danna and me in the restaurant at six thirty, as promised. He had asked for the afternoon off because of a family thing he needed to attend, and I'd assured him he could go. From a cloth shopping bag, he extracted four little metal cans plus a knobby piece of ginger, three limes, and a bunch each of mint and cilantro.

"Mustard seed, cumin seed, turmeric, and garam masala," he announced, pointing to the cans.

"Yum." Danna rubbed her hands together. "Awesome. Plus cilantro and mint."

Turner tossed both bunches of herbs into a colander and ran them under water for a few seconds. "They get chopped and added after the potatoes roast, along with lime juice."

"You know some people can't stand cilantro?" Danna asked. "It's like a genetic thing."

Turner frowned. "That's right. I forgot."

"It's true. Some people say it tastes like soap." I nodded. "Maybe leave it out?"

"Or we can have it chopped and ready, and when we take the order, we can ask if they want cilantro," Danna suggested.

"That's a great idea. Okay with you, Turner?"

"Sure. You add it last, anyway."

"We're lucky the power is back on, even though I made do last night," I said. "Did you lose electricity at the maple farm, too?"

Turner nodded as he washed his hands and donned an apron. "But we're used to it. Happens all the time, even when there isn't a storm."

"The potatoes are all ready for you," I said. "Fortunately, this old stove works with a match." And I'd gotten an early start on baking the biscuits and doing other setup this morning, because I knew Turner would be joining us in the cook space during the first hour and a half. The meats were all out and ready to grill, and pitchers full of pancake batter and beaten eggs stood ready, like breakfast sentries at attention.

"Girl, can you mince garlic for me?" Turner asked Danna. "And Robbie, same with the ginger?"

Danna nodded and set to work. I peeled the ginger, sliced it crosswise, cut the slices into narrow strips, and chopped the strips as finely as I could.

Turner emptied the container of potatoes into an enormous mixing bowl. He tossed them with oil, turning the potatoes with a big spoon. He set more oil to heat in my biggest cast-iron skillet. When the oil was hot, he measured in the seeds and stirred until they popped. He added the ginger and garlic and stirred for a scant minute, then mixed in the garam masala, turmeric, and salt and stirred for another minute. He mixed the seasonings into the potatoes and spread it all onto two big, rimmed baking sheets before sliding them into the oven.

"That already smells heavenly," I said.

"Don't you use curry powder, too?" Danna asked.

"Seriously?" Turner asked, with an expression that matched his tone. "You call yourself a cook? Don't you know that what you call curry powder is simply a mild, sanitized spice mix like garam masala but less interesting?"

Danna wrinkled her nose. She glanced at me. I nodded confirmation.

"I give," she said. "I did not know that. I plead Hoosier! And I think I need to apprentice myself to you, man." She grinned and gave a mock bow, rolling one hand in front of her head in obeisance.

"All is forgiven." Turner nodded his head regally. He washed his hands and stashed his spices where I kept the ones I most often cooked with. "Just so you have some around should the need arise, Robbie."

"Or should you need to make more during the morning, as I suspect." I checked the clock. We had only ten minutes until opening. I laid a dozen rashers of bacon on the cool edge of the griddle and made sure all the omelet add-ins were in their respective containers: grated cheddar, sliced mushrooms, diced ham, and diced red and green sweet peppers—what old-time Hoosiers in these parts called mangoes.

"So, no new murders overnight?" Danna asked as

she stocked the condiment caddies that went on each table.

"Geez, let's hope not," I said. "Baking cake and prepping potatoes by candlelight was enough excitement." I mentally crossed my fingers, since the excitement of finding the slip of paper had been surmounted only by the fear induced by a silly cat trapped in a cabinet. I didn't want to share either of those. "Although Mike Stiverton dropped by."

"The lady who drives the big machines?" Danna asked.

"Exactly. She's a single mom to two boys, twins, and she wanted me to ask Adele to cool it on the protests."

"Ha!" Danna said. "As if."

"Right. I said I would, but I know it won't have a snowflake's chance in Hades of changing Adele's mind. I don't blame Mike for trying. She needs the work."

"Speaking of twins? My sister and me, some people call us Irish twins, even though we're kind of obviously not Irish," Turner said.

"Because you're only a year apart or something?" I asked.

"That's right. My mom has said how hard it was when we were young, to have two so close together. But twin boys? That's gotta be tough."

"Robbie, how'd the cake come out, anyway?" Danna asked.

"Freaking delicious, that's how. It's in the walk-in except for one piece." I withdrew a plate from the fridge below the counter where we stocked things like milk and juice. I sliced the square piece in half and offered one to Turner and the other to Danna. "Cake for breakfast. It's not iced yet, but it will be."

"Ooh," Danna said after she'd tasted it. "Sweet but—"

"Not too sweet," Turner finished.

Danna worked her way through her half piece in short order.

"That was what I was going for," I agreed. "I confess I reduced the jam and sugar a bit from Adele's recipe, and I plan to do so in the icing, too. She's going to demand royalties when she sees how popular this special is. Remember, it's to serve during lunch. I don't know what would happen if we started serving cake for breakfast."

Danna, who was now bustling around making sure every place setting had its silverware roll, grabbed one in each fist and banged them on the nearest table, chanting, "Cake for breakfast, cake for breakfast!"

I laughed and headed for the door, stepping out on the porch. Not only had the storm washed the world clean, it had also cleared away the humidity for the moment. The air was cool, dry, and quiet. I soaked it up for a moment, then reached to flip the CLOSED sign that hung from a chain on the door. It had been ten months since I'd first turned the sign on my dreams to OPEN. I was more than grateful to still be doing it.

Chapter 23

By eight thirty, a half dozen weekend regulars from the university in Bloomington, as well as my usual cast from South Lick, occupied tables. Several customers had already raved about Turner's potatoes. One professor had engaged Turner in a lengthy discussion of the subcontinent, saying he'd been on annual research trips to Kerala in the south for years. Turner had responded with his own stories of visiting Jalandhar in the north with his family.

Buck, who had come in around eight and grabbed his usual table at the back, was a different story.

"Spiced potatoes from where?" he asked, wrinkling his nose.

"From India, Buck," I said. "Turner learned it from his grandmother, Sajit's mother. They're good. You should try some."

"Can I sample me one bite? I'm not all that fond of foreign food, mostly."

I brought him one piece of the crispy spiced potato on a little plate. "Here."

He forked it into his mouth with a face that expected to dislike it. As he chewed, the look slid away. He glanced up at me with surprise. "Say, that's tasty.

Sure, order me up a full portion, plus, you know, pancakes and sausage and maybe two scrambled. I don't suppose you're serving up some of that cake you was baking last night, are you?"

I laughed. "Not until lunchtime. Do you like cilantro?"

He peered at me. "Never heard of it. What is it?"

"Haven't you ever eaten at a Mexican restaurant?"

"Sure. Never saw nothing on the menu called cilantro."

"Never mind. I'll go put your order in." Sans cilantro. All I needed was for Buck to be one of those people who hated it.

I had just handed the slip to Danna when the bell jangled, admitting Fiona Closs. I approached her.

"Good morning. Will you be dining alone?"

"Yes. Good morning." She didn't smile and seemed to be all business. She wore pressed white Capris and a sleeveless black top that matched her canvas slip-ons, and she carried a slim leather briefcase.

"Follow me, then." I sat her at the last open table, a small one not far from Buck's.

Adele burst in through the door. Vera tailed her as Adele marched up to Buck. I hurried over to hear what was up. Because something clearly was.

"Now listen here," she said to him, folding her arms. "There's sabotage going on, and I want you to get to the bottom of it."

Sabotage? I could almost see the smoke curling up from her ears. I'd rarely been around Adele when she was mad, but when something steamed her, she was a force of nature. Diners at the closest tables stared. Danna and Turner both watched, too.

"Just set down here, Adele, and calm yourself." Buck pointed to the chair next to him. "You, too, Vera."

Adele looked around like she wanted to slug somebody. She finally pulled out the chair and sat.

"What all do you mean by sabotage?" Buck asked.

"Somebody got one of my sheep tangled up in barbed wire," Adele said, outraged. "I had the dickens of a time untangling her this morning. She near broke her leg, struggling so."

"That's awful, Adele," I said. "Your poor sheep." Anyone who hurt an animal—big or small, smart or stupid—should be put away for a long time.

Vera nodded. "It's true. I saw it with my own two eyes."

"The animal probably got herself caught up in your fencing," Buck offered in his lazy drawl.

"Buck Bird, I do not use barbed wire on my farm!" Adele's face was red by now.

True. She used only electric fencing, not barbed wire. My gaze drifted over Adele's shoulder to Fiona. I didn't think Adele had even seen Fiona when she stormed in, or she might be giving her heck right here and now in view of all my customers. My aunt had told me she hadn't met Fiona yet, but had studied her picture and her background.

The developer appeared to be focused on the small open laptop in front of her, but my Spidey sense told me she was listening intently. I flashed on the strands of barbed wire surrounding the clearing at the building site. What I wouldn't give to be beamed up there right this second to see if any of the wire was missing.

"It's a threat, plain and simple," my aunt continued to Buck and everybody else within earshot. "And

I think it's obviously in retribution for my efforts to stop that fool resort from going in."

Vera again nodded her agreement. "I heard a engine in the night. It was around one fifteen, after the rain stopped. Addie was snoring in her room, but I heard it clear as a bell."

"Why didn't you notify the police about the trespasser?" Buck asked.

Adele rolled her eyes. "Don't be ridiculous. I live on a public road. You want I should call in every car and truck that goes by? Admittedly, it's lightly traveled, but it's a town road, nevertheless."

"There was no note or anything?" I asked. "You know, to . . ."

I glanced at Buck. He set his chin in his hand but slid a finger casually over his lips. He was telling me not to talk about the note I'd found upstairs. I gave a little nod and left my sentence hanging.

"A note?" Adele sounded incredulous. "What, on the sheep? No, Robbie, there wasn't no note."

"I don't rightly know what I can do about it, Adele," Buck said. "I can have an officer patrol your road tonight. But short of floodlights and a camera, I can't see how you're going to nab whoever did that to your poor animal."

I didn't like the way this was going. What if the person didn't stop with sheep next time? What if Adele herself was the next to be attacked?

"I've a mind to set out there all night tonight with my rifle." Adele banged the table. "Nobody messes with Adele Jordan's sheep. And I mean nobody."

"I think we all know that, Addie," Vera said. "Now calm yourself down."

If Buck or I had said that to Adele, she would have

gotten even more indignant. Vera seemed to have a private line to Adele's emotions.

Adele inhaled and let out an exasperated breath through her lips, but she didn't make any more demands on Buck.

"Adele, please come on over to the station after you've et your breakfast and fill out a report for us," Buck said. "Just so's it's all on the up and up, like."

"I will."

"Now, I, for one, am hungry." Vera glanced at the Specials board. "Ooh, Indian potatoes? I'll take me some of them, please, Robbie, and two fried eggs, over easy. What'll you have, Addie?"

"What's this about Indian potatoes?" Adele's face lit up.

I pointed to the board. "Turner made a recipe he learned from his grandmother, except he left out the hot pepper. You'll love it, Adele."

"It'll bring me to mind of my service trip to India with Samuel. Order me up some spicy potatoes, will you, sweetheart?" She smiled up at me. "And eggs like Vera ordered, too, plus a side of pancakes. I got me a hunger all of a sudden." Now she was smiling. "I'll take a bottle of hot sauce to go with them tubers. The hot pepper young Turner left out is some of the best part."

Good. This was the Adele I was used to, not the storming fury of a few minutes ago. Still, if the attack on her sheep was only the beginning, I had to figure out how to protect her. I didn't know what I'd do if I lost her.

Chapter 24

Even an hour after she'd arrived, Fiona kept glancing up from her phone to look at the door. It was if she'd planned to meet someone over breakfast, despite her having told me she was eating solo. Nobody joined her. I flashed on what she'd said about Gregory and his law practice when Lou and Gregory had ridden up to the resort site that day after our swim. I went over to clear her dishes and offer her more coffee.

She covered her mug with her hand. "No, thanks. I've had enough."

"Can I ask you a question?"

She blinked but didn't say I couldn't.

"When you met Gregory DeGraaf up at the resort site, that day I was there in my van?" I waited until she nodded before continuing. "You said you'd heard of some of his cases. What were they? I'm curious."

She tossed her head. "He was a skilled but unscrupulous lawyer. He twisted the facts to win his environmental lawsuits, primarily against resort projects like mine."

Was that true?

"He was well known among real estate developers."

Fiona cleared her throat. "And not in a good way. May he rest in peace." She focused on her phone again.

I hoped he was, indeed, resting in peace, wherever that was.

Adele and Vera lingered over their own meals for a long time, chatting first with Buck and then with whomever strolled by. Since Adele knew nearly everyone within a twenty-mile radius, that kept her plenty busy.

Buck stood at about nine o'clock and left a few bills on the table.

I met him near the door. "They gave you weekend duty, huh?"

"Cops work every day of the week, Robbie."

"I noticed you were in uniform." The short-sleeved, summer version of it.

"I left money on the table to cover my meal. I don't want you thinking I'm running out on the tab, now."

"Buck, get real." I set fists on waist. "Since when have you ever not paid way, way more than you owe us? You're one of our most generous regulars. You could get away with not paying for a week, and I wouldn't care. I mean it."

He chuckled. "I s'pose you're right. I have a thirst to see you succeed here, Robbie. You're a real fine person. This place has become a community anchor, and that's no joke."

My eyes pricked, and my heart swelled as if it was going to burst into a happy dance. "Thank you," I whispered, all I could manage. "It's what I've wanted all along."

"Then you done good."

An urgent question burst into my pink bubble of

contentment. Popped it, actually. I lowered my voice so only he could hear me. "Wait. Will you make sure Oscar and his people check alibis for their persons of interest for, you know, last night in the wee hours? I really want to know who did that cruel thing to Adele's sheep. Because it was effectively an attack on my aunt. You saw her reaction."

He gave one deep nod. "Going over to the station to request exactly that. And if you-know-who won't check on where them folks were all night, I will."

"Bless you, Buck."

"You'll remind that aunt of yours to come in and do her report?"

"Sure." I smiled at him and watched him make his way toward the door.

The Babsons came downstairs, and Adele gestured for them to join her and Vera. Buck waved to me and clapped his hat on his head. He put a hand on the door handle, then stepped back and held it open for Martin Dettweiler, whose arms were laden with a big, shallow, closed cardboard box.

"Mr. Dettweiler, would that be a honey delivery?" I asked.

"Indeed, it would, Ms. Jordan. Where would you like me to deposit it?"

The cooking area was busy and occupied, and this delivery was destined for resale, anyway. "How about on my desk?" I led the way.

He set down the box of Dettweiler's Mennonite Honey and pried open the top. "There you be. Twenty-four eight-ounce jars, sixteen minis—which are four ounces—and ten pints."

"Perfect. What do I owe you, sir?"

After he told me the amount, I sat and wrote out a business check.

"Thank you very much," Martin said. "Here is a stack of my business cards, too, as you requested." He handed me a set of cards neatly bound in a rubber band.

"Great. Can I get you some breakfast?"

"Thank you, no. I have eaten, and my daughter awaits outside with the horse and buggy."

Yes, he was one of those who eschewed modern technology, at least until it came to buying pre-glued labels by the page. But the label on every jar was hand lettered, perhaps by the daughter.

When Martin spied Adele in the restaurant, his face lit up. "I'll just be a minute. I must speak with my partner in crime. Perhaps you wouldn't mind informing Lydia, my daughter?"

I watched as he beelined it to Adele. Who else but my aunt would be a partner in crime with a devout Mennonite? I glanced out the front window and spied a teenage girl in a prairie dress slouched in the buggy's driver's seat, her nose in a book. She wouldn't care if her father took a few more minutes inside, and the roan mare in her harness looked patient, too.

I turned back to my customers, where Martin had come up behind Adele and said hello. While I watched, she twisted in her seat to greet him, but instead apparently saw Fiona sitting behind her. Adele jumped to her feet and glared at the developer. I hurried toward them. Not that I had any great desire to become involved, but the way Adele's temper had been a little while ago, I wanted to be close by to prevent her from unleashing her rage on Fiona. A farm woman and her animals were not trifles to be messed with.

"You're the one. Admit it, Fiona. You're the one!" Adele's finger shook as she pointed it.

Uh-oh. Martin froze, looking from Adele to Fiona. I was about a yard away when Fiona looked up from her computer.

"Good morning, ma'am. I overheard that one of your livestock suffered an injury last night. I'm very sorry to hear it. What do you raise? Merinos, Suffolks, Rambouillets?"

Whoa. If Fiona had been the culprit last night, she was doing an expert job at acting like she wasn't. Made me wonder if she had had a prior career on the stage, she seemed that sincere.

Adele's face relaxed, like she'd done a one-eighty flip from Jekyll to Hyde. "Excuse my manners. My name's Adele Jordan, and, yes, I raise about four dozen Merino and a smattering of Cheviots, too. You sound like you know your ovines pretty darn well."

"Yes, ma'am. I grew up on a farm in eastern Nebraska. My daddy ran several thousand head of sheep. I know them quite well." Fiona stood. "I'm Fiona Closs. I don't think I've had the honor of meeting you in person yet." She extended her hand and shook with Adele. "I know you don't approve of my development, but I've been hoping we could talk about it. Maybe come to some kind of middle ground? Please, join me." Fiona gestured to the chair next to her.

"Martin, do we have business to conduct?" Adele asked him.

"No, ma'am. I merely wanted to wish you a good morning."

Emily Babson had been following the back and forth like it was a Wimbledon final match, but Wayne was immersed in his phone. Emily leaned over to Vera and murmured something. Vera nodded and smiled.

"And good morning to you, my friend. All righty, then." Adele glanced back at Vera, who pointed to Fiona's chair. Adele sat. "I appreciate the gesture. Fiona. Why, yes, we do have a good deal to talk about. I have to say this, any lady who knows her sheep has got to have something good going for her."

Fiona dipped her head in agreement. "That applies fully, and then some, to you yourself, Ms. Jordan."

Adele snorted. "Oh, Christ on a cracker, Fiona. Call me Adele and be done with it."

Chapter 25

I wasn't sure I'd have believed it if I hadn't been there, but Adele and Fiona sat for nearly half an hour, heads together, murmuring about this and that. Not a harsh word was said, at least not at a volume I could hear.

Meanwhile, Martin had chatted with Vera and Emily for a few minutes before leaving. He cast a couple of disbelieving glances at Adele, finally shrugged, and departed. Maybe this was the end to South Lick's big demonstration against the resort. Was Fiona practicing a "make friends with your enemy" tactic, or trying to throw up a smokescreen around Gregory's death at the building site? All I knew was that we hadn't had a turbo-charged display of personal fireworks in the store, and for that I was grateful. After the Babsons ate and returned upstairs, Vera grabbed today's paper, which a customer had left behind. She looked perfectly happy doing the crossword puzzle in ink. A woman after my own heart.

I checked the time. It was nearly ten, and, true to form, business was in a lull.

"Take a break, Turner, and then you, Danna," I

told my employees. I bused a few tables and reset them, topped up two coffees, made change for a table of white-haired men, and picked up discarded crayons under a vacated booster seat.

One of my wisest purchases to date had been a box of paper place mats featuring simple puzzles and pictures, plus a supply of four-crayon boxes that ought to last me at least a year. Better to keep the kiddos busy and happy than have them screaming and running around, their boredom disturbing other customers. Although, these days, many of the younger set lost themselves in digital devices of one kind or another, even the toddlers. Children could barely make polite conversation with grownups anymore—half of whom were on their own phones. My upbringing had, of course, included computers and other digital devices, but Mom had insisted we spend time together away from screens, especially at meals. I was more than grateful for that but felt like a twenty-eight-year-old crabby granny sometimes.

I didn't see any customers who looked in need of attention, and all the empty tables were ready for the next round of diners. I brought out the two sheet cakes from the walk-in, then checked the caramel icing recipe. It was easy enough to whip up, and I could keep an eye on the restaurant while I did.

I was deep into stirring a saucepan full of butter, brown sugar, and milk when the door opened to someone new. I raised my eyes to see Oscar poised in the opening. Backlit, he stood there with his hands at his sides and those cowboy boots a foot apart like he was about to draw twin six-shooters and mow down the bad guys. All he was missing was the ten-gallon hat and the bolo tie. Okay, and the guns, too. In my opinion, lacking the guns was a very good thing, although he was a cop. He probably had a firearm in a holster under his jacket.

Fiona stood, apparently oblivious to Oscar's entrance. She shook Adele's hand, dropped a couple of bills on the table, and made her way unhurriedly toward the restroom at the back. Except that she appeared to be the bad guy Oscar was aiming for. He spied her and left the doorway, clomping toward her. He'd almost reached her when she slid into the ladies' room and shut the door. Even I could hear the lock snick shut. Smart lady.

I shook my head. Who was I to congratulate someone for evading the law? Oscar lurked near the restroom door, leaning against a table with his arms folded. I returned my focus to the stirring at hand. After the ingredients were melted and merged, I took the pan off the fire and beat in vanilla and powdered sugar until it was a spreadable glaze. I dug my wideblade vintage frosting spreader out of the drawer, ran warm water into a small bowl, and went to work. With any frosting, but especially with a glaze, using a wide blade and wetting it frequently were key for creating a smooth, attractive finish with pretty swirls in it.

By the time I'd finished icing both cakes, Fiona still hadn't materialized. Oscar had taken to pacing. I was surprised he hadn't accused me of spiriting Fiona away, but maybe that was unfair.

I glanced at Danna, who sat at a table working her way through an omelet. I made a subtle "what gives?" gesture with my hands, eyes, and shoulders. She mirrored the gesture right back to me.

We both knew there wasn't a second egress from the bathroom. Or . . . *uh-oh*. There wasn't a second door, *per se*, but the restrooms were in the oldest section of the building. The double-hung windows measured three and a half feet by six feet. I happened to know that their raising and lowering systems worked perfectly because I'd restored them myself. I'd swapped in new ropes, cleaned the weights, and cleared out the channels. Top and bottom sashes in both restrooms slid up and down easier than cutting butter, and the ground outside was only a few feet below the windowsill. Fiona could have simply slipped out, and since that was the back wall of the store, who would have seen her?

I wiped my hands on my apron and beckoned Oscar in my direction. "It looks like you were waiting for Fiona Closs. Am I right?" I asked him.

"Yes, I was." He nearly spat out the words.

I lowered my voice to deliver the bad news, explaining about the window. "So maybe she didn't want to talk with you?" I ended.

He glowered at me as if I had restored the windows for the sole purpose of allowing Fiona's escape. In a moment of grace, Adele moseyed up at that very moment.

"Oscar, my man." She clapped him on the shoulder.

The detective cringed and shrank away from the human contact.

"Listen." I held up both hands. "Why don't I go in and check? I'll make sure, if Fiona is in there, that she's okay. I have the master key." Because, really, Fiona could very well still be in the bathroom playing possum, or having extreme gastric distress, or even be dead of a heart attack or an overdose. How did I know?

Adele nodded, so off I went, grabbing the key from my desk drawer. I knocked on the restroom door several times, with Oscar and Adele hovering a few feet away.

"Ms. Closs? Fiona? Are you in there?" Radio silence. "Anybody in there?" I called. Zip. Out came the key. By now all ten people still in the restaurant had fallen silent. I turned the key and pushed open the door.

To flapping café curtains, a wide-open sash, and not a Fiona to be seen.

Chapter 26

Why did I feel like life had gone off the rails? For starters, Detective Thompson appeared to be angry with both me and Adele, and it was only eleven o'clock. He'd stalked up behind me to inspect the truly empty bathroom. The dancing pancakes wallpaper was devoid of life. So was the tiny wall cupboard in the corner where I kept cleanser, paper towels, a plunger, the toilet brush, and extra TP. The room didn't include a closet or a laundry chute.

And it wasn't like I'd whispered in Fiona's ear, "Escape out the window." I was sure Adele hadn't, either. Or had she? Either way, it wasn't my fault Fiona was smart enough—and agile enough—to notice the window and make a discreet departure. It also wasn't like nobody could find the businesswoman, either. Good luck with trying to get away from a state police detective. Was she desperate or merely impatient?

Oscar planted his hands on the windowsill and leaned to see where his prey had gone. He kept his back to me and speed dialed someone. He spoke so softly I couldn't catch what he said. He didn't seem happy with whatever transpired in the conversation and jabbed the phone to disconnect.

"I might advise you in future," Oscar said when his call was done, "to keep your ground-floor windows locked."

"They are locked," I said, "to anyone trying to get in from the outside. But it's easy to undo the lock from the inside."

He sat on the sill, ducked his head, and hung one leg over to climb out. Except the toe of his boot caught on the sill on his way out, and he fell most ungraciously into the leaf mold below. When he brushed himself off and stood, his waist was at a level with the windowsill, and his neck was redder than a dish of beets.

"Ms. Jordan." He bit off each syllable.

I waited politely to hear what else he'd say. Instead he turned on his heel and disappeared. Coming around the front to continue the conversation would have been my guess, but I could see the front door from where I stood. He didn't reenter the store. *Huh.* I felt bad for the guy. He was doing valuable and much-needed work fighting crime. He was an officer in the state police, and not a young one, which meant he'd been through rigorous training and had, by now, years of experience under his belt. So why did he come across as either a buffoon or odd and disgruntled? Maybe he was in an unhappy marriage or suffered from clinical depression. He also didn't seem to enjoy human contact that much. He could be on the high-functioning end of the Asperger's spectrum, I supposed.

And then there was the Adele-Fiona conundrum.

Did Fiona's growing up on a sheep farm—if that was even true—absolve her of being the opposition?

"Hon," Adele said. "You all right?"

"I'm fine. Just thinking." I faced her where she stood in the open doorway. "What I want to know is what went on with you and Fiona earlier. You were upset as anything with her, then all of a sudden you two were best buds. What did you talk with her about?" My words made me sound almost jealous. I wasn't, of course, but I sure was confused. "I thought you regarded her as the evil enemy. Maybe even suspected her of hurting your sheep."

"I guess we found common ground. It don't mean I'm going to stop my opposition to her project, as she well knows."

"It seems like you all have abandoned your march." I leaned against the sink. "That action you'd planned?"

"We did, or at least for now, like. The lawyer's death put a crimp in the plan. Didn't want to disrespect him or nothing."

"And you don't suspect Fiona for the barbed wire?"

"Probably not," Adele said, but she didn't meet my gaze. "She sure acted like she was as upset by it as I was."

Oh? I'd never known my aunt to be gullible. I guess there's a first time for everything. Fiona seemed too smooth by half, if you asked me. Except nobody had. And of course, someone else could have planted the barbed wire.

A customer appeared at the open restroom door, and the thin lines of her eyebrows went way up when she saw the two of us hanging out in there like we were teenagers gossiping about our love lives.

"Sorry, ma'am." I ushered Adele out before me. "It's all yours."

The window shut with a *thunk* a moment after she closed the door. It occurred to me that maybe I should secure the bottom of the window and only allow the top to be opened and closed. I could toe-nail the lower half to keep it closed. South Lick usually felt like a pretty safe community, but at times like now, with a murderer out there? Not such a secure harbor.

"I need to get back to work, Adele," I said. "But remember, Buck wants you to meet him at the station to fill out a formal report."

"I'm on it." She gave me a thumbs-up and a quick hug and headed over to collect Vera.

While we'd been yakking in the bathroom, two couples and a family of six had made their way in, and they all looked hungry. Turner was almost done with his break snack of a grilled cheese sandwich, and Danna had just finished adding Southern Jam Cake and Hot Dogs with Everything to the Specials board for lunch, even though it was only ten thirty. We still had plenty of potatoes in the warmer, so she left that up. I approached the newcomers, addressing them all together. "Good morning, and welcome to Pans 'N Pancakes."

Both couples seemed well-groomed and comfortably situated financially, with the women sporting neatly manicured hands, plentiful jewelry, and well-dyed and styled hair. The family, on the other hand, included four stair-stepped children ages four to seven, or so it appeared. None of them, including the parents, were particularly well-styled. But the kids were well-behaved and seemed well-loved, judging from the smiles on the mother's and father's faces, and that was all that counted.

"Mommy, look," the smaller of the middle two girls said, pointing at the Specials board. She screwed up her face and concentrated to figure out the words. "Hot dogs . . . wuh . . . wih . . . with eh-ver . . . ever-ree . . . with every th-th—"

"With everything," said her older brother, and he was kind about it, not mocking. "Hot dogs with everything."

"Good reading, kids," I said, smiling.

"What's everything, ma'am?" the boy asked in an eager tone. "Do you have pickle relish?"

"Of course, we do. And chili, and cheese, and all the usual stuff like ketchup and mustard."

His face lit up. Actually, all the kids' faces did. The beginning reader whispered to her sister, "I want cheese on mine." Her sister whispered back, and the two of them giggled. Clearly there was something funny about cheese on hot dogs.

"Don't you guys want breakfast food? It's not even eleven," the mother said.

"No, we want hot dogs," the older girl asserted. Nods from the other three echoed her desire.

"Hot dogs, it is," Mommy said with a smile.

I always liked to get child diners seated and occupied as soon as possible, for their own benefit as well as that of the more mature and unrelated diners. "There's a big table for all of you over there in the corner," I told the parents, pointing. It sat eight, but that way the six of them wouldn't be crowded.

"Thank you, miss," the father said.

"Daddy, I have to go!" the littlest child wailed, clutching his privates.

I didn't say anything but pointed to the men's room.

Daddy said, "Let's do it, buddy." He scooped up the kid, and strode in that direction.

"Ooh, Southern Jam Cake," one of the well-groomed women said after she checked out the Specials board. She tapped her husband's arm. "That's what your mama always used to make, isn't it, hon?"

He beamed. "It surely is. Does it have caramel icing?"

"Absolutely," I replied. "Isn't that sort of required?"

He nodded enthusiastically.

"I hope you all enjoy it," I said. "Please, sit wherever you'd like."

His wife leaned in and spoke in a low voice. "We heard the man who was murdered was staying upstairs here." Her eyes were wide. "Aren't you afraid the killer will come back?"

I shook my head. "No. The person wasn't killed here, so the murderer has no reason to pay us a visit. I have good security measures in place, and the authorities are working hard on the case."

The other woman spoke up. "Didn't you have a murderer staying up there earlier in the summer? I'm surprised you can get any guests with that kind of history."

I sighed inwardly. Of course I didn't like people associating my name and Pans 'N Pancakes with these brushes with violent death. I smiled anyway. "It hasn't been a problem. Please, don't worry. I'll give you a couple of minutes to decide on your orders. Menus are on the tables." I headed to the coffee pot. I could almost tell now which diners were going to ask for coffee before lunch. These were four of them, despite their interest in gossip. And with any luck, not a one of them was a murderer in the guise of a well-off, middle-aged Hoosier.

Chapter 27

By noon, the place was hopping. I'd never been gladder that Danna had ordered triple the number of hot dogs she'd thought we would need, because they were flying off the grill. Labor Day wasn't until nine days from now, but folks seemed eager to get a head start on the holiday, murder or no murder. The cake was proving super popular, too.

Turner left at noon as agreed, and I realized how much I had come to rely on a fully staffed restaurant. Ever since I'd hired Turner, none of the three of us had gone home completely exhausted, at least not on a normal basis. Today was clearly not going to be normal.

At twelve thirty, Wanda slid into a just-vacated two-top. A couple had been browsing the cookware shelves, but they hadn't said they want to eat, too, so I let Wanda have the table. On occasion, people did come in solely to shop. Danna hurried over and bused the table, wiping it down before resetting it for one.

I carried the coffee pot to Wanda. I knew her preferences.

She leaned back and inhaled audibly. "I could smell them frankfurters all the way over in Nashville,

Robbie. Nothing like your basic hot dog to take the edge off."

I laughed. "Glad to serve." I poured her coffee. "Thanks."

I peered at her. Something was different about her appearance. But what?

Ah. "Hey, you cut your hair." I'd met her last fall, and every time I'd seen her since, except once, she'd worn her strawberry blond locks pulled back into a severe bun. Now she wore it in a straight bob, parted at the side, falling just below her ears. It was a much softer look for her and flattered her big green eyes. Wait. Was she wearing eye makeup, too? I felt a little like my world was one of those snow globes that had been shaken up and rearranged, despite it being eighty degrees outside. Plain Wanda was kind of a staple around here. Good for her for changing it up. "It's a really nice style," I added. "Seriously. I approve." It was a brand-new cut, too. It hadn't been like that when she was in a few days ago.

She blushed but pretended she hadn't. She shook her head a little and cleared her throat. "Thanks. You're busy here today, aren't you? Must be good for the old bottom line." Today she wore her tan uniform, complete with the deputy sheriff's badge on her full chest. Wanda was not a slender woman. At least the sheriff's office seemed to offer a women's uniform option, so a curvy figure like Wanda's didn't have to fit into the straight lines of a man's uniform, as had been the case when Wanda was an officer with the South Lick police.

"Looks like a working lunch, so I won't offer you a margarita." I tried to keep a straight face.

Wanda knew as well as I did that I never served

hard liquor, and not even beer or wine during the hours I was open, unless someone brought their own.

"Cute, Robbie. Actually, I finished my shift a few minutes ago." She frowned. "Have you heard any news about the lawyer's death yesterday?"

"I haven't heard a thing, and I know it's only been a little over twenty-four hours. But you know better than I do, the more time that passes, the less likely it is that the killer will be caught. Right?"

"That tends to be the rule, true."

"An odd thing happened a couple of hours ago. Oscar Thompson was in here, and he seemed to want to talk with the developer of the resort, Fiona Closs. He hadn't quite gotten to her, although she, apparently, had figured it out. She managed to make a speedy getaway through the bathroom window." I pointed to the restroom door. "I don't know if that means she's guilty or what."

Wanda seemed to have tuned out my reply. She was smiling at the table and tracing little shapes with her finger. Were they . . . hearts? She glanced up at me. "So, can I get two dogs with everything? And I mean everything."

"Of course."

"Oh, and someone will be joining me for lunch."

"Got it." I hurried over to the wait station and brought back a second place mat and silverware roll. "Do you want me to bring your order as soon as it's ready, or hang onto it until the other party arrives?"

Wanda opened her mouth, thought, and closed it. "Uh, I'll wait."

I had the feeling she'd been about to tell me how goldarn hungry she was and to bring her food ASAP. Interesting that she'd chosen delayed gratification.

The next few minutes flew by, with Danna cooking and me doing everything else: taking orders, conveying them to Danna, delivering food, taking money and making change, and clearing tables. I barely looked up until I saw someone join Wanda. I took a second look, this time staring. The second party was none other than Oscar Thompson, who had morphed into a normal-looking man in his forties. No ball cap, no black suit. No cowboy boots, as far as I could tell. He wore a dark green polo shirt tucked into belted khakis, with dark hair dampening his collar. Now I really was living in a tossed-about snow globe. Or maybe an alternate universe. Except, even in my universe, detectives were as entitled to romance as anybody else.

I headed over to their table with my order pad and a big smile. They didn't need to know I brought a thirsty curiosity, too. By the time I arrived, Oscar was holding Wanda's hand across the table. A tall paper bag twisted closed at the top also occupied the tabletop. It looked suspiciously like a bottle of wine or bubbly.

I cleared my throat. "Hey, there, Detective. Welcome back. I already have Wanda's order. What can I get you for lunch?"

He blinked, and focused, as usual, past my ear. "To begin, we'd like you to open this bottle and bring two stemmed glasses. For my meal, I'll have what she's having."

The order of a man besotted. No wonder he'd cleared out in a hurry earlier. Wanda nudged his hand.

"Please. If you please." He smiled at my ear, and then gazed straight into Wanda's rosy-cheeked face.

At least he was capable of eye contact when he felt like it. Which he clearly did with the woman who had captured his dysfunctional little heart. I immediately scolded myself for being judgmental, but I could only hope his heart would grow and blossom like the Grinch's had. Judging from right now? Oscar's heart was definitely looking a couple of sizes larger. My only worry was the still-unsolved case. Was a man struck by Cupid's arrow going to be able to focus on his work?

Chapter 28

Phil strolled in a half hour later. Oscar and Wanda still appeared to be thoroughly enjoying their chilled Pinot Grigio and their loaded hot dogs, as well as each other. It seemed odd that Oscar would go off the clock when there was still a murder to be solved. I supposed everybody needs time out from work, even detectives, but I did wonder who besides Buck was on duty tracking down alibis, questioning suspects, and the like.

The family with the polite children had enjoyed their meal, paid, and departed. Beyond that, I'd lost track of who, what, and when, not to mention why and how. All I knew was the where—here. Danna cooked and tossed dirty dishes into the dishwasher when she could, and I did the remainder. What worried me was that my knee pain had resurfaced, right when I'd been plotting a bike ride with Lou later this afternoon, and I had zero time for the standard RICE—rest, ice, compression, and elevation. So I hobbled around and made do.

The one thing I hadn't lost track of was how popular the Southern Jam Cake was. The clock read only twelve thirty, and, despite my cutting the sheet cakes into a two-inch by two-inch square per serving—the smallest pieces I thought I could get away with— the dessert special was almost gone.

"People are lovin' them some jam cake. Save me a piece, will you?" Phil asked, surveying the damage. "Give me the recipe, and I'll quadruple it next time."

"Hey, you got time to do a popularity assessment of a special dessert, dude," Danna said, "you got time to be, like, useful."

He merely smiled, washed his hands at the deep sink, and slipped a clean store apron over his head. "Where can I be of best use, Dame Danna?"

She grinned at her former babysitter. "Wheresomever thou shalt observests a need, Sir Phil."

I raised an index finger. "Despite her best attempts to fracture Elizabethan English beyond repair, Danna means for you to get your sweet rear end busy clearing tables, bub," I said with a smile.

"Aye, aye, ma'am." He gave me a mock salute and headed off to several tables in need of both clearing and cleaning.

Me, I headed over to the lovebirds to see if they wanted anything else. "How'd those dogs go down?" I asked Wanda.

She barely glanced up at me, and Oscar's gaze didn't budge from her face. "Delicious, Robbie. Thank you."

They'd either eaten the very messy lunch neatly and one-handed, or had resumed holding hands as soon as was logistically possible.

"We might have a couple of pieces of Southern Jam Cake left if you're interested."

The mention of cake got Oscar's attention. "Yes, ma'am, two please." He cocked his head to look at me, and it was as if he'd finally realized where he was. He scowled.

I smiled and scooted out of range, hoping desperately that we still had, in fact, two last pieces of cake, besides the one set aside for Phil. We did, but I commissioned Danna to take the plates to Oscar and Wanda.

Danna returned smiling and rubbing her hands together. "Officer Wanda and Detective Thompson, is it?" She grabbed a whisk and held it to her mouth as if it was a microphone. She turned her back to the restaurant and lowered her voice to a dramatic tone. "Lovebirds Across the Ranks. Will there be conflict or conjugal relations? Tune in next week, same time, same station."

I covered my mouth to keep from laughing out loud. "Hush, you. I think it's sweet. Everybody deserves love."

She sobered and nodded. "You're right. That was mean of me. All those lessons we had in school about bullying, and how to counter it, you'd think I would have learned."

I was ashamed to think I'd felt the same kind of amusement at this budding romance between the two normally brusque law enforcement officers.

When the rush finally eased up, I said to Phil, "You came in to eat, no? Tell me what you want and go sit down."

"If you say so." He slid off the apron and tossed it in the hamper. "I'm hungry enough for two dogs, loaded, and a double dish of coleslaw."

"It's yours." I elbowed Danna out of the way and told her to take whatever kind of break she needed.

Five minutes later, I brought Phil his lunch. He was so focused on his phone, he barely registered my delivery until I cleared my throat.

"Sorry, Robbie." His brows knit together. "Adele's planning another meeting." He read his phone's screen. "It's going to be here, at seven thirty tonight." He glanced up at me. "Cool. Are you joining us?"

Here? "Me? No, I hadn't planned to. In fact, this is the first I've heard the group is planning on meeting here. Unless . . ." I patted my back pocket. No phone. *Uh-oh.* Where in heck was it? I thought back. Sometime during the morning, I had used the facilities, and I'd learned from one very unfortunate experience a few years back to take the darned phone out of my back pocket before I sat. "Never mind. Adele probably texted me, and I didn't see it."

Phil set his phone on the table. "After I eat, I'm headed home to bake brownies, and I'll make enough extra to supply you for the next couple of days."

"You're the best, Phil. So, who else will be at the meeting tonight?"

"Adele and Vera, of course. Martin. Don. Me. And I think Lou might be coming, to sort of stand in for Gregory."

My Lou? Of course. Who else? I realized with a pang I hadn't touched base with her since yesterday. Was it only yesterday? *Sheesh.*

"Are you planning another action, or rescheduling the march?" I asked.

"That's really up to Adele," Phil replied.

Adele seemed to have a lot of power in the group, or else everyone was somehow in agreement. She was definitely in charge.

"Enjoy your food, then, and I'll see you in a few."

"Thanks, Robbie," Phil said, but he addressed his phone when he spoke.

"You're welcome," I murmured. Now, where in the world was my phone? I felt disconnected from my world, like an astronaut on a spacewalk whose lifeline to the mother ship had been severed.

Chapter 29

I emerged from the restroom to see Lonnie Dinnsen surveying the few tables that were still occupied at around one thirty. He frowned at what he saw, checked his watch, and frowned some more. Without Turner, Danna and I had run our rear ends off keeping up, even with Phil's help for that short period. Things had calmed down by now. Danna's arms were deep in a sudsy sink, and I'd had time to take a much-needed break.

I walked up to him. "Afternoon, Lonnie. Are you here to eat?"

"I guess so." He gazed down at me, mopping sweat off his brow with a folded red handkerchief. "I mean, sure. Of course." He gave a little laugh.

"We have plenty of empty tables, as you can see, so sit anywhere you want."

"Did a lady come in here? Tall, blue eyes, looks a little worn down?"

I flashed on the woman up on the hill. "Do you mean Yolene Wiley?" I asked.

"I do." His face lit up, accentuating deep blue eyes.

"No, I haven't seen her. In fact, I don't think she's ever been in."

He frowned again. "Then how did you know who I meant?"

"I met her the other day. I drove by her house when I went to look at the building site, and I stopped to chat with her. Actually, she waved me down."

"I see." Lonnie nodded once.

"Was she supposed to meet you here?"

Danna ran water and clinked metal in the sink, while outside a siren ululated in the distance. A breeze brought in the late-summer buzz of cicadas. I waited while he seemed to struggle with how to answer.

"Yes." He left it at that but didn't look at me when he said it. "Okay, then. I am hungry, so I may as well eat."

"Coffee?" I asked.

"No, thanks, although I'd love a big glass of co-cola."

I'd learned that when someone ordered co-cola, they meant any flavor of soda pop, not only Coke. Use of the term marked Lonnie as coming from farther south than here, although he didn't have any drawl to speak of.

"We have Pepsi, root beer, and ginger ale," I said.

"I'll take a ginger ale, thanks. Large, with ice, if you don't mind."

"Coming right up." I found our biggest plastic glass, scooped out ice, and filled the glass with ginger ale from a big bottle. Maybe one day I'd invest in one of the soda dispensers that larger restaurants had, but I wasn't quite ready for that step.

The cow bell jangled as I was taking the soda over to Lonnie. Speak of the devil. Yolene herself pushed through, sighted Lonnie, and made her way over to the table. She plopped into a chair across from him.

"Dang fool car tried to quit on me halfway here." She was breathing heavily, and her hair lay limp from the heat. "Sorry I'm late."

I took the last few steps and set the soda down in front of Lonnie. "Welcome to Pans 'N Pancakes, Yolene."

She looked up with surprise. "Well, hey there, Robbie. That's right, this here's your outfit. Glad I finally made it down."

"I am, too." I handed them each a menu. "Can I get you something to drink to start?" I asked her.

"I'll have what he's having, except make it Coke."

"Pepsi okay?" Some people were very particular about the difference between Pepsi and Coke.

"Sure, I don't care none." Yolene batted away the thought. "Just something cold, sweet, and bubbly's all I want. I got me a thirst something wicked. It's hotter than Satan's sauna out there."

It was hot in here, too, despite the cross breeze. The cooler air ushered in by last night's storm had kept on moving, it seemed, and we were back to the heat-and-humidity swamp typical of late August in the Midwest.

Yolene leaned toward Lonnie as if to share a confidence. She glanced up at me and leaned back. "I was going to share some news with my buddy Lonnie here, but I reckon you already know it, Robbie. A man was killed at the resort yesterday. It's terrible." She shook her head. "Some girl on a bicycle found him."

Some girl? Lou was thirty and had harbored hopes of a relationship with Gregory. She wasn't just some girl on a bicycle.

Lonnie looked pointedly at Yolene and blinked. To my eyes, it looked like he was trying to send her a message. She scrunched up her nose like she wasn't getting it.

"Yes, it's very sad news," I said. "You shared a table with him only two days ago, wasn't it, Lonnie?"

"What?" He seemed startled I was still there. "Yes, I ate with him. Mike and I did. He seemed like a very nice gentleman. May he rest in peace."

"I'll get that drink." I turned to go. Nice or not, Lonnie and Mike had been upset with Gregory on Thursday. Lonnie's last words just now had sounded rote and not a bit heartfelt. After I scooped the ice into Yolene's cup, I glanced back. The two conferred with their heads together. Yolene made an angry-looking gesture. What I wouldn't have given to be a fly on the wall. Or a ladybug on the table. Anything to hear what was up over there. Because something clearly was.

Chapter 30

Danna went home at around three, after we were
finished cleaning up. I headed over to my desk to
play a CD of opera arias. Mostly I streamed music,
but Mom had given me these CDs, and I couldn't
bear to part with them. I stared at my phone on the
desk. *What?*

"Silly phone, is that where you've been all afternoon?" I pocketed it. I didn't remember leaving it
here, but we'd been busier than a one-armed wallpaper hanger, as Buck was fond of saying. I had store
laundry to start, breakfast prep to do, and calls to
make. I'd have loved to relax out on my patio with a
beer and a puzzle instead, but first things came first.

I hoisted the hamper of napkins, towels, and dish-
rags and headed into my apartment. I could get the
gang at the meeting tonight to make silverware rolls
for me, but first the blue cloth napkins had to be
laundered. I could do breakfast prep during the
meeting, too. I had no desire to become involved in
whatever idea they'd cooked up, but that didn't mean
I didn't want to know what they were planning.

When the machine was chugging away, I did open
a beer and poured it into a glass. I knew my knee

wasn't up to a ride, and it was really too hot to be out exercising, so why not? I grabbed an ice pack, sat in the shade on my little patio out back, and propped my leg up as I'd done the other night. I applied the ice to my knee, applied some beer to my mouth, and pressed Lou's number. Birdy headed over and bumped against my leg until I scratched his head.

"Hey, Lou," I said when she connected.

"Hi, Robbie." She sounded breathless.

"Are you out riding?"

"Yeah, why?"

"I was going to ask if you wanted to go for a ride with me, but today my stupid knee is giving me problems again. I'm really sorry I haven't touched base with you since yesterday. It's been nuts here. How are you doing?"

"If you mean, am I still grieving the violent death of a man I was starting to adore, yes, I am. What a waste, Robbie." She fell silent.

"I know. He really seemed like a great guy." Unless he wasn't, and we'd both bought the story he was selling. Maybe he had something shady in his past, and that's why he was murdered.

"I still can't believe it." Lou sniffed, then blew out a breath. "That's why I'm riding my heart out in this heat. I've probably lost five pounds in sweat alone."

Not that she had any need to lose even an ounce. Unlike me, the woman had nearly zero body fat.

"I get it, Lou. So, Phil told me you might be coming to a meeting at the store tonight?"

"I am. Adele asked if I wanted to join their group. I hope you don't mind."

"Of course not. Have a good ride, and I'll see you tonight."

We said good-bye and hung up. I traced a figure eight in the moisture on the pint glass of lager. A mockingbird showed off its songs from a branch of the old elm behind my barn, and it had had all spring and summer to learn a new repertoire of tunes. First, the bird sounded like a song sparrow. Then a cardinal. It ended up mocking a cell phone ringing. I glanced at my phone. Nope. That was all bird.

My thoughts were as scattered as the mockingbird's songs, like a deck of cards dropped on the floor. Some face up, some face down. Some red, some black. A spade followed by a club followed by two hearts and a diamond. No order to any of it.

I assumed Oscar and company were researching Gregory's background, but it couldn't hurt for me to do the same. I tapped his name into my phone and followed links here and there. His Facebook page said he was forty and single. He belonged to the Central Indiana Bicycling Association, the club he'd come to South Lick with. He'd won several high-profile legal cases. He'd been married for a couple of years but was now divorced. I didn't see any evidence of children. I sat back. It could be his killing was unrelated to the resort project. Maybe the ex had followed him there and killed him, or had hired someone to do the deed. Stranger things had happened.

"What do you think, Birdy?"

In reply, he eyed me, coiled his energy, and jumped into my lap with the little chirp that had given him his name. I knew if I uprooted myself and went in to get puzzle-making supplies—clipboard, graph paper, and a sharp pencil with a good eraser—I could sort through the facts and put them in as much order as I was able. But for now? Beer, ice, and cat made for way too cozy a situation to disrupt. So, I made a mental puzzle, instead.

Clue: August murder victim. Answer: Gregory DeGraaf.

Clue: Means. Answer: Strangulation.

Clue: Motive. Answer: Keep resort project moving forward.

I paused. Or was that the motive? Maybe Gregory had an entire dark side, a sordid history nobody knew about. Anybody he'd ever wronged in his law career could have come after him. Or that difficult ex-wife. I sure hoped the homicide team was looking into all possibilities. I shrugged and moved on.

Clue: Opportunity. Answer: Dark of morning, at isolated site.

Clue: Suspect One. Answer: Fiona Closs McGill.

Clue: Suspect Two. Answer: Lonnie Dinnsen.

Clue: Suspect Three. Answer: Yolene Wiley.

Clue: Suspect Four. Answer: Micaela Stiverton.

I cringed at the last one. Single mom of young twin boys? Why would she risk her life and her kids' future to kill someone? I couldn't see it. And yet she needed the job, badly, it seemed.

I mentally added Clue: Suspect Five. Answer: Unknown. Which wasn't any answer at all.

The buzzer from the washing machine interrupted the quiet of the afternoon. I gently lifted Birdy off my lap and went to shift the load into the dryer. I very much wished Abe was home to hash through my thoughts with. He'd turned out to be an excellent sounding board before, when I was puzzling through an issue. He was a good listener and often saw things from a different angle than I did.

I texted Abe, asking if he had time to talk, but got no reply. So much for that idea. He probably hadn't even heard about the murder. That still wasn't something appropriate for a text message. While I had my phone out, I ought to touch base with Adele. I was a bit annoyed she'd arranged a meeting at my place without asking me if it was all right. As it happened, I didn't have a single other thing going on tonight, so of course, it was fine. The store was a lot more centrally located than her sheep farm. But I did occasionally host an after-hours gathering for a club or other group. It kept my dinner-chef skills honed and was a way to bring in some extra cash.

After I got Adele on the line, she said, "Oh, hon, I've been meaning to call."

"I hear you're holding a meeting here tonight," I said.

"You don't mind, do you, Robbie?"

"It's fine. The only thing I minded was not being asked before you scheduled it. But, as it happens, the store will be empty."

"I got carried away. I won't do it again," Adele said, sounding suitably chastened.

I laughed. "I'll have penance for you and your group to do."

"Penance?"

"By way of rolling silverware. I'll have a fresh load of napkins all ready for you."

"And we'll be happy to oblige. See you a bit before seven thirty, then."

We disconnected. They'd better be happy to oblige, or there would be no more meetings in Pans 'N Pancakes.

Chapter 31

I stood at my prep counter that evening, listening to the group's conversation as I cut butter into the dry biscuit mix. The anti-resort gang tossed around ideas for continuing to protest the resort, pushing thoughts of solving the murder out of my mind for the moment.

"I like the idea of a silent vigil," Martin said. "We stand with arms linked at the entrance to the road that leads back to the building site."

Emily clattered down the stairs, cheeks pink. "I'm sorry I'm late."

Emily? Vera and Adele must have convinced her to join, too.

"Not a problem, hon," Vera said. "Pull up a chair and grab a bottle."

Adele sipped from a beer bottle. She'd brought a couple of six packs for the meeting, and a bag of Tell City pretzels. She pushed a bottle over to Emily. "We were discussing the idea of a vigil out on the road to the resort. My question is, how will people know why we are there?"

If this had been daytime, I would have left the front door open to allow the breeze to come in through the screen door. But since I wasn't open to the public—

and we were drinking, to boot—I kept it closed and locked. I took a swig from my own beer as I worked. The group was working, too, as a lovely pile of blue napkin rolls was rising, and the pile of flat napkins was diminishing along with the clean silverware in the dishwasher basket.

"You could make sandwich boards, or at least signs that hang from around your neck," Lou suggested.

Interesting that Lou was still saying "you" rather than "we." I took that to mean she wasn't totally convinced she wanted to be part of the effort.

"Good idea," Martin said. "I will say, we need to keep whatever we do peaceable. You know what Gandhi said. 'Nonviolence and truth are inseparable and presuppose one another.'"

"I don't know. I think we should be more daring," Vera said. "I'm willing to chain myself to a tree so they can't cut any more down. That would be preventing violence."

"I'll be at the next tree over," Adele said, giving her friend a high five.

I winced. I didn't really understand how any of these ideas would achieve the desired result, especially chaining themselves to trees. Shouldn't they be lobbying the planning board?

"I spoke with Barb Bergen recently," I chimed in. Seven heads twisted to look in my direction. "She's chair of the South Lick Planning Board."

"Barb, the cashier at Shamrock Hardware?" Phil asked.

Don O'Neill nodded. "Barb's a good egg. She's worked for me for years. It's the planning board that would do the final sign-off on the resort," he explained.

It occurred to me for the first time that Don was

active in this group, but he was also Barb's boss. Was that a conflict of interest? Would she have to recuse herself from the board's vote on the resort vote in case Don had influenced her decision?

"Barb told me they were still waiting for the okay from a few other agencies," I said. "Like the state's environmental commission or whatever it is, and I think the highway department, too. But she didn't sound all that certain that her board would approve the project, even if they got the go-ahead from those other groups. So you could be jumping the gun here."

Phil studied me, nodding slowly. "I think Robbie might be onto something. We find out when the board meets, and we show up with informational fliers, pointing out all the reasons the resort shouldn't be built."

"And then keep the pressure on," Lou said. "Call each member and offer to meet one-on-one with them."

"Or do that before they meet," Emily added.

"But we don't want to be so annoying that we turn them against us," Adele said.

"What about the idea of getting some of the supporters to come over to our side?" Vera asked. "Maybe that lady who drives the big trucks would consider changing her position. What do you think, Robbie?"

"Mike?" I shook my head. "I sincerely doubt that. She said she really needs the work. Actually, I doubt any of the supporters I know of would abandon their positions. The developer least of all." I focused on my biscuits again, stirring eggs into the middle and adding the milk. I kneaded it lightly, formed a disk, and wrapped it. I headed into the walk-in to store the dough and to grab fruit I needed to cut up for tomorrow.

When I came out, the seven of them were huddled more closely together around the table, speaking in low tones. Rolling silverware had ceased. Lou glanced over at me with an uneasy look. What were they up to that they didn't want me to hear?

Adele sat up straight. "Well, that's that then," she said in a too-loud voice. She clapped both hands flat on the table, then leaned back and drank her beer. "I sure love me some Hoosier lager, don't you, Vera?"

"Yup."

"What are you guys up to?" I looked from Adele to Lou to Martin and on around the table.

"Nothing you have to worry your head about, Robbie," Don said.

"Now let's get these rolls done so we can get out of Robbie's hair." Vera grabbed another napkin and a set of flatware. The rest of them followed suit.

"I appreciate the help," I said.

Twenty minutes later the rolls were done, people had their marching orders, and I still didn't know what the secret had been. I kissed Adele good-bye.

"Please don't do anything crazy," I murmured.

"Now, Roberta, would I do that?" Adele mustered her best innocent look.

"Yes, of course you would. But stay safe, please?"

She hugged me. "I promise."

Good-byes went around, with Adele and Vera the first ones out the door. Emily headed back upstairs. Only Phil remained when Adele burst back inside.

"Well, I never!" Her face was red, and she was breathing fast.

"You never what?" I asked. "What's the matter?"

"Come and see. And bring that phone of yours so we can take a picture of the evidence."

Evidence? I shook my head, but hurried out after her, clattering down the steps, with Phil close behind. The others stood around Adele's truck. Martin shook his head and pointed at something. When they heard us behind them, the cluster parted.

"Well, would ya look at that?" Phil said.

I gasped. Adele's little red pickup truck perched low on the pavement. Lou's phone's flashlight app illuminated the reason. Every one of Adele's tires was flat. And a knife stuck out of the front left tire's sidewall. The threat was unmistakable.

Chapter 32

I'd said I would call 911. I'd encouraged Adele and Vera to go back inside and sit down and told everybody else to go on home. Adele had gotten a hug from every single one of them.

On his way out, Martin had murmured, "That's a hunting knife, you know."

"Thanks. I didn't think it looked like it belonged in a kitchen."

Now I paced back and forth on the porch, on the phone with a South Lick police dispatcher. "Yes, I said a knife." Was she being willfully thickheaded? Dim on purpose? "All four tires have been slashed." I swiped my forehead. It was well after nine and had to be about a thousand percent humidity. "We need an officer to come down and investigate as soon as possible."

"What's the address, ma'am?"

"It's the country store in South Lick, Pans 'N Pancakes. Nineteen Main Street."

"Someone will be there as soon as possible. Please do not touch the vehicle or the . . . knife."

I could almost hear her roll her eyes. "Thank you." I punched the phone icon to disconnect. I didn't

care if she didn't believe me. I knew a knife when I
saw one.

I trotted down the stairs and knelt in front of the
knife, shining my phone flashlight on it. The handle
was wooden and curved where fingers would grasp it.
Gold capital letters spelling SOG were embossed into
a dark metal plaque on the side of the handle. Was
that a monogram or the knife's brand? And whose
was it?

I knew a lot of people hunted around here, including Don and Abe, Corrine, and Adele herself for
that matter. I'd never gone out shooting with her or
anyone else, and had no idea how common this
brand of knife was, or who it might belong to. It
would be our bad luck if the vandal had worn gloves.
Any criminal worth his or her stuff would protect
against leaving fingerprints or DNA, of course.
Someone obviously knew this was Adele's truck. I
would be truly surprised if it was a different someone
than whoever tried to injure her ewe. I shuddered at
the thought of her being followed here.

I stood and walked all the way around the vehicle.
It had been a pretty brazen act, to stick a knife into
Adele's tires right out here on Main Street. Sure, I
was at the edge of town, with woods across the street
and behind my barn, too. If the streetlight hadn't
been on the fritz, something I had reported to the
town repeatedly, it would have clearly lit up half
the truck. Since the group had come in before it got
dark, I hadn't turned on the store's porch light until
my friends started to leave. Both sides of the truck
would have been in relative darkness after the sun
went down. But there was ambient light around, including from inside my store, and occasional traffic.

I'd say cars passed in front of here every few minutes, even in the evenings.

A car drove by and gave a little beep, so I waved, although I hadn't seen who it was. That was what small-town life was normally like. People were friendly. They helped each other. They greeted store proprietors standing outside at nine o'clock on a Saturday night, even when they were checking out a knife in the side of a tire.

A police car finally rolled up, red and blue lights flashing but no siren splitting the night. A fresh-faced, young officer I'd met last fall emerged from the driver's side.

"Evening, ma'am. Robbie Jordan, correct?"

"Yes."

"Patrolman George Mattheos. You called in an instance of vandalism?"

I pointed to the truck. He glanced at it and whistled. I was glad it wasn't a body he had to look at. Back in November, he'd turned positively green at the sight of one in my store. But maybe he was more experienced now.

"It's all four tires." I shone my phone light on the knife. "And there's the knife."

He squatted, pulled out a slim camera, and snapped pictures of the knife in situ from both sides. "A SOG, huh? That's not a cheap knife, by any means." He rose and photographed each tire, finishing with a shot of the truck from the rear so it included the license plate. Indiana requires a plate only on the back of vehicles.

"Is the truck registered to you?" he asked.

"No, to my aunt, Adele Jordan. She's inside. Want me to get her?"

"In a minute. I understand this building belongs to you."

"Yes." I didn't think I'd ever seen him in here for a meal. "You should come for breakfast or lunch someday. It's one of Buck's favorite restaurants."

"Lieutenant Bird has mentioned it once or twice." George struggled to keep a smile off his face.

"I bet you mean twice daily."

He finally laughed. "Yes, ma'am." He focused on the flat tires again. "What time do you estimate the tires were damaged?"

"Adele and Vera arrived at seven o'clock tonight, maybe a few minutes before. They had a group meeting here."

"What kind of group?" He had now brought out a phone and was quickly thumbing information into it.

"It's, uh, a group of friends." I didn't want to go into the anti-resort cause for the meeting, or that the group even existed. "Anyway, seven of them were here talking from seven until about nine, or whenever it was that I called this in."

He checked something. "That would have been at twenty-one-oh-seven, ma'am."

I wished he'd quit addressing me as "ma'am." I doubted I was more than five years older than him. But it seemed to be part of police culture—or southern culture—or both, to use "ma'am" or "sir" whenever possible.

"I gather you didn't witness the act," he said.

"None of us saw or heard anything. At least I don't think anyone did."

"I'd like to speak with your aunt now, if possible. Is she elderly?"

To him she would seem that way. "She's in her

seventies, but she isn't frail or anything, and she definitely has all her faculties. She was mayor of South Lick some years back."

His eyebrows went up. "Mayor Jordan? My father tells stories about her."

"One and the same. Come on in." I led the way up the steps into the restaurant.

Adele and Vera sat with two coffee mugs. I suspected Vera's held hot tea and Adele's a few fingers of Four Roses from my not-so-secret stash of Kentucky bourbon. George removed his hat and introduced himself to the ladies.

"I'm Vera Skinner, from Indianapolis." Vera smiled. "I'm down here visiting my old friend, Adele."

"Set right down here, young George." Adele patted the chair next to her.

George's neck turned pink, but he sat.

"How's your daddy? He used to help me with the sheep way back when he was younger than you are now."

"He's fine, ma'am."

Adele peered at him. "Are you out of high school, son?"

"Adele," I scolded. "Of course, he is. Officer Mattheos is a patrolman in the police department. That's why he's here."

She snorted. "I'm pulling his leg. You don't mind, now, do you, George?"

He cleared his throat. "No, ma'am. I am very sorry about the vandalism to your vehicle. I'd like to ask you and Ms. Skinner a few questions, if you don't mind."

"Why should I mind?" Adele asked. "I want y'all to catch whoever is doing these awful, unlawful things." She gave a little start, then smiled at her clever wording.

"Things, ma'am?"

"They didn't tell you about my ewe?"

"Your you, ma'am?" George looked hopelessly confused.

The kid clearly wasn't familiar with sheep. I jumped in.

"One of my aunt's female sheep—a ewe, E-W-E," I spelled, "had been tangled up in barbed wire during the night. Adele doesn't use barbed wire on her farm out on Beanblossom Road."

"I certainly do not," Adele maintained. "And I filed a report with your department, sonny. Anywho, I figure this tire attack and that sheep attack had to be carried out by the same person."

George thumbed away at his phone. He looked up again. "But you didn't see the perpetrator of either instance of vandalism?"

"No, I did not." Adele shook her head. "I wished I had. I woulda taken 'em down with my trusty Marlin, believe you me."

George cleared his throat again at the mention of her hunting rifle. "Did you happen to see either act of vandalism, ma'am?" he asked, looking at Vera.

"Not a dang thing, unfortunately."

"Thank you. My next question is for all of you. Who do you think might have had reason, however misguided, to think you had wronged them in some way and deserved retribution?" On the second "you," he pointed to Adele.

Adele and Vera exchanged glances. Guilty ones, in my estimation. George looked at me. I flipped open a hand in the direction of Adele. This was her question to answer, not mine.

It was Adele's turn to clear her throat. "You might

have heard, young man, that some of us are rightly
upset about that proposed new resort up to Greasy
Hollow. We had a protest all planned, and I'm
proud to say I'm the ringleader. What with poor
Mister DeGraaf losing his life to the hands of another,
we have regrouped and altered our plan of attack,
so to speak. So the folks you should oughta be
looking at for the vandalism are the people eager to
have that blight on the landscape get built and be up
and running." She ticked them off on her fingers.
"Fiona Closs."

"Her legal last name is McGill." I spelled it for
George even as Adele looked surprised. Did she not
know, or was she surprised I knew? We could work
that out later.

Adele went on. "Micaela Stiverton, who goes by
Mike. Lonnie Dinnsen. No idea if that's his full
Christian name or not. And Yolene Wiley, who lives
on up next to the property Fiona has already started
to raze."

George focused on his notes app, but drops of
sweat popped out on his forehead from the weather
and maybe from the stress of all this information
coming from someone who'd known him when he
was in diapers. He finished entering what Adele had
said. "Anyone else?"

Adele threw back her head and laughed. "Ain't
that enough, son? But yes, I s'pose folks unhappy with
me in my wayback past could have returned to try and
harm me. I don't really see why they would, though."

"What kinds of things happened in your past,
ma'am?" George asked.

Adele batted away the thought. "You may's well ask
what didn't happen. I just mean not every Tom,

Dinah, and Harry loved what I did as mayor. But enough people did, so I served five terms, and that's a fact."

Patrolman George stood. "I thank you all for your time this evening, ladies. I'll start the investigation and will let you know how it goes. In the meantime, I'd suggest not traveling alone at night. Lock your doors at all times when you're inside. Just to be safe."

"Yes, sir," Vera said.

Adele patted her right hip as if it held a holster and winked at me. I knew she carried a gun for self-protection. I didn't personally agree with the practice, but it was her life, and it was all legal and above board.

"I'll need to see the truck's registration before I go, please," George said.

Adele tossed me the keys, which by some miracle I caught. "Say hey to your daddy, George."

He blushed again and got out of there as fast as he could.

Chapter 33

Seven o'clock on a Sunday morning had never been so problematic. In a nod to the fabled habit some favored of sleeping in on the weekend, I opened the restaurant an hour later on Sundays. Not that I ever got a chance to practice that mythological custom. On Sundays, I allowed myself to stay in bed until, wow, six thirty. Doing that only made me feel rushed and like I'd missed part of the day. Even a dark part.

But today was not going well at all. My head hadn't cleared from the events of the last few days, with murderous questions hanging over all of us. I had a pretty good idea that Adele, along with her demonstrators, was about to get into hot water with the authorities, despite the attack last night. I'd loaned her my van to get Vera and her home after the officer had left. We'd get a tire repair person over here today if we could find one who worked on Sundays.

In addition, I knew another low-pressure system was moving in, evidenced by my clogged sinuses and my aching knee. To top it all, Turner had texted me half an hour ago that he wouldn't be in today and possibly not for the rest of the week. The woman he called *Dadiji*, his Indian grandmother who had taught him to make the spiced roasted potato dish, had entered hospice care in Indianapolis. She wasn't expected to last the week, so he and his family were heading up there to keep the death vigil.

Nevertheless, I was nothing if not a responsible business owner. By ten past seven, the first pot of coffee had brewed. I'd rolled out and cut the first pan of biscuits. The oven was preheated, and sausages sizzled gently. I'd washed the antique waffle maker, crossing my fingers as I plugged it in. I'd written NATIONAL WAFFLE DAY on the Specials board and had mixed up the batter.

But where was my uber-responsible, second-in-command, Danna? I texted her, including a note about Turner's absence, and asked if she'd be in soon. I waited, but no response zipped onto my screen, so I stashed Carmen and kept working.

I put the decaf on to brew as a text dinged in. Expecting it to be Danna, I was surprised to see Abe's avatar.

He'd written,

Good morning, Sunshine. Wishing you a glorious day.

Aww. Did he know how to make a woman smile, or what? I tapped back,

Love you, handsome. A little hectic right now, but I know it'll improve.

Next up on the pre-opening checklist was one of Danna's regular tasks, the condiment caddies. I hauled the tray out from the walk-in and restocked the packets and mini jars of jam as fast as I could. Still no sign of the dreadlocked volleyball champion otherwise known as my right-hand woman. At least the silverware was all rolled. I'd just finished setting the last table when someone rapped on the door. I checked the clock. Sure enough, it was eight already.

I hurried over to the door, favoring my knee as much as I could, and flipped the lock. Buck turned his hat in his hand and looked as worried as I'd ever seen him.

"Uh-oh. What happened now?" I turned the sign to OPEN and stepped back so he could enter. "Is Adele okay?"

"As far as I know, she is, Robbie. It's just, I got some bad news for you."

I waited, certain I looked as worried as he did. When he didn't speak, I said, "Are you going to tell me what it is?"

He heaved an audible sigh. "Danna got herself in a automobile accident."

My hand flew to my mouth. "Is she all right?"

He nodded slower than he ever had, which was saying something. "She's alive."

"Thank goodness." I let out a breath.

"But she's banged up pretty bad, I'm real sorry to say. Cuts and bruises, and mighta broke her arm. They were taking her to X-ray when I left the hospital. I told Corrine I'd head over here and tell you myself."

"Her head's okay?"

"No brain damage, nothin' like that."

"Whew." That was a huge relief. Cuts and bruises healed. Even broken arms mended. But brains often weren't so responsive and could take months of rehab to bounce back, if ever. "Wait. How did it happen?"

"She'd been out in the woods visiting that fella of hers, Isaac. Looked like her vehicle slipped on a curve due to the wet road and the dark."

Wet road? I peered out the door. Sure enough, the sky had lightened enough for me to see it was raining, but I would have been able to hear the patter and smell the clean scent of rain even if it were still dark. I'd been so involved in my own woes this morning, I hadn't even noticed.

"So no other car was involved? It was a single-car accident?"

"That would be correct. But believe you me, we're going to get her vehicle all checked out," Buck went on. "Want to be sure there wasn't none of that sabotage going on, like's been happening with Adele."

My eyes went wide. "Do you think that's what it was? Danna isn't even part of the anti-resort group."

He shrugged. "Dunno. I'm sure it was simply a accident." He cleared his throat. "I'm powerful hungry, though. Can I get me some breakfast while I'm here?"

"Of course. I'm alone, though, so when others come in it might get kind of nutty in here."

"Where's young Rao?"

I wrinkled my nose and told him where Turner had gone. "I would hire a temp, except I tried that last year. They only do office jobs. You don't happen to know a good short-order cook with some free hours, do you?"

"Can't say I do. But anything I can help you with, you let me know, okey-dokey?"

"Careful, I might take you up on that," I said, as five more people entered the store. "I just might."

Chapter 34

I was too busy to dwell on either Danna's injuries or Adele's safety. I'd already written WAFFLES on the Specials board, and several people had sounded excited about being able to order them. I didn't need the extra work of preparing waffles, but I didn't really want to set up a make-your-own station. Somebody getting a finger burned on the antique waffle iron would be big trouble—for them and for me.

Phil hadn't picked up when I'd called to ask if he could come help. I didn't want to exhaust Adele and Vera, and I knew Adele did her sheep chores in the mornings, anyway. Despite the rush, I took one more minute to text Lou and ask if she had time to rescue me. I relaxed for a few seconds when she replied: **Be there in an hour.** Which meant she was going to ride out. I'd have to make do until then, which wouldn't be until nine thirty.

"Yes, ma'am, I'll be with you in a minute," I called to a customer. I had explained to each diner as they came in that I was seriously short-staffed due to circumstances beyond my control. So far, nobody had walked out in anger. Now, I lifted the waffle iron lid too late. All four sections were way too brown and crisp. I forked the waffles onto a plate and ladled another pool of batter onto the iron, easing the lid down. The little light was supposed to signal when it was done. I hoped it worked next time. I hurriedly flipped pancakes, pushed around omelet ingredients, and turned rashers. Where were my two extra sets of arms when I needed them?

This time, the waffle was perfect. I delivered four breakfasts and poured coffee. I carried two OJs in lidded cups with straws to Mike Stiverton's twin boys. She and the kids had come in a little while ago—accompanied by Lonnie. He'd had one boy by the hand and seemed very much a part of the family. I hadn't known for sure he and Mike were a couple.

"You sure look busy this morning, Robbie," Lonnie said.

"You can say that again. Both my assistants are out. I have help coming but not until nine thirty. Who are these cuties?" I asked Mike, who hadn't smiled once since they'd arrived.

Mike frowned and stared at the table for a minute without speaking. "These are my sons, Jimbo and JonJon. Boys, this is Ms. Jordan. This is her restaurant." Her voice was tense, curt.

"Please call me Robbie, boys."

The kids were about as identical as they come, with curly red hair and freckles. One wore a green shirt and the other a red one of the same style, possibly the only way people other than their mom could tell them apart.

Green-Shirt piped up. "Robbie, are you the chef?"

His childish speech made my name come out like "Wobbie."

"She's not wearing a chef's hat, she can't be," Red-Shirt whispered to his brother.

"Don't bother her, boys," Mike said in an annoyed tone. "She's busy."

I laughed. "I'm not too busy to answer his question. Yes, I'm the chef. This baseball cap is my version of a chef's hat." I glanced around at three tables needing attention and heard a sausage pop on the grill. "And I'd better get back to cooking right now."

Lonnie exchanged a silent communication with Mike. She rolled her eyes and folded her arms, but he stood, anyway.

"I'm happy to help," he said. "I'm pretty handy at the grill. When I was in high school, I used to work as a short-order cook up to the café in Morgantown."

I stared up at him, stunned. "Are you serious?"

He bobbed his head once, down and up.

"Then you are a saint and a martyr, both, man. Sure you can spare him?" I asked Mike.

She shrugged. "Whatever. He doesn't listen to me, anyway."

Ouch.

Lonnie touched Mike's shoulder, but she twisted away from his hand. Both boys now studiously colored their place mats.

It was too bad the couple seemed to be having a bad morning, but I wasn't going to refuse the offer of improving my own bad morning. I beckoned to Lonnie. "Follow me."

A minute later he'd washed his hands and was aproned up, even though the store apron on such a big man barely covered his midsection. A spatula in both hands, he took over the grill.

"Here's the bell to ring when an order is ready, okay? And you can see, this is where we stick the order slips." I gestured to the carousel.

How I'd ever thought that either he or Mike was a murder suspect was beyond me at the moment. Now I could attend to clearing a vacated table here, pour coffee over there, and take the orders at the six-top in the corner. Lonnie and I were both beyond busy, but the pace was no longer insanity-inducing. What it did was leave me some mental space to worry about Danna. I hoped Buck was right about her brain. I hoped she wasn't in too much pain. And, selfishly, I hoped she would heal quickly and be back to work soon.

It was still rainy and raincloud-dark outside, so I had all the lights on in the restaurant. At around nine o'clock, I'd just added a couple of plates to the dishwasher and switched it on when the cord to the waffle iron made a little zapping sound. The lights in the half of the store that included the grill flickered. And went out.

Wonderful. Exactly what I didn't need this morning.

The buzz of conversation rose up like a swarm of honeybees. Amid it was a little voice saying, "Mommy, it just got darker. Is it nighttime?"

I raised both hands and my voice. "No cause for alarm, folks. I think we blew a fuse." I glanced at Lonnie. At least the grill and the stove ran on gas, so he could keep cooking. "I think we lost the waffle iron, too. Breaker box is in the basement. I'll be right back."

He unplugged the waffle iron. "Go."

I ran downstairs. Sure enough, the breaker for that side of the store was flipped. I'd never been more glad that I'd had the whole building rewired after I'd bought it. It was all modern and up to code. I flipped the breaker back and ran my hand down the line, making sure nothing else had jumped to the wrong side. All the rest were where they should be.

I hurried up to the restaurant, the lights back on. I erased WAFFLES from the Specials board as Lou clomped in wearing biking clothes, completely soaked from the rain. I went to the door to meet her, where she grinned, holding up a plastic bag of dry clothes.

"Go change in my apartment. Lonnie volunteered to staff the grill until you got here, and it's a good thing he did, too."

"Awesome. BRB." She clomped away.

I surveyed the restaurant, where for the moment I wasn't needed. I made my way back to Lonnie.

"That's your relief, my friend Lou," I said.

"I've been enjoying myself."

"Breakfast is on the house for you, Mike, and the boys."

"Thanks. Hey, did you get your phone yesterday?"

I tilted my head. How did he know? "I found it on my desk. Is that what you mean?"

"Yeah. I saw Fiona up at the building site. When I said I was coming down here, she asked me to return it to you."

After she'd slipped out the window.

He went on. "She has the same model and said she picked up yours in the ladies' room by mistake."

"So that's where I left it." Even though I couldn't remember doing that. "I appreciate the favor. It is a pretty common model."

"You were busy, so I left it on the desk. I meant to tell you, but I forgot."

Lou emerged from the back in dry jeans, a T-shirt, and tennies.

"You haven't eaten," I pointed out to Lonnie. "Make yourself whatever you want."

"I will, thank you." He poured a disk of beaten egg and started four sausages.

A couple of minutes later he was eating with Mike and the kids. I took over at the stove and Lou handled the front of the house, as restaurants called it. For Pans 'N Pancakes, it was the everywhere else of the house. I flipped and poured, sautéed and assembled, toasted and flipped some more, but my thoughts were on my phone. Fiona had had possession of it for a few hours, and I'd never gotten around to password protecting the device. Did I have anything on there I would rather she not have read? Lonnie could have done the same in the time he'd had it. I didn't have a minute free to check now, but as soon as I closed this afternoon, that would be top on my list.

Chapter 35

We blessedly had a lull at around eleven. Emily and Wayne hadn't come down for breakfast, which seemed a little odd. They were either really sleeping in or had taken themselves elsewhere to dine.

"Grab something to eat and sit down while you can, Lou." I glanced out a window. The sun was shining, so I headed to the door to open it and let air come in through the screen. "Whoa," I said. A guy was hooking Adele's truck up to a flatbed truck. She must have phoned them. I stepped out onto the porch and greeted the guy.

"Good morning, miss," he said, peering up at me. "An Adele Jordan called for me take this beauty and give 'er a new set of tires."

"Perfect. Thank you. Any idea how long it will take?"

"Should have it back in an hour. Two, tops."

"Great. Thanks for doing it on a Sunday."

"Hey, for Mayor Adele? I'd do a lot more than this, and gladly."

I smiled. Adele's reputation as firm and fair preceded her, as always. I pressed her number on my phone. As it rang, I admired the sparkle of sunlight on the washed-clean trees across the road. Steam rose up from the pavement, though, signaling a return of the humidity along with the light.

After I greeted Adele, I said, "The guy is taking the truck now. Said he'd have it back by, let's see, one o'clock at the latest."

"That's what he told me, too. We'll come in for a bite of lunch about then and return the van. Much obliged for the loan, Robbie."

"Of course. No more vandalism overnight?"

"Not a whiff, I'm happy to say. See you in a bit, hon."

Good. I was glad I'd have my van back, because I wanted to visit Danna after we closed. She and Corrine lived way across town, and it was a little far to walk. I could pick up some flowers on the way, too. I went back into the restaurant, where Lou was digging into a Kitchen Sink Omelet loaded with everything and then some.

I grabbed a couple of unclaimed sausages and made a pancake sandwich with them before I joined her.

"You work hard at this, girlfriend," she said. "I'm beat, and I've only been on shift what, two hours?"

"You get used to it. We have a break like this pretty much every morning, which helps. And I've had two on staff since last spring. The extra person makes all the difference because we can spell each other. Having them both out at once is unfortunately a perfect storm kind of thing." At least my knee had eased up considerably, feeling almost normal.

"How long will Danna be laid up?"

"I don't know. I'll find out this afternoon. And I'm not sure when Turner will be back, either. It sounded like it depended on how long his grandmother hangs on." I took a bite of my lunch.

"What are you going to do?" Lou asked. "I mean, I'd keep helping, except I have research and teaching I have to do, and a dissertation I'm supposed to be writing."

"I know, and I wouldn't expect you to provide emergency assistance beyond today. I really appreciate you rescuing me." I thought as I chewed. "I think if Turner isn't back by Tuesday I'll stay shut for another day or two." My bottom line was in pretty good shape. I could absorb a couple of days without money coming in. "I'll play it by ear." My gaze fell on my phone on the table next to me. "Lou, remember when we first met Fiona Closs up at the building site?"

Lou nodded, but the light went out of her expression. "When Gregory and I rode up there."

I nodded.

"You know, I barely knew him," Lou said. "But whenever I think about him losing his life at such a young age, relatively speaking, and in such a violent way, I want to cry all over again."

"I'm sorry." I reached out a hand across the table to squeeze hers.

"I'll be all right. It was such a shock, that's all." She stared at the table and tapped it. "I wonder if his ex-wife did it. Gregory said she was difficult." She looked up, sniffed, and sat up straighter. "What if she followed him here? Or hired a hit man to kill him out of spite?"

I nodded slowly. "That had occurred to me, too. What makes you think that?"

"No real reason. Just brainstorming. I've learned that leaving myself open to possibilities, to creative thinking, can let new ideas rise up."

"I know what you mean. Did you tell Oscar?"

"No, I just thought of it."

"I'll mention the idea to him next time I see him. He might have already checked into her."

"I suppose."

"So, I had a question I wanted to ask Fiona Closs. You said you'd joined a gym she belonged to. I thought I might drop by there this afternoon, see if I can find her."

"It's the Hard Knocks Gym. It's on the way out of Bloomington heading in this direction." Lou explained how to find it going from here. "She seems to have a boyfriend there, too. Maybe it's her trainer, but they seem a little more cuddly than that."

"Cuddly?" I asked. "That's not a word I would ever associate with Fiona."

"I know, right? She is sweet with him. Anyway, good luck with your question. She sure didn't seem that receptive to talking about her weightlifting the other day."

"That's okay. Weightlifting isn't what I want to ask her about."

A couple pulled open the screen door.

"Come on in," I called. I stood and washed my hands. No, weightlifting wasn't at all what I wanted to talk with Fiona about.

Chapter 36

"Miss?" At a few minutes past one o'clock, a burly man at the far end of the seating area waved the air like he was cleaning a window.

"Just a second, sir," I called back. I barely rescued a short stack of flapjacks from burning. The toaster held four pieces that had popped up two minutes ago and were now too cool to butter. Half a dozen order tickets gazed longingly at me from the carousel.

Lou was busing tables as fast as she could, and delivering food when it was ready, but we simply weren't keeping up. Two women who had been waiting for a table for twenty minutes had left in a huff a minute ago. I'd lost track of how many times I'd apologized. And to top it off, the humidity had zoomed back up, so the restaurant felt like a great big fragrant steam bath. And not in a good way.

From behind me came the clomp of cowboy boots. I glanced over my shoulder. *Oscar.* Exactly what I didn't need. Why wasn't he out solving the murder? I checked a ticket, then dished up two bowls of potato salad. I laid three hamburger patties and three rashers of bacon on the grill and started over on four new pieces of bread in the toaster.

"Any news, Detective?" I asked without looking at him.

"Not to speak of." He cleared his throat. "I was hoping to have a word with you."

Really? I shook my head and sprinkled grated cheese on an omelet. I added sautéed peppers and onions to another. "I won't have time until after two thirty."

"It's about—"

I twisted to my left. "Oscar, I can't," I snapped. "Got it? Take a glance around. Does it look like I have time to do anything except take care of my customers?"

He held up both hands and took a step back. "I'll wait until later."

"You do that," I muttered. I grabbed the new, still-warm toasts and applied butter. Turned sausages and bacons. Flipped burgers. Folded omelets. Dished it all up and slammed the Ready bell. Rinse and repeat. I shouldn't have lost my temper like that. He was just trying to do his job. And the sooner he solved the murder, the sooner people wouldn't wonder about a murderer being in my store or B&B.

Out of the corner of my eye I glimpsed Adele and Vera bustle in. Adele spoke with Oscar near the door. He sat in the waiting area as Adele hurried toward me. Was he really going to wait there until two thirty?

Without a word Adele washed her hands and threw on an apron. She leaned over to kiss my cheek.

"Cavalry's here, my dear. Where can I best be of use?"

"Work with Lou? And thanks." *Whew.* Adele had saved my bacon, literally and figuratively, more than once. I didn't know what I'd do without her in my life, and I didn't even want to contemplate that possibility.

By the time Buck ambled in ten minutes later, the man who'd waved his hand was happy. Three tables' worth of diners had clean, set places at which to sit. I was getting caught up on the tickets. Vera pitched in, too, putting on two fresh pots of coffee. Buck waved a greeting and took a seat next to Oscar.

"We brought your van back, Robbie," Vera said. "And as we drove up, that nice man returned the truck with all new tires, plus he ran it through the car wash."

Like many Hoosiers, she pronounced "wash" to rhyme with "borscht" minus the *T*. I had picked up some of Adele's colorful phrases in my four years in Brown County, and some of Buck's in the last year, but I hadn't started adding an *R* to wash.

"You want me to cook for a while, hon?" Vera asked. "I hate to say it, but you look like you been rode hard and put up wet."

I winced. Something about that particular colorful phrase rubbed me wrong, even though I was sure I looked as frazzled as my waffle iron's electric cord. I took a deep breath.

"Just for a few minutes so I can get to the restroom? Thanks so much, Vera." I smiled. She'd helped out in the restaurant once before, so I knew she could handle the grill. I tossed my apron in the bin and headed for the door labeled SHE ALL, a goofy label Phil added when he'd help paint the interior before I'd opened last fall. The men's room bore a sign reading HE ALL to match.

I wasn't in there long, but by the time I came out, the last of the regular customers waiting for tables had been seated, and Adele was gesturing for Buck and Oscar to occupy the sole empty two-top. I scooted over to Lou, whose arms were laden with dirty dishes.

"Dump those and take a break," I said. "Looks like we're on top of the rush."

"Finally. And thank goodness for your aunt and her friend."

"Right? They're the best."

A woman hailed me for more coffee. I donned a clean apron and grabbed the just-brewed caf and decaf pots. "You're still okay here?" I asked Vera.

"Just dandy, Robbie."

I made the rounds of mugs, ending at Oscar and Buck, where Adele was jotting down their orders.

I cleared my throat. "Sorry about earlier, Oscar. We were kind of imploding here. I still don't have time to really talk until we close."

He squinted up at me and pushed his glasses back up the bridge of his nose. "I understand. Officer Bird and I will conference here."

"Conference, nothing," Buck snorted. "We're gonna have us a decent lunch and put our heads together, that's what."

Oscar pressed his lips together but didn't comment on Buck's rephrasing. Oscar was back in his version of full-detective mode today, right down to the boots and up to the Colts cap.

"Buck, any results from checking Danna's car or the road?" I asked.

"Nope. Not yet, anywho." He glanced at Oscar. "Robbie's employee got in a single-car accident this morning. In case it might have bearing on your case, and in light of the incidents of vandalism this week, I asked for Danna's vehicle to be looked over, make sure there wasn't no tampering with it."

Vera dinged the bell. A recently seated man held his paper menu aloft like he wanted to order.

"Excuse me, gentlemen. Duty calls." I hurried back to the cooking area to deposit the coffee pots and continue with the myriad tasks of a successful restaurateur. Every time I glanced at Oscar and Buck, though, they were talking with somber, serious faces. That didn't look good.

A few minutes later, their orders were up. Adele and I arrived at the same time after Vera dinged the bell.

"I'll take these over, Adele." I glanced around. We really had gotten on top of the rush. It was one thirty and nobody new had come in after Buck. We even had a clean empty table and no wait line. "I know you and Vera didn't come in to work. It looks like we're okay for now, if you want to knock off. Both of you." I made sure Vera knew she was included.

"I confess to a bit of hunger, but we'll keep on it for another little while. What do you say, Veerie?" Adele asked her old friend.

"I'm quite enjoying myself." She beamed as she used both spatulas to push around a pile of sautéing vegetables.

"All right, then," I said. "I can't even say how much I appreciate the help. You really saved us."

"Go on with you, now," Adele said. "It was easier than falling off a potato truck short a tailgate."

I loaded up Buck and Oscar's orders and headed their way. I set down a double cheeseburger, potato salad, and an order of biscuits and gravy in front of Buck and gave Oscar his bowl of chicken soup with crackers and a dish of fruit salad.

"Oscar, when do you think you'll be done with my B&B room upstairs? The one where Gregory was staying."

"We're finished with DeGraaf's room. We have cleared it of his personal belongings and attempted to remediate the residue of our fingerprinting material."

"Good. I have new guests coming tomorrow night, and I don't really want police tape across one of the doors."

"Check. I believe we have removed it."

"Got time to set a minute now?" Buck asked me.

"I think so." I pulled over a chair from the empty table next to us and gazed at Oscar. "I wanted to tell you that my friend Lou had talked with Gregory DeGraaf about his ex-wife. Apparently, the ex is a bit nuts. Lou had the idea that maybe she killed Gregory. Or hired someone to do it. Like a hit man."

Oscar sputtered into his spoonful of soup. When he'd recovered, he said, "A hit man? What kind of movies do you girls watch?"

Girls. The term grated. I cleared my throat. "What would you call it? A hired killer?"

"It doesn't matter, but rest assured we are checking into Genevieve DeGraaf, and you can tell Ms. Perlman that." He pronounced the name JEN-eh-veev.

"Okay, thanks. Wait. Genevieve is her first name?" I glanced up at the ceiling, up where my B&B rooms were.

"It is," Oscar said. "Why?"

I lowered my voice. "This might be total coincidence, but Vera Skinner said she saw my B&B guest Wayne Babson being very affectionate with a woman in public a couple of months ago. It was in downtown

Indy, and Wayne was calling her Genevieve, but saying it like 'jeh-neh-vee-EHV'."

"That is interesting information, indeed. Thank you for sharing it. I have spoken with Mr. Babson, but I see I need to arrange a follow-up interview. And with Ms. Skinner, too."

"Wayne seems like such a nice guy. Do you think the ex might have convinced him to kill Gregory?" I asked.

"I think nothing, Ms. Jordan. I follow the information where it leads me."

"Oscar was sharing his bad news when you brought our food." Buck took a giant bite out of his cheeseburger.

I frowned and waited.

"Turns out the alibis of our various persons of interest for the time in question are pretty shaky," Oscar said.

"That's unfortunate," I said. "Who are you looking at?"

"Fiona Closs, or McGill. She lives alone near Martinsville, with no one to vouch for her. Can't find a neighbor to say either way if she was seen going out or was at home." Oscar ticked the names off on his fingers and kept his voice low enough for only Buck and me to hear. "Yolene Wiley. Also lives alone, and next door to the would-be resort, to boot. And Lonnie. Dinnsen and Micaela Stiverton appear to be involved romantically, and say they were together. Now I'll need to check into Wayne Babson, as well."

I was amazed he was sharing this with me, but I wasn't going to question it. "What about Mike's twin boys?"

"Robbie, they're four years old and unreliable

witnesses at that age," Buck said. "But anywho, they was at their grandma's that night."

I wrinkled my nose. "None of that sounds very good. That means you can't rule out any of those people, right?"

Buck nodded.

"And you haven't found any evidence, you know, like at the scene, that might lead you to someone?"

"We might have a partial print from the victim's neck." Oscar shook his head. "It's not much to go on."

"You can get fingerprints from skin?" I asked.

Buck and Oscar both nodded. It was kind of cute, sort of a Mutt and Jeff routine.

"In some cases," Oscar said.

Adele caught my eye, pointing to a diner in need of attention.

I stood. "Good luck. And thanks for sharing, Detective."

He cleared his throat. "If you happen to encounter any information you believe might be useful to the case, I would appreciate a call at your earliest convenience. I know of your past, ah, successes in this general area." He again addressed my ear, but my left one this time.

"You can count on it. I have you on speed dial in my phone." I headed for my customer. Glory be and hallelujah, as Adele sometimes said. Detective Thompson actually wanted my help.

Chapter 37

I sat in my van at three thirty that afternoon, about to head over to see Danna. Corrine had called at three o'clock to say she and Danna were home from the hospital. The store was closed and cleaned, and I'd cleaned up, too. A breeze blew the scent of something baking through the van's window. The chug of a lawnmower vied with nearby children shrieking to the sound of splashing. The soundtrack of summer anywhere.

Before I left, I needed to see if I had any text messages or e-mails that could land me in hot water with Fiona, if she'd, in fact, taken my phone on purpose, or with Lonnie, if he'd taken a look, too. I had two bad phone habits. No, make that three. One, my device wasn't password protected, so anyone picking it up could look at my life. Two, I never deleted texts. Three, I was always logged into my e-mail. All those made my life a lot easier, but greatly reduced my privacy if my cell phone was lost or stolen.

I swiped through texts to Oscar and Buck. Nope, nothing in the last week or two. We'd either talked in person or on the phone. E-mail? I didn't use it as much as I used to, and was sure I hadn't sent or received anything from the police about Gregory's murder. *Whew.* One thing I could cross off my worry list.

I started up the van and was backing out, but was still in the driveway when I hit the brakes. I'd also done Google searches on my phone. I sat there, thinking back. Yes, I'd been on the patio researching Fiona herself. Which didn't make me guilty of anything, but still. If she'd really taken my phone to snoop, she could easily find the trail of my searches. I banged the steering wheel with my hand. I couldn't do anything about it now except make darn sure I had my phone with me at all times from now on. And watch my back. I took a minute to add a password on the spot.

"Ouch, girl," I said to Danna twenty minutes later. I'd grabbed a bunch of yellow and white alstroemeria on my way, which I'd handed off to Corrine.

Danna's left arm rested in a blue sling, and the left side of her face was scratched and bruised. She half-reclined, supported by pillows, on a long couch in the family room of the house she shared with her mother. A big TV across from her showed a baseball game in progress—the Reds versus the Red Sox, it looked like—but the sound was muted. I sat in the leather recliner Corrine pointed me to.

"You look like you lost a fight with a bear or something," I said to Danna.

"I sort of did." Danna nodded. "I still don't know what happened."

Corrine hovered, the worry on her face echoing

Buck's a few hours earlier. "Buck said you slid because of the rain."

"But Mom, I drive that road in the rain all the time. I swear I wasn't speeding. So why did I end up in a ditch this time?" Danna shifted her position and winced, sucking in breath through her teeth. "Is it time for a pain pill?"

Corrine checked her watch. "Close enough." She hurried into the next room.

Danna closed her eyes for a moment. Where her face wasn't beaten up, it was pale. She opened her eyes again. "I'm totally sorry to desert you like that, Robbie. I really don't know how it happened this morning. And this sucks." She looked down at the sling.

"Don't worry about it. You focus on getting better. So, what was the diagnosis?" I indicated her sling. "Did you break your arm? Dislocate your shoulder?"

"Hairline fracture of the ulna. They can't really set it, but I'm not supposed to use it for a while. I don't know for how long. Mom got the details before we left the hospital. Anyway, it means I won't be back at work for a few weeks, at least."

"I'll manage. You get better. Turner actually wasn't there this morning, either."

"He wasn't?" Her light eyebrows headed toward her hairline. "Why not? What did you do?"

I told her about Turner's grandmother. "I don't know if he'll be back by Tuesday or not. But Lonnie Dinnsen pitched in for a while this morning, and then Lou came and handled the front, so I could cook. Adele and Vera helped later. It all worked out." An air conditioner hummed in the window. I was almost too cold in my sleeveless dress and sandals.

"Lonnie is that big dude who works at the music park?" Danna asked. "He's the one who was kind of arguing the other morning with the guy who was killed."

"That's right. Turns out he used to work a grill in Morgantown when he was in high school."

Corrine brought in a pill and a tall mug of water with a bendy straw in it. "Here you go, sweetie."

Danna gave a little laugh. "I'll get sorta wacked out in a few minutes, Robbie. I'm warning you." She popped the pill and took a long drink of water. "Love me some drugs. Hey, are they any closer to catching whoever killed the lawyer dude?"

"I don't know," I said. "Not that I've heard. Corrine, do you have any inside intel?"

Corrine perched on the arm of the couch at the far end from her daughter. "I do not. It'd be awful nice if old Oscar got his rear end in gear and made an arrest. Not good for the town to have somebody on the loose, so to speak."

"Not good for anybody," I said.

Danna's eyes drifted shut. Time for me to go. When I stood, Corrine did, too. She beckoned to me, so I followed her into the kitchen. The room was decorated in cozy country style, with fruit-bedecked wallpaper, gingham curtains, ball jars wrapped in checkered ribbons holding whisks and wooden spoons, and what looked like a varnished reclaimed barn board countertop.

"I have to tell you, Robbie, I am suspicious about my girl's accident." Corrine spoke in a near whisper, leaning against the counter with arms folded. "She's a good driver. Sure, it was dark and raining, but to miss a turn she knows like the back of her pretty little hand?" She shook her head, hard. "Didn't happen. I told Buck in no uncertain terms I want him to check out her car for tampering, and that section of road, too. Somebody could have spread grease on it or some such thing like that."

"But why attack Danna?"

"I don't know. It's not like she was involved with anything. Not the resort, not the investigation." She shook her head hard, her big hair flying.

"I can't think of a reason, either. Anyway, Buck was in the restaurant a couple of hours ago, but he didn't have any news about the car or the road yet."

"I swear, Robbie, something fishy is going on."

"But what kind of fishy? I mean, you must have heard about the attack on Adele's sheep and then on her truck last night."

"I did, and I was shocked to hear it."

"And you also know Adele's the ringleader against the development. It doesn't excuse the vandalism, but there's a reason for it in somebody's sick mind. Danna, though? She's been minding her own business, as far as I know."

"That's what she says, and I raised my daughter to be truthful. Well, we'll see what ol' Buck turns up. Mark my words, Robbie. I mean to get to the bottom of this. Because nobody attacks Corrine Beedle's little girl. And I mean no one."

Chapter 38

Lou's directions to the Hard Knocks Gym were good ones. I pulled into a nearly full parking lot and parked next to a battered green pickup. Musing as I drove on why someone would attack Danna had netted me exactly nothing. It had to have been a simple accident. Either that, or something had already been wrong with her car.

I wouldn't have thought a gym would be so popular on a summer Sunday afternoon, but then, what did I know? I wasn't a gym person. I got my workouts on my bicycle, and as soon as I arrived home today, a long hard ride was my plan for the last daylight hours, now that my knee was better. Even though I didn't think I had anything on my phone I wouldn't have wanted Fiona to read other than my search history, I still wanted to check her out. Maybe she would act guilty about the phone or mention something she could have learned only from my phone. I didn't have any particular plan of how I was going to approach her, but I could wing it.

I was almost at the door of the low, windowless building when it swung open. Yolene Wiley burst through, the skin on her face mottled, her hands clenched into fists. She stopped short when she saw me and blinked.

I wouldn't have pegged her as the gym type, given her smoking and a body that wasn't in the prime of physical fitness, but then again, what do I know?

"Hi, Yolene. Did you have a good workout?" I smiled.

"I don't work out, Robbie." She wore red Capris and a blue blouse, and didn't carry a gym bag, either.

So why was she here? It seemed rude to ask her. I laughed. "I don't either, at least not in a gym. I came to see if I could find Fiona here."

"She's here, all right." She crossed her arms and pinched her mouth with the expression of a person who had tasted a bite of too-old catfish.

"You don't seem all that pleased. Was she rude to you or something?"

"Or something." Yolene barked a harsh laugh. She sent an errant pebble flying with the toe of her loafer as if she wished she were kicking Fiona down the parking lot and into outer space. "She don't understand that folks like me, we're living on the edge. All's I asked her for was a small advance on the sale of my land." She gazed at the door, and then shook her head like she was shaking off the conversation.

"So she hasn't actually bought the land yet?"

"She has the core parcel under agreement from somebody else."

Fiona must be clearing what Yolene called the core parcel, which could be as small as half an acre. "I gather she said no to the advance?"

She made a face like she'd smelled a couple of scared skunks. "You gather correct, Robbie. Not only that, she laughed at me."

An advance on the sale of property for a resort that hadn't yet gained final approval to even be built. I didn't blame Fiona for refusing Yolene, but there was no call to be rude about it.

"That's no good," I said.

"It ain't been my day." Yolene covered her mouth and coughed her deep, rattling cough. "That weirdo detective was asking me all kinds of rude questions, too."

About her alibi, no doubt. "He's a good detective."

"He don't got no call to be poking his nose into my business." She glared at me and set her big fists on her waist.

I held up both hands. "Actually, he does. But you didn't kill Gregory DeGraaf, right?"

"'Course I didn't." She lifted her chin and stared out at the road. "What a thing to say."

"Then what's the problem? He won't be able to find any evidence that you did. You answer his questions. And that's it."

"It's not exactly like that. Anyway, I best be going." She stepped gracefully past me, then stopped and turned back. "Say, that burger you cooked up the other day was real delicious. I'm going to make a practice of dining at your cute store after I get my money."

"Thanks. I'm glad." I watched her head for the green truck parked next to my van. So, it was hers. Now that I thought of it, the vehicle was the one I'd seen at her house. What I hadn't seen that day was the long-gun rack hanging in the cab's rear window.

I pulled open the door to the gym, but in my brain

was the way Yolene had not looked me in the eye when she denied killing Gregory.

Once inside, my brain had nowhere to go but here. Loud music with a steady beat played. A buff man in a tank top, exercise pants, and heavily tattooed arms stood behind a counter. Beyond him was a room full of bodies hard at work. Weights clanked. A jump rope slapped a mat repeatedly. A man lifting impossibly huge weights grunted. Mirrors lined the walls, and the smell of sweat permeated the air.

"Can I help you?" the guy behind the desk asked. He looked me up and down.

I had changed into a swingy sundress after work, and I wasn't carrying a gym bag. Mine was no more workout attire than Yolene's had been.

"Did you want to buy a membership?" He picked up a brochure.

He had those rings called gauges set into his ear lobes, the ones that looked like something an African ethnic group did. No matter the name, it made me feel a little nauseous to look at them, the same way tongue piercings did.

"No, thanks," I said. "I'm looking for Fiona McGill. Or Closs. I'm not sure which name she goes by here." I peered into the room but didn't spy her.

He pointed to a drinking fountain on the far wall. "There she is."

And so she was. "I'm going to say hello for a minute, okay? I won't be long."

When he nodded, I hurried over while she was taking a break.

I cleared my throat. "Fiona, hi," I ventured.

She straightened and turned. Her skin gleamed

with sweat, and there was a lot of skin. She wore a red sports bra and stretchy black shorts that were no more than trunks, barely extending down the tops of her thighs. Black knee socks sprouted out of flat, low-profile exercise shoes, and a black headband held back hair damp from her efforts. I tried not to stare at her muscled abdomen, her thick strong thighs, or the defined muscles of her shoulders and arms.

"Looks like it's my day for visitors," she said.

"Yeah, I ran into Yolene in the parking lot."

"So what brings you here, Robbie? Unless you were following Yolene?" She raised a single eyebrow.

"What? No, I wasn't following her. As I said, I ran into her outside."

Fiona nodded as if she didn't believe me and folded her arms, which made sinews on her neck stand out. "I know your reputation as an amateur detective. Do you have evidence against Yolene for the murder?"

I stared at her. "No, I don't. And I'm not a detective, really. I came here because I wanted to thank you for returning my phone," I said. "Lonnie told me this morning he left it on my desk yesterday."

"Sorry about the mix-up. Your phone looks exactly like mine." She lifted a shoulder and dropped it. "He was up at the site bugging me again, so I asked him to take it back to town when he went."

"What was he bugging you about?"

"A job, what else? He thinks I should hire him on now to prevent any more crime from happening up there."

"He'd have to camp out around the clock to ensure that, wouldn't he?"

She snorted. "That's not going to happen. I bet he killed that lawyer himself just to make his case."

Yikes. Talk about going to extremes. "You do?"

"I do. And I told the detective as much." She scrunched up her face. "Do you know him, that Thompson? What a kook." She and Yolene had at least one thing in common: a bad opinion of Oscar.

"I know he's good at what he does."

"Yo, McGill," a man called from across the gym. "You coming back or what?"

She waved her index finger at the guy. "Sorry, Robbie. I have to get back to my practice. There's an important competition next week."

"Good luck. And thanks again." I leaned against the wall and watched as she lay on her back on a bench, her head nearly under a bar on a stand, her feet on the ground on either side of the bench. The bar held thick, two-foot-diameter disks on either end. A man with biceps the size of my thighs—and I have a cyclist's muscular quadriceps—stood at the head. Fiona tensed her abdominal muscles and lifted the bar off the stand as the man guided it. She lowered it nearly to her chest and pushed it up again. Her back arched and her legs shook with the effort. She was serious about lifting and way strong enough to strangle someone. Maybe it wasn't any different from me being serious about pushing myself on the hills.

I thanked gauge-guy and headed out. As I drove home, I realized I hadn't learned a thing about what Fiona might have gleaned from my phone. My suspicions were probably baseless, and it had happened exactly like she said it had. She picked up the wrong phone, and when she realized her mistake, she returned it.

Then I thought about Fiona's claim that Lonnie might have killed Gregory to highlight the need for security. She hadn't sounded like she was going to take him up on his suggestion of an early hire. I hoped a man's life hadn't been senselessly lost over such a plan.

Chapter 39

By five thirty, I was out on my bike, doing what I loved nearly best in the world. I pumped up a hill, cruised along a flat section, and coasted down a slope that seemed to last forever. To my relief, my knee seemed to be holding up fine. I slowed as I rode by the funky log cabin owned by a woodswoman who carved whimsical statues out of tree trunks. A goofy-looking bear she always decorated for the season stood at road's edge. Right now it wore a red bikini top and had a beach towel wrapped around its waist, with a paperback mystery tucked into a big paw and a floppy straw hat on its head.

Usually, riding cleared my mind and was the best de-stressor ever invented. Today, though, I couldn't shake the thoughts of Gregory's murder, still unsolved as far as I knew. At least Oscar had been talking to people like Yolene and Fiona, as well as Lonnie and Mike. Mike sure had been out of sorts this morning. Because she and Lonnie had had a disagreement? Or she was worried she'd be out of a job? Or maybe she was tense because she was trying to avoid being arrested for murder. Lonnie had been congenial and generous, offering to help cook, but the seed of suspicion Fiona had planted was a stubborn one. Would he really have killed a man to show the need for security at the resort site? Was he that hard up for work?

I slowed for a crossroad that didn't have a stop sign, checked both ways, and rode on. With a start, I realized I was on the road to Isaac's, where Danna must have had her accident. Had the police found anything suspicious on the road? The sun had come out before noon, so they should have been able to check. I slowed way down as I rode, but I couldn't see any grease. It would help if I knew where she'd gone off the road, but I didn't.

Or . . . maybe I did. I braked to a stop. Low vegetation to the side of the pavement was matted and tamped down here, where it wasn't elsewhere. I climbed off my bike, laying it down. Yes, tire tracks had left prints in the ground. The road here was on a kind of berm, and it sloped down on this side a few feet, with woods several yards away. Danna had said she'd slid into a ditch, but it wasn't exactly that. I turned my back to where her car had gone and squatted, peering at the road's surface. My biking gloves were fingerless models, really more pads for my palms. I swiped a finger across the pavement and rubbed it against my thumb. It wasn't oily or greasy, so I remounted and pedaled on. It was a stretch to imagine why anyone would sabotage the road or Danna's car, anyway.

After another twenty minutes, I came to the turnoff for the resort. I could do one more steep climb, look around up there, and then head for home. I still had nearly an hour and a half of daylight, and

I seriously doubted a murderer would be lurking at
the building site. First, I texted Lou and Phil where I
was headed, just in case, then I put my head down
and drove the power of my legs into the pedals.
When I got to Yolene's, I glanced over, but her green
truck wasn't there, not that I had planned to stop in.
This was an exercise ride, not a social tour.

I was breathing hard from the ascent, but I was
almost to the site. I rounded the bend and slowed
on the dirt road. The chain was across the entrance
again. This time, yellow police tape stretched the
width of the opening, too. I rode up to the chain and
got off my bike, leaning it on the post. If Fiona really
wanted security, she should erect a tall fence with a
gate and keep the gate locked. That chain was a barrier in name only. Maybe she expected the ring of
woods and the single strand of barbed wire to keep
people out. The trees, mostly deciduous with some
evergreens mixed in, weren't that densely packed.
Anybody could wander in from any direction.

The tape was easy to cross, too. Gregory was killed
almost three days ago. Could the police still have evidence here they were looking for? Feeling only mildly
guilty, I ducked under both barriers.

Despite sweating from my ride and the still-warm
air of the day, I shivered. The last time I'd been here,
Gregory had been alive and well. The last time Lou
had ridden up here, she'd found him dead. I leaned
against a tree and patted its solid, rooted trunk, a
comfort in the face of human evil. That evil had been
physically present right here only two days ago. The
trees would live on until they fell from disease, natural disaster, or heavy machinery, as was the case in the
clearing. Gregory had no more life to live.

I started to pick my way around the perimeter of the clearing. I wished I knew exactly where at the site Lou had found his body. I could search the area for evidence the police might have missed, as they had in Gregory's room. Except this was way too big of an area to search without being able to zero in on a few square feet. Stumps and cut brush still remained around the edges, and where the wood had been cleared away, the ground was uneven from large tire treads and the work of some large machine. I didn't really know one big construction vehicle from another, but I'd heard words like excavator, backhoe, and front loader, in addition to the old standby, bulldozer. Which one or ones they'd used here was anybody's guess.

I wasn't sure why I was walking. A tribute to Gregory, maybe, bringing human kindness back to the place where it had gone missing. I hummed an aria softly and tried to walk without my feet making a sound, so I wouldn't disturb any birds in the vicinity.

As I walked, I spied something white nearly hidden under a branch and squatted to check it out. My eyes narrowed. It was a cigarette butt, white and tan. Surely Fiona didn't smoke, not with her athleticism. But Yolene did. I reached out my hand to pick it up but snatched my fingers back in time.

The police tape. Maybe they were still searching up here. Maybe this was a clue, a piece of evidence. I had no business touching or disturbing it. I maneuvered my hand into the zippered pocket in the back of my shirt. I drew out my cell phone and snapped a couple of shots of the butt, then stood and took a picture across the clearing toward the entrance, so I could explain to Oscar where I'd found the smoked cigarette. I took a minute to text the photos to him.

> Saw this cigarette butt at the building site across
> from the entrance. Not sure if it's important
> but thought you should know. Yolene Wiley is
> a smoker.

Yolene also lived down the road and had a keen interest in the resort project. Simply because I found a cigarette butt here didn't mean it was hers. And if she'd been the one to drop it, it didn't mean she dropped it after murdering Gregory. At this point, I didn't care if Oscar thought I was being foolish by sending him stuff like these pictures. I was simply trying to be a good citizen. I resumed my walk.

I was halfway around, when the hair on my arms stood up and my scalp prickled. I halted. And listened. I didn't think I'd heard anything to justify feeling so alarmed, and I still didn't. So what was spooking me?

Slowly, I turned toward the entrance. It was as empty as I'd left it. No vehicle. No bike except mine. No person had appeared. Still, I felt sure someone was watching me. It was an exceedingly creepy feeling. I'd added a 911 speed dial button on the main screen of my phone last year. In case I needed it. Was now one of those times? My throat was thick, but I tried to swallow down my nerves.

"Just walk calmly back to your bike," I whispered to myself, "and ride home. That's all you have to do." The phone was a reassuring weight in my hand. I could fake a call. I'd tried that the last time I'd been confronted with a murderer, but the killer had seen through me. I didn't want to call the police for real unless I had a reason to. Surely, I was imagining that a person was hidden, observing me. Wasn't I? Otherwise I was in deep trouble. I cleared my throat and fake-tapped some numbers on the phone. I held it to my ear and kept walking. The trees weren't the cavalry or anything, but they felt like good backup, so I stayed close instead of walking straight across the middle of the clearing.

"What?" I said out loud. "You're driving up to the resort site, Buck? Good idea. I'm up there now, but I'm about to get on my bike and ride home."

I pretended to listen, nodding a couple of times as I walked. I was a quarter of the way around from the cigarette butt and maybe two minutes from my bike.

"Okay, great. I'll probably pass you on the road. Make sure you wave." I nodded some more. Nearly there. The hairs on my arms had not stood down from high alert.

A crack resounded behind me. I screeched and dove for the ground. I lay there, heart jackhammering in my chest. I twisted to look. Nothing. Nobody had emerged from the woods holding a weapon. No more cracks.

I brushed myself off. I stood, blew the dirt off my phone, and held it to my ear again.

"No, nothing's wrong." As I gazed at where the sound had come from, a fat squirrel leapt onto a dead branch on a white ash tree. As he leapt off, the branch cracked and fell. That was the crack I'd heard. Not attempted murder.

"Well, would you look at that? It was only a branch." I laughed, but the sound was weak, even to my ears. I said my fake good-bye, stored the phone, and mounted my bike. I forced myself not to rush, not to reveal the nerves that had me nearly unhinged. I bumped along the road to Yolene's house, with the green truck back in the driveway. I didn't see Yolene.

As I wheeled down the mountain, I vowed to never, ever again go alone to a deserted hilltop crime scene.

Chapter 40

My ride, terrifying noises notwithstanding, had given me a hunger for a big salad. I would be dining alone again tonight, since Abe was still away, although he'd texted me that he would call later. In hot weather, sometimes a fresh California salad with avocado and grilled shrimp topped by a sesame-orange dressing was the only food that called to me.

The small supermarket in South Lick was surprisingly well stocked, even though its name of Quicky Mart always made me think of the convenience store on *The Simpsons.* By now, I knew the owner of this real one—unlike on the show, he wasn't named Apu—well enough that he let me park my bike inside, so I didn't have to weigh myself down by carrying a lock on my rides. Before I went in, I texted Buck—for real—that I thought someone might have been watching me up at the resort site. He could act on it or ignore as he wished.

I clomped my bike shoes over to the produce section, hoping against hope I could find a perfectly ripe avocado. The avocados were on the end of an island holding bins of tomatoes of all sizes on one side and various citrus fruits on the other. I glanced up to see Barb down at the other end, with a full cart of groceries. Her arms were folded, and she shook her head at a tall woman with her back to me. A woman with short, red hair under a yellow ball cap, who looked a lot like Mike Stiverton.

"No," Barb said. "I told you, Ms. Stiverton. There's a process, and it's out of my power to rush it through. I might be the chair of the planning board, but I'm not the governor."

Mike turned away in frustration, rubbing the back of her neck, her jaw clenched. She caught sight of me.

"Robbie, come help me talk some sense into this woman." Mike gestured me over. "She isn't listening to me."

I approached the two.

"Robbie, good to see you," Barb said. "Will you tell Ms. Stiverton that approvals take time? I can't rush them along." She smiled politely.

"And you tell her we need that project to go forward, and soon," Mike urged.

"Hang on, ladies." I held up both hands, palms out. "I don't know the first thing about the planning board, but I do know neither of you is particularly hard of hearing. Sounds like you've both expressed your views already, am I right?" I waited for each of them to nod.

"But there has to be something you can do, Ms. Bergen," Mike said to Barb. "My rent is due, and Fiona won't pay me for the work I've already done until the project is signed off." Mike's cart was not laden. It held a gallon of milk, a box of store-brand cereal, a loaf of squishy bread, and a package of hot dogs. "Also, I thought Fiona gave a big donation to the no-kill shelter. Don't you run the volunteers there? I thought it was like your favorite charity."

Barb blinked. Her polite smile didn't waver, but her eyes were no longer taking part, and her nostrils flared ever so slightly. "You may tell Ms. Closs that bribery will get her exactly nowhere. If she wishes to support the cause of homeless animals, I applaud her. But it does not, and will never, affect how I conduct the business of the town. Now, if you'll both excuse me, I need to get dinner on the table. Good evening, Ms. Stiverton, Robbie." She maneuvered her cart around Mike and headed for the checkout counter at the front of the store.

Watching her go, Mike's shoulders slumped.

"I'm sorry, Mike."

"It's not your issue. I can't seem to get ahead." She gazed at me. "I had a lot riding on that job."

"Maybe it's time to look for another one?"

She set her hands on her hips, her face suddenly livid. "Where do you get off telling me what to do? What do you know?" She stepped into my personal space. "You have a successful business. You don't have kids, or a worthless piece of manure for an ex-husband who doesn't contribute a penny to their care and feeding."

I took a pace backward and dislodged a lemon with my elbow. It fell and rolled toward Mike's feet. She ignored it, instead taking another step toward me. She wagged a finger in my face.

"You have it easy, Robbie Jordan, and don't you forget it. Taking over our country store and making it into your chi-chi restaurant. Coming in here in your expensive bike clothes like you own the town. Well, you don't. I was here before you, and I'll always be here. I'm only trying to keep my head above water, which gets harder every year."

Whoa. "Our" store had been a wreck that was about to be closed when I took it over, and since I'd opened, I'd heard only positive words about how good it was for the community. I did my best to serve decent, wholesome food, not chi-chi at all. It wouldn't do any good to tell her to calm down. That kind of admonition almost always backfired. And telling her how hard I worked to make the restaurant a success wouldn't go over well, either.

"I know I'm very fortunate." I sidled sideways with the oranges and grapefruits to my back, to put some distance between us. I grabbed a grapefruit as I went, not sure if I was going to need something to defend myself with. "And I hope your situation improves soon, I really do." Mike must be scared with the prospect of no job and a family to take care of. I cleared my throat and glanced around. Several other shoppers were staring at us. I looked back at Mike. I opened my mouth but shut it again. I didn't have anything left to say.

She shook her head in disgust and strode off, pushing the meager collection of inexpensive foods for her family. If she was so bad off, how could she afford to eat breakfast at my store more than once? Lonnie must have treated her the first time, and I'd comped all their meals when they'd come in with the boys. I replaced the grapefruit. It wouldn't have been much of a self-defense weapon, anyway.

Wanda appeared at my side, in her sheriff's uniform. She was carrying a red onion and a big ripe tomato in a blue plastic shopping basket. "Everything okay here, Robbie?" She kept her voice low and gazed after Mike.

"Yeah, sort of. Did you hear all that?"

She nodded. "That girl's had a tough few years."

Oscar appeared behind her, carrying a pound of hamburger and a package of buns. Looked like a couple of somebodies were going to have a cozy cookout.

"Hi, Detective," I said.

He acknowledged me with a nod of the chin but didn't return my greeting.

"Mike's smart, but life keeps throwing her punches," Wanda continued. "She was even going to college. Then her pappy died, and she had to go to work to help support her younger siblings. She trained as a heavy equipment operator but had to step down for a while when she was carrying the twins."

"Sounds like the boys' father isn't much help," I said.

"No, he is most definitely not much help at all. We all went to school together back in the day. He was a jerk then, and he hasn't changed. Never did know what she saw in him." She made a *tsking* sound. "And now she's having trouble finding work."

"She seems desperate," I said. And desperate people sometimes did desperate things.

Chapter 41

I sat at the round table in my kitchen with a brain full of thoughts as the day's last rays of sun slanted through the west-facing window. My salad had been everything I'd wanted it to be and then some. But the joy in tasting perfectly grilled shrimp and avocado with sections of clementines over mixed greens? It was tinged with the memory of my encounter with Mike. She had gone from pleading to dejected to furious in the space of five minutes. Wanda had confirmed how tough life was for Mike. Was it tough enough to drive her to murder to keep a job?

I stared at my plate and forked up the last shrimp with a piece of sweet seedless citrus. Birdy, who had been dozing with ears alert, popped open his eyes.

"What do you think, Birdman?"

He trotted over to his dish and lapped up the last morsels of his wet-food treat. He looked up at me hopefully, but I shook my head.

"Sorry, buddy. That's all you get." I popped the final piece of avocado into my mouth. In my opinion, there was no more perfect food than this, but then, I was a Californian. I admit to being biased. I set down the plate for Birdy to get every speck of shrimp flavor off it and poured myself a second glass of a buttery Alexander Valley chardonnay. It was time for a puzzle, especially since I didn't need to do breakfast prep. Thank goodness for my weekly day off. Tonight, I was going to create a puzzle, not solve somebody else's. I assembled a clipboard, a sharpened pencil, a ruler, and the pad of graph paper I always kept at hand.

I started with the mental puzzling I'd done yesterday. Had it been only yesterday? I yawned. My days had been packed lately, but I forged ahead. I knew my mind wouldn't calm down enough for me to sleep if I didn't get all my thoughts about the murder organized and on paper.

I started with headings of CLUE AND ANSWER and started to jot down what I knew. I could do the grid later. In the CLUE column, I listed VICTIM, MEANS, MOTIVE, OPPORTUNITY, and SUSPECTS. In the ANSWER column, I began with Gregory DeGraaf as the victim. While there was no question about the fact that he had been the victim, I wondered again, why him in particular? Adele was a much more public opponent of the project. I was immensely relieved and grateful she had not lost her life to a killer, but that same killer had to have a reason he or she picked Gregory instead.

Perhaps his death was unrelated to the resort. Gregory easily could have enemies from past cases he'd taken. He'd only become involved in the anti-resort group the day before. Was his death what they called a crime of opportunity? The murderer could have heard about his joining the protest group. Maybe Fiona maintained an e-mail or instant message group where the various people interested in the project could communicate. I didn't know how anyone outside the protest group would have learned of Gregory's interest, but it was certainly possible. My brain idly moved to espionage. Perhaps Adele's group had been infiltrated by someone who pretended to want to stop the resort, but who was actually in Fiona's back pocket.

"Let's stay connected with reality, Jordan," I scolded myself. I didn't have a reason in the world to think someone was spying on Adele and her gang. Not that any of her group—all friends of mine except Emily— would be secretly working for the other side.

It didn't really matter how the murderer had learned of Gregory's involvement. When he happened to show up at the building site alone, a person who had every reason in the world to be at the site could have stepped out of the woods and ended his life. I shuddered, imagining it.

I added Strangulation next to MEANS and stopped. Putting your hands around someone's throat and choking them to death was a method anyone big and strong enough could use. It didn't have to be planned, unlike poison, or a gun, or other more complicated ways to kill people that I'd read about. Little bits of arsenic in your husband's eggs every day for months. Liquid nicotine in a cup of coffee. Mixing heavy doses of acetaminophen and hard liquor. All of which required deciding to kill someone and obtaining the necessary tools to carry it out. Strangling someone? Could be a snap decision.

Now I stared at the word MOTIVE. The motive overall had to be to keep the resort project moving

forward. Why else kill the lawyer engaged in helping
the opposition? But the individual reasons for wanting him gone depended on who did the deed. I
erased the word MOTIVE for now and moved on to
OPPORTUNITY. That was easy. An isolated construction
site on a dark morning.

Now for SUSPECTS. And back to MOTIVE. I copied
the SUSPECTS entry three more times and added a
number, a slash, and the word MOTIVE to each.

SUSPECT ONE/MOTIVE:	Fiona Closs McGill Fear of losing her investment
SUSPECT TWO/MOTIVE:	Lonnie Dinnsen Security job
SUSPECT THREE/MOTIVE:	Yolene Wiley Money from land sale
SUSPECT FOUR/MOTIVE:	Mike Stiverton Construction job

I tapped the pencil on the pad of paper. For the
first three suspects, the benefit of the resort was ongoing. Fiona could recoup the money she'd put into
the project. Lonnie could have full-time gainful employment instead of seasonal. Yolene would have
money to live on and be able to get out of debt. But
Mike? After the resort was built, she would again be
out of a job, unless she could slide into maintenance
manager or something. Maybe she and Fiona had
already talked about that.

But what about Wayne Babson? Had Oscar inter-
viewed him again? Oscar had said he was going to want
to speak with Emily, too. Wayne, unlike the others,

didn't have any reason except malicious intent to sneak out in the dark of the morning to a building site. Surely Emily would know if he had. And if she hadn't already learned of his affair, she likely knew now. Otherwise Oscar wouldn't have a reason in the world to suspect Wayne. I realized I hadn't seen either Wayne or Emily all day. Usually my B&B guests popped in for a meal or to ask a question.

I jumped when Carmen buzzed. I peered at the display and smiled. "Hey, handsome," I greeted Abe.

"Hi, sugar," he said. "How are things?"

"Crazy. Sad. Exhausting."

"Whoa, really? Are you all right? What's going on?"

I blew out a breath. "I'm fine. But Abe, one of my B&B guests was murdered Friday morning."

"In one of your rooms?"

I heard the concern in his voice. "No. Out at the proposed resort site."

"The so-called Closs Creek?"

"Right. Lou was the one who found his body, and life has been wild ever since. Adele has organized a group opposed to the resort, and one of her sheep was attacked Friday night, plus all four of her tires were slashed right in front of my store last evening. Four people seem kind of desperate for the project to go through. The man who was killed was a lawyer, and he was helping Adele's anti-resort gang."

"And you're probably looking into the murder. I'm really sorry I'm not there to support you, hon."

"I appreciate that. I know Detective Thompson is doing his best, but as far as I know he hasn't made an arrest in the case. He's looking at anyone who might have had a reason to kill Gregory, and apparently none of them has an alibi." I told him about Danna and about Turner being out, too. "So it's been a zoo here. I'm glad I have tomorrow off."

"You're going to stay safe. Keep your door locked. Not do anything risky, right?"

"Girl Scout's honor." I drained my glass of the last sip of wine. "I guess I did one thing kind of stupid today. I went for a walk around the clearing at the resort site. At one point, I could swear somebody was watching me, even though I couldn't see a soul."

"Hmm." Abe fell silent for a moment. "I know those woods pretty well. I think there's a path that goes up the hill from the side opposite the access road. Do you know Greasy Hollow Road?"

"Sure."

"It dead-ends at a wide spot in the creek. We used to ride our bikes to go fishing there when I was growing up. My buddy and I explored all the woods. As I recall, the path leads up from that spot but on the other side of the creek. An old guy had a hunting blind up there, and he always kept the path cleared."

"Does anybody live out there?"

"Nobody did when I was a kid. Not sure about now, and, of course I don't even know if the path has been maintained."

"Well, I can tell you one thing. I'm not going up there alone again. It creeped me out."

"Sounds like a plan. Listen, Robbie, I better go. We have homework for tomorrow."

"I didn't even ask how you are. I'm sorry."

When he laughed, the pang of missing him hit me hard. I loved that laugh and the man who owned it.

"I'm fine. This course is super intensive, though. Only two more days. I'll be home Tuesday night."

"Go study. I miss you buckets."

We exchanged phone kisses and disconnected. Nope. I would not be doing anything risky. Girl Scout's honor.

Chapter 42

"It's a go, Robbie! The march is on, this morning at nine." Adele's voice on the phone sounded more excited than I'd ever heard her.

I yawned. "That's good." It had been too hot to sleep well, and now at seven thirty I was already dragging.

"You gonna join us or what? We need all the support we can get."

"Adele," I began, then paused, searching for the most diplomatic way to refuse. I didn't get the chance.

"Roberta, you need to learn how to do an act of civil disobedience." Her words rushed out. "Now, listen up. We're going to all meet up at your store at eight and go from there."

What? "I'm closed today."

"I know that. I'll put the coffee on and such. You go ahead and unlock the door. Maybe soaking up some of our energy will convince you. Anyway, see you in a few minutes."

"A few minutes?" I screeched. "Are you on the phone while you're driving?"

She laughed. "No, silly. Vera's driving. All righty, then. Bye-bye."

I stared at the disconnected call. I'd better get into

the restaurant and get ready for the unstoppable tsunami named Adele Jordan. At least I was washed and dressed, with shorts and a T-shirt being my at-home summer uniform for my day off. I'd done my morning sit-ups and downed my first cup of coffee.

"Come on, Birdy. I need reinforcements on my side."

He paused in his bathing, with one foot up over his head, to regard me. Food apparently not forth-coming, he resumed the task at hand. But when I unlocked the door from my apartment to the store, he streaked by in a black-and-white flash.

I started coffee. It would have been generous to also start a batch of biscuits, but this was my day off. Coffee was all they were getting.

True to her word, Adele was at the door four min-utes from when she'd called, with Vera grinning right behind her. I glanced behind them at the back seat full of hand-lettered placards reading things like NO TO CLOSS CREEK, KEEP BROWN COUNTY BEAUTIFUL, SAY NO TO THE RESORT, and DEPORT THE RESORT!

"Come in," I said. "The coffee's on."

Adele kissed my cheek and bustled in.

Vera held out a wide, shallow box. "Donuts."

"Thanks." I was a bit too fond of a donut every now and then.

"This is so exciting, don't you think?" Vera's cheeks were pink. "A real political action."

"If you say so." I left the heavy door open, so the morning air could come in through the screen. I hoped people not part of the protest group wouldn't also come in and then ask for breakfast.

By eight o'clock the gang was all there, coffee and donuts at the ready, and I'd locked the door behind them so your average person on the street wouldn't think I was open for business.

Emily and Wayne trotted downstairs. On my days off, I offered my guests a self-serve breakfast menu. I set cereal, yogurt, and fresh fruit out on the counter, as well as bread and the toaster. I started coffee for them and let that suffice. This morning, Wayne helped himself to cereal, yogurt, and fruit and headed to a table to read a newspaper as he ate.

Emily sat with Lou, Martin, Phil, Don, and Vera around my biggest table, with Adele standing at the head. I perched on a two-top nearby, my feet on a chair. I checked Emily's face. She didn't look any different. Certainly not like she'd been weeping over her husband's infidelity. She poured herself a cup of coffee and took a cinnamon-sugar donut.

Adele spread a paper map out on the table. "Here's the plan, people. We'll drive to this spot where the road to the resort branches off." Adele poked her finger at the map. "We park and then march out onto Route 46 with our signs. It's a nice straight stretch there, and we'll be able to see cars coming from both directions. Vera and I got the signs all ready. We'll hold them up and stop traffic."

"Do you still have news people coming?" Martin asked.

"*Brown County Democrat*'s all I could get," Adele answered in a tone that implied the bigger newspapers were fools not to cover the event. "They said they'd send out a photographer, though, so maybe we'll go all viral and such."

Martin nodded in all seriousness. I suppressed a

smile. I doubted either of them actually knew what "going viral" meant.

"I, for one, am glad to be part of this demonstration," Emily said. "Who needs another resort if it comes at the cost of harming the environment?"

"Right on, girl." Vera gave her a high five.

Don's brow was furrowed. "What if the drivers get mad at us? Or a resort supporter comes after us?"

"Son, we simply sit on the pavement and smile." Adele modeled the smile. "Do you really think somebody's going to try and run us over?"

Don nodded, and the expression of worry didn't leave his face.

"Or what if someone is going too fast to stop?" I asked. "People tend to speed down that section of the road."

Adele gave me the stink eye. "Robbie, I said it's a long straight stretch. Vehicles will be able to see us in time."

Phil was big-eyed. "We could hold our signs by the side of the road, instead. So people could see us but not get mad at us."

I wondered if the *idea* of a protest march was more attractive to him than the reality of it. Was this the first time most of the group had understood the plan? I was also reconsidering my decision not to go. I had no interest in stopping traffic, but I could offer to be their support person from the sidelines. Because what if somebody did come after them? What if a car threatened to make them move? It was my day off, I could spare the time. On the other hand, it might be unwise of me to show up, even on the sidelines of this fight. I could alienate a lot of customers.

"I, for one, am glad to put my body in the road," Lou said, sitting up tall and lifting her chin. "We owe that much to Gregory."

"Yes, we do, hon." Vera nodded. "He was a true martyr."

Really? I hated that he'd been killed, but a martyr for the cause? The cause of stopping a commercial enterprise? Hardly the right term.

"Adele, don't you need a parade permit or something?" I asked.

All heads turned my way like they'd forgotten I was there.

"Do you think they would have given us one, Robbie?" Adele asked. "You know the mayor supports the resort going in."

"She says she's trying to be fair to all of South Lick's residents," I said.

"Anyway, no, we don't have no permit." Adele crossed her arms.

Phil chimed in. "Speaking of permits, I heard the planning board is announcing their decision today."

"I heard that, too," Adele said. "It had better be good news. I was hoping for another day to let the news of our action filter out. Irregardless, we're going. And we'd better get a move on, people."

"I'm coming," I said. Whether it was a wise choice or not. They were going to want somebody neutral in the wings in case they needed help.

Adele's face lit up like it was still the Fourth of July. "I'm pleased to hear that."

I held up a hand. "I'm not going out on the highway, but I'll be providing support from the side of the road." And hoped I didn't have to call an ambulance.

Chapter 43

I brought up the rear of the rag-tag band. They all seemed thrilled. Except Don, who alternated between rubbing his arms, running a finger along his collar at the back of his neck, and looking around as he walked. All the signs of a worried man.

Adele held her sign high. She chanted, "What do we want?"

"Resort has to go!" the others responded.

"When do we want it?"

"Now," they shouted.

Rinse and repeat. Me, I kept my mouth shut. I was here strictly in a supporting role. We'd parked twenty yards from the state route along the berm of the road leading up the hill and to the resort. The sun beat down bright from a cloudless sky as we walked, making me glad I'd grabbed my San Francisco Giants hat before I'd left.

We reached the highway connecting Bloomington in Monroe County with the Brown County seat of Nashville. Cars whizzed by. Adele had been right. There was a decent stretch without a curve in either direction, so vehicles coming upon the group would have time to stop.

"All righty. Everybody ready?" Adele asked.

Everyone nodded his or her head except Don.

"Don O'Neill, what in tarnation are you doing out here if you're not with us?" Adele scolded.

Don always looked a bit worried. This morning, his shoulders slumped, his right knee jiggled, and worry carved new lines in his face, as if the emotion had taken over his entire body. "I believe in your cause, don't get me wrong. But what if—"

"What if nothing." Adele didn't let him finish. "It's going to be fine, my friend. Nothing's gonna happen. Come on." She grabbed his hand.

He shook his head but let her lead him closer.

Adele addressed the group. "Now, I want every other person to face the opposite way, so vehicles coming from either Bloomington way or South Lick and Nashville can see us and our signs."

"Yes, ma'am," Phil said with a big grin. He'd clearly gotten over his own concerns. "I'll lead us as soon as it's clear. Move fast, gang, so we can block the whole road while it's empty."

Another car whizzed by, and another. Phil looked both ways. Far down the road toward the west, a truck had just come around the bend.

"Go!" Phil shouted.

And they went. Phil strode most of the away across and faced west, the Bloomington side. Vera was next facing Nashville to the east. Lou west, Martin east, Emily west, Don—gently prodded by Adele—east, and she finished the line facing west. Each of them held a sign. I perched on a boulder well off the road and waited.

Adele started the chant again. "What do we want?"

"Resort has to go!"

"When do we want it?"

"Now!"

Lou raised her sign and jogged it up and down. Vera followed suit. A white-haired woman emerged from the only house nearby. She wiped her hands on her apron and plopped into a rocking chair on the covered front porch to watch the show.

The pickup truck from the west arrived first. It flashed its lights as it grew nearer. The demonstrators on the far side of the yellow line didn't budge. The truck pulled up and the driver honked. I glanced in the opposite direction. Three cars in a row approached. The first one, a red Honda, pulled to a stop. The others followed suit because they had to. A woman climbed out of the first car wearing a big smile.

"Can I stand with you? I'm on your side."

"Of course you can. And welcome!" Adele gestured to the spot next to her.

"I'm with all y'all," the woman on the front porch shouted. She gestured with two thumbs up.

Vera smiled and waved back. "Thanks, hon!" she called.

I had only been expecting opposition. It hadn't occurred to me that the group could encounter supporters, too. The cars behind the Honda weren't in favor, though. Horns blared. More vehicles stacked up on both sides of the line. More horns sounded. The driver of the pickup climbed out and stood with fists clenched in a stare down with Phil.

"What the devil do you all think you're doing?" the man snarled. "People have to get to work. You can't up and stop traffic."

Phil simply smiled at him and didn't engage in

conversation. Was that part of nonviolent passive resistance? Probably.

From behind me I heard a vehicle approach. Yolene out on an errand or somebody from the resort site? I twisted to see a big white pickup approach. The way the line of protesters stood, they also blocked the road up to the building site. The truck braked to a stop next to me and Lonnie stuck out his head.

"Hey there, Robbie." He pulled his brows together. "What the heck is going on here? I have somewhere I have to be."

I lifted a shoulder and let it drop, looking at the highway. "It's my aunt and her anti-resort group. They seem to think this was the only way to get attention." I glanced back at Lonnie, whose neck was flushed and jaw was set. *Uh-oh.* "I'm only watching," I hurried to add.

As I watched, he lifted a long gun off a rack hanging in front of the back window of the truck's cab. He loaded it and slammed the truck's door. "This is wrong six ways from Sunday." He took a step toward the demonstrators. "They can't get away with blocking the road."

Double uh-oh. "Hey, Lonnie? There's no need for guns. I don't think they plan to stay out there much longer."

"No, you can bet your sweet rear end they won't be."

He turned his head. A siren in the distance grew louder. It was coming from the east, so from either South Lick or Nashville. I would text one of the protesters to warn them, but with all this noise, nobody was going to stop to check a phone.

Another vehicle approached from behind me. This time it was Yolene. She drove around to the left of Lonnie's truck, nearly clipping me where I sat on the rock, and pulled up only feet from Adele at the end of the line. Yolene leaned on her horn. Adele smiled sweetly and waved as if they were passing on a country back road. The cacophony of angry car horns was deafening, especially with Yolene's so near.

"Get on outta my way, you effin' idiots," Yolene yelled.

Nobody moved, although Emily's eyes went wide. At least Yolene hadn't taken her own weapon out. Lou appeared to be deep in intellectual conversation with the first man. A woman with a decent-sized camera slung around her neck approached the group. She wore a khaki vest with six patch pockets over a black T-shirt. She snapped a few pics from the east. That was going to be quite a picture. A young African-American, an old lady, a graduate student, a Mennonite complete with flat-brimmed hat and suspenders, a petite early retiree, a local businessman, and another senior citizen, with a middle-aged woman beside her.

"Howdy, miss. Would you be the reporter?" Adele asked the photographer.

The woman nodded. "Reporter and cameraperson, both." She pulled out a small notebook and pen from one of the many pockets, and Adele proceeded to explain the cause and give her the names of the marchers amid the din of car horns.

"Thanks," the reporter said.

"Don't you want to hear the other side?" Lonnie strode toward her, rifle and all.

"Sure, I do," she said. "But could you put that away, please? It's the reporters' union protocol. We don't interview people holding weapons."

Lonnie shook his head. "It's my constitutional and God-given right to defend myself. I'm not putting this gun away until all these fools clear out."

Defending himself? Against what? Nobody was threatening him.

"As you wish. Have a nice day, sir." The reporter strode around to the other side and photographed the demonstrators facing that way. It looked like she'd included angry Lonnie-with-gun in the shot. She headed back in the South Lick/Nashville direction, pausing to take a long shot that included all the cars.

I liked the newspaper's protocol. Last fall, I'd had to ask a customer to return his shotgun to his vehicle after he'd brought it into the store. He'd told me he was carrying legally. I'd told him that was fine, but not in my restaurant. Luckily, that had been the end of it. He was about to go hunting and had wanted coffee badly enough to comply.

A state police SUV arrived at the end of the line from the east and parked on the shoulder. Wanda emerged and hurried toward the blockage. I knew the resort was within the South Lick border, but down here must be unincorporated territory. Or maybe Wanda got called because we were on a state route. It didn't much matter. This protest was clearly about to come to an end. Adele had gotten her visibility, including news coverage. I doubted she would mind.

Except it all blew up. Lonnie lifted his gun and fired it above the heads of the people in the road. The Honda driver who had joined the protest screamed. Lou cowered. Don fell to his knees, his hands in the air. Emily crouched, shrinking her head into her shoulders. Phil cried out but shielded Vera with his body. Martin stood with his hands in prayer position and his eyes closed. Wanda broke into a run, her own gun in hand.

"What do you think you're doing, Lonnie Dinnsen?" Adele demanded. She pointed her pistol at him.

Where had she had that weapon secreted? I felt frozen to my boulder. Should I do something?

"Stand down," Adele demanded. "We have a right to protest."

"And I have a right to drive away from here, which you are preventing." He lowered his gun to point at the ground but looked ready to lift it and fire again at the drop of a hat.

Wanda finally arrived, breathing hard. "All right everybody, this party's over. Put away those weapons." She glared at Lonnie and Adele until they complied. "Anybody hurt?" she called out in a loud voice as she looked up and down the line.

Don lowered his arms and got to his feet. Lou stood, too, and Martin opened his eyes. Emily and Vera straightened, but Phil sat down hard, grabbing his lower leg with both hands.

"I was hit," Phil called out, waving one hand in the air.

Lonnie had fired high, but I'd heard of bullets ricocheting off objects and wounding people. Vera knelt in front of him and offered a bandanna for the wound.

Wanda checked Phil. She spoke into a radio near her shoulder, asking for an ambulance. "Looks like it grazed the calf. He's conscious and aware. Bleeding is being stanched."

"We was protesting in peace out here until this clown decided to stir up trouble," Adele said.

Lonnie scowled at her and opened his mouth.

"Dinnsen, go," Wanda ordered. "Go sit in your truck and unload that weapon. It was darn stupid to discharge your firearm. MacDonald there has cause to file charges. Now. Adele, I'm serious. Call off your group and clear out, or I'll arrest the lot of you. You're disrupting the safe flow of traffic and frankly giving me a big old headache."

Lonnie obeyed Wanda. I was a little surprised that he did. I watched Adele. She probably wanted to get arrested to make more news.

Vera walked toward Adele and took her arm. "Come on, Addie. I've had enough excitement to last the rest of the decade."

Adele gazed at her. She looked past her at the group, all of whom were looking back, waiting for her decision. "All righty, folks. Let's move on out." She waggled her hand, gesturing them toward her.

Martin helped Phil up and slung Phil's arm around his neck to help the injured man walk back across the highway toward us, the red bandanna tied around his leg below the knee. I winced. It was probably unwise to move him, but they had to get off the road.

Wanda blew out a breath and holstered her gun. "Thank you." She stalked behind Phil and Martin, shaking her head and muttering something about damn fools.

I hurried over to the two once they were on the side. "You okay, Phil?"

He nodded from the ground where he sat. "It hurt like heck, but I think this bandage is doing the trick."

Once the group was off the highway, Wanda held up a hand in both directions. She pointed to Yolene to make her turn but raised both hands to stop Lonnie. She directed the highway traffic to resume.

Yolene yelled an obscenity at the group as she swung left. I cringed, but Adele ignored it. I hoped she was happy with her action. She might have simply made more people angry. And none of it mattered. The whole decision was up to the planning board. Not Adele, not Fiona, not any of them.

Chapter 44

The march had indeed been enough excitement for the rest of the decade. The din of the car horns, the shock of the gunshot, Phil's injury, the arguing—that kind of stuff wasn't for me, even though Adele clearly thrived on it. Well, except for Phil being wounded. Nobody thrived on that. We'd all waited by the side of the access road until the ambulance came for him. The bullet had grazed his calf, and the EMT assured him he would be fine, but that they needed to clean and stitch up the area. Lou volunteered to follow him to the hospital and give him a ride home afterward.

"Did you have the effect you hoped to, Adele?" I asked as Vera drove her, Emily, and me home at ten thirty. Vera had brought her car so we could all fit in it, since Adele's truck only carried two, three in a pinch, and only if the third was on the slim side.

"I should say so." Adele banged her hand on the dashboard for emphasis. "A number of drivers witnessed our commitment. We picked up a new convert to the cause, and we got us some news coverage."

"You also did a good job of riling up Lonnie and Yolene," I pointed out.

"All's well that ends well," Adele replied.

"It didn't end so well for Phil, and it could have been much worse," I protested from the back seat. "What if Lonnie hadn't fired high? What if one of the cars got fed up and rammed through the line?" I shuddered to think about it.

"You're right, Robbie, and we're all lucky nothing worse happened," Vera said. "I confess I quite liked all the excitement. But now I'm ready for some quiet. Maybe even a nap."

"Me, too," Emily said. "Except Wayne and I are leaving by noon. I can always nap at home."

After Emily and I climbed out of the car and waved good-bye to Adele and Vera, I turned to my guest. "Did Detective Thompson get in touch with you or Wayne yesterday?"

"He surely did. We were touring all that great architecture in Columbus, and the detective kept calling and calling. We finally cut short our afternoon and came back."

"Columbus is pretty amazing, isn't it?" The town of under fifty thousand to the east of here was ranked one of the top ten cities in the country for architectural innovation and modern art. Architects and artists with names like Saarinen, Pei, Berke, Tinguely, and Chihuly were among those with works in the town. "What did Oscar want to talk about?"

"He kept asking about the early morning of the day poor Mr. DeGraaf was killed. He made us sit in separate rooms, too. I told him my husband was in bed with me until eight o'clock Friday morning. No two ways about it." She lifted her chin a little, even as her cheeks pinked. "We're here on a getaway. We made the most of our time, and I didn't mind telling him so."

"And he let you both go, so he must have been mistaken about something." About Wayne sneaking out to kill Gregory?

"That's exactly what I told him." She extended her hand. "Robbie, it's been lovely being your guest. We'll be sure to tell all our friends, and we'll be back, for sure."

"I appreciate that, and thanks for choosing Jordan's B&B. You'll get your final bill in your e-mail." I did all-electronic credit card billing and receipts.

"Now I'd better get up there and pack. You know men—they're hopeless at it." Emily's laugh followed her around the side of the building.

Good. Oscar apparently hadn't seen the need to let Emily know about Wayne's infidelity. I felt bad for Emily. She seemed like such a nice person. Maybe Vera had misinterpreted what she saw between Wayne and Gregory's ex. If she hadn't, I hoped it had been only a one-time mistake.

I enjoyed being quietly alone for the next few hours, although I didn't need a nap. I played with Birdy, ordered in breakfast and lunch supplies for the next few days in the hope I wouldn't have to close because of lack of staffing, and did the restaurant laundry. I also cleaned and made up Gregory's room, since Oscar had given me the all clear, and I had new guests arriving tonight. The detective's people had done a pretty good job of removing all the messy fingerprint powder. Lou and I had arranged to go for a ride and a swim later in the day, which I was looking forward to.

My mind wasn't so quiet. I gravitated toward my

pad of graph paper. But I hadn't learned much new about the murder other than that Lonnie Dinnsen carried a gun in his truck and wasn't afraid to use it. That Yolene knew a full complement of obscenities. And that Wayne seemed to be in the clear.

I texted Turner, asking if he would be back tomorrow but didn't get an immediate reply. I thought I might make a chocolate chip muffin for a breakfast special as a kind of riff on *pain au chocolat*, the French puff pastry wrapped around a piece of dark chocolate. But if Turner wasn't going to be here to work with me, I wouldn't be able to open. Still, muffins kept pretty well.

I headed into the restaurant. Busying my hands with cooking often allowed new ideas to bubble up into my consciousness. When my cat perked up and trotted after me, I said, "Yes, Birdy, you can come, too." I hauled butter, eggs, and milk out from the walk-in, grabbed a couple of big bags of mini chocolate chips, and fired up the wide oven. I mixed the dry ingredients—flour, baking powder, salt, and sugar—then broke the eggs into a well in the middle and used a fork to stir them in, thinking as I worked. I wondered if Oscar would tell me anything about his progress. I imagined Wanda had already relayed the news of the protest and about how Lonnie had fired his gun. With that kind of temper, which I hadn't seen in him before, he could easily have gotten into an argument with Gregory and throttled him.

I added oil and milk and mixed it in with a light touch, then stirred in the chocolate chips. Yolene had been pretty upset this morning, too. As had Mike been yesterday in the grocery store. Yesterday. Had I learned anything I should have passed along to Oscar?

I'd told him about the cigarette butt I had found, but I didn't know if he'd followed up on it or not. Maybe I should tell him about Fiona's donation to the cat shelter, and about her suggestion that Lonnie might have killed Gregory to highlight the need for security. And about the old road Abe mentioned.

I filled my fabulous no-stick muffin tins and slid them into the oven before washing my hands and setting a timer for twenty minutes. I composed a text to Oscar about the donation, Fiona's suggestion, and the road. At the end, I added,

Any chance you could tell me your progress in the case?

As I hit Send, the phone dinged with an incoming text. Oscar couldn't have even gotten mine yet. My eyes widened when I saw the contents of a message from Adele.

Planning board meeting to decide at two pm! Meet me at Town Hall?

I checked the clock. One thirty. I had to wait until the muffins were out, but if I moved fast, I could make it down to Town Hall in time. I tapped out my answer.

See you there.

Chapter 45

I hurried toward the wide granite steps of Town Hall. "Barb," I called out when I spied her ahead of me. I was a bit breathless from speed walking over here.

She turned and waved, but she wasn't smiling. She carried a thick red binder and wore a red linen blazer to match. "I'm surprised to see you, hon. You aren't here for the meeting, are you?"

I caught up with her a moment later. "Yes, I am. I only now heard about it. Isn't it odd to hold it during the day? I thought boards usually met in the evening."

"Normally we do." She pulled open the heavy door and gestured for me to precede her. "But the final two state reports came in this morning, and the mayor asked us to hurry the heck up and expedite our decision. Especially given that crazy demonstration this morning." She raised one eyebrow.

I wondered if the afternoon meeting was also part of an effort to keep the public from showing up.

"She wants this issue put to bed, what with everything that's been going on." Barb gave her head a little shake as fine lines carved into her forehead. "We on the board are in a real uncomfortable position, you understand. But we're going to take ourselves a vote and stand by it."

"I'm sure it isn't easy." I followed her up the marble steps, which dipped in the middle from a century of feet going up and down. Barb wore black flats that clicked on the treads, and her slacks of the same color swished in the quiet. On the second floor, Corrine stood in the doorway to her office, conferring with a man in a suit. The air smelled, as it always did, of old wood, old paper, and a hundred years of municipal governing—with an overlay of the perfume Corrine always applied too heavily.

Corrine caught sight of Barb and me. "There you are, Barb. Good, y'all can get started. Howdy, Robbie." Madam Mayor wore a black-and-white patterned dress with her four-inch red stilettos, putting her height well over the six-foot mark.

I smiled. "Have you seen Adele?"

Corrine gestured with her chin to an open door across the hall. "She's in there already. Along with half the town, seems like. It's that dang open-meeting law. Got to let in every single soul who wants to be there."

Barb bustled through the door and made her way up to the table at the front of the meeting room. I stood against the back wall to watch what might turn into fireworks. Buck ambled in and stood next to me, his hands behind his back, elbows out, eyes on the crowd. A crowd was exactly what it was. On the left side of the aisle sat Adele and Vera, along with Martin. On the right, I spied Fiona next to Mike and Lonnie. Yolene sat a couple of rows back from them on the

same side. Other townspeople had heard of the
meeting, too, apparently. Nearly every seat was filled.
The air was filled, too, with a low rumble of conversation and a buzz of anticipation. Adele and Martin
had their heads together, and Mike seemed to be arguing quietly with Lonnie. Fiona's back was straight,
as always. She kept her eyes on Barb.

Barb used a sheet of paper to fan herself but didn't
shed her power jacket. The large windows on both
sides of the room were open, even though any breeze
was a warm one. This old building hadn't been mod-
ernized with central air conditioning. Sort of like my
store. Some of the offices, like the mayor's, had
window AC units. Not the meeting room, unfortunately. I was glad I'd changed into a summery skirt
and sandals while my muffins had baked.

Two men and two women sat on either side of
Barb, one being the man who'd been talking with
Corrine a minute ago. I recognized several who came
into my restaurant to eat occasionally. Each person
had a stack of papers in front of him or her, and
Barb's binder lay open. One woman flipped through
a stapled sheaf, maybe the state agency report Barb
had referred to, and made notes on a legal pad. The
town clerk sat at a small table to the side with an open
laptop in front of him.

"All righty. Let's us get started here." Barb rapped
her fingers on the table until the room quieted.

Corrine slid in and took up a position standing on
the other side of me. I was surprised she didn't have
an official role in the meeting, but, then, I didn't
know much about town government.

"This meeting shouldn't take long," Barb began.

"Thank y'all for taking the time out of your day. The reports that arrived this morning were distributed to the members of the committee. Each of you had time to peruse them?" She looked to her right and her left.

Each member of the board nodded or raised a finger in turn.

"Good," Barb said. "Speaking for myself, I found the environmental summary a big mess of trouble, and the state highway department's prediction of increased traffic wasn't no bed of roses, either."

The man in the suit nodded. The woman who had been taking notes did, too.

Fiona stood. "May I speak to the traffic study, Madam Chair?"

Barb shook her head. "No, Ms. Closs, you may not. This here is not a public hearing."

"But we have a solution for—"

Barb cut her off. "We've had several public hearings, as you well know, because you attended every single last one of them. This here's a meeting with the purpose of coming to a decision. You, and everyone else in those chairs, may witness the meeting, but you must keep your sweet mouths shut. Anyone preventing our board from acting will be ejected from the room. Lieutenant Bird is here to enforce that." She made eye contact with Buck, who nodded.

Fiona sat with an unhappy thump. She leaned over and muttered something to Lonnie. Adele and Vera started talking, too, and the buzz of conversation rose again.

Barb lifted her binder and let it fall. "Quiet!" She waited until everyone had complied. "I do believe the weight of these two state reports, along with our prior deliberations, leads us to reject the construction of the Closs Creek Resort. Any one of you on the board here opposed to the decision?"

One of the men lifted his hand. Barb looked at each board member in turn. No one else raised a hand.

"Let the record show that the South Lick Planning Board rejects the resort project by a vote of four to one."

"No!" Yolene cried, jumping to her feet. "You can't."

"Ms. Wiley, you will kindly sit down and be quiet," Barb directed.

Yolene didn't budge. Buck took a step forward. Fiona shook her head, and Mike sank her face into her hands. Adele fist pumped the air and hugged Vera, then high-fived Martin.

"If you please?" Barb said to Buck.

He nodded and headed for Yolene.

"None of you understand!" Yolene shouted. "There's real people out here. We need that project."

Buck reached Yolene and put his hand on her shoulder.

Corrine murmured, "That's a big old crying shame. Town would have benefited real good from the resort." She shook her head and walked out.

"We have an additional matter of business before us," Barb went on.

Buck escorted Yolene, red of face, to the back of the room. When they reached the door, she spied me.

"You nosey parker, you." The corners of her mouth drew down in disgust. "You've been everywhere lately, butting in, asking questions. I'll be glad if I never see you again."

I held up both hands but didn't say anything. Buck ushered Yolene out and closed the door behind him.

"Ms. Closs," Barb read from a sheet of paper. "For cutting down trees at the site without approval, the board levies a fine of five thousand dollars against the resort management, to be paid to the town before the last day of the present month."

Fiona's rigid posture did not slump, and she didn't say a word, but she couldn't have been happy about the fine.

"In addition, we require you to level the area and sow native wildflower seed on the site," Barb said. "The trees are gone, and that's a crying shame, but there ain't no reason the people of the town need to be left with a dang eyesore because of your bad judgment."

A murmur of approval rolled through the room.

"Is there any more business before the board?" Barb polled the members. "If not, this meeting is adjourned." She pushed back her chair and stood. "Go on home now, folks. The show's over."

Or was it? The venomous look Fiona shot Adele made me want to take my aunt away on a long trip to keep her safe. People started making their way out. I stood in place and waited for Adele. Lonnie had an arm around Mike's shoulders as they plodded toward the door. Lonnie paused when he saw me, exactly like Yolene had.

"You happy now?" he asked, his tone low and stern. "Now that your aunt got her way?"

"I'm happy all the tension and disagreeing is over. But I really didn't have a ball on either side of the game."

"As if!" Mike stared at me. She blinked and shook her head. "Let's get out of this cesspool, Lonnie."

I guessed I was guilty by association. But I spoke the truth. It was going to be awfully nice if things calmed down around town. If only Oscar could put the murderer away, all would be right with the world.

Chapter 46

I coasted my bike to a stop in front of the barn behind my store. I was refreshed from my swim and visit with Lou and physically exhausted in the best of ways by a hard, fast ride.

"I'm glad for the planning board's decision," Lou had said after I'd explained it to her. "At least Gregory's death wasn't in vain."

I'd agreed, and we'd whiled away the rest of the time talking about everything and nothing, as good friends do.

Now I tucked my bike into the back hall of my apartment, exchanged my bike shoes for a pair of flip flops, and grabbed the broom. The B&B rooms for my new guests were ready, but I wanted to make sure the outside stairs were swept while it was still light. I headed around the back of the building to the east side.

And gasped. The broom fell from my hands. The set of steps, which I'd made from pressure-treated wood only last spring, was now splashed with crimson. The color stretched from where I stood to halfway up. And it looked fresh.

Who had ruined my stairs? Who would do such a

thing? And why? And was that . . . I leaned forward and sniffed. *Whew.* It was red paint, not blood. I ran an index finger through it. It had been applied within the hour, I'd guess. Somebody must have taken an open can and hurled the paint upward, which was why it ran only halfway up.

I gazed to my left, but a massive pine tree stood sentinel, blocking the view of the street. I hurried around to the front of the store. Would I find more red paint there?

But the front was perfect, not marred by a vandal. The person must have chosen the side because it was hidden from view. I walked back to the side and stared at the damage, arms folded on my chest, my shock turning to anger. The vandal had to be one of the four resort supporters, upset about the planning board decision. But why target me? I'd been a bystander. If anything, I'd thought the cause of providing employment to locals was a good thing.

Wait. I nodded slowly to myself. I'd added a light, but I'd also added that security cam on the landing at the top of the steps. With any luck, this afternoon's footage from the camera would identify the culprit. The cam software was supposed to send an alert to my phone when it sensed a human-like figure. I pulled out my phone from my biking shirt. Sure enough, I'd gotten an alert at five forty-five when I'd been out swimming or riding home. It was six thirty now.

I had B&B guests coming in a few hours. It was too late to either paint the whole set of stairs or sand off the red. I didn't want to have to explain it to them, but I was going to need to. Their instructions already said to park in the side lot where I stood. There was no way they wouldn't see the damage, even after

dark, because I'd posted a motion-controlled light
when I'd built the second egress. Maybe I could tell
them I'd dropped a bucket of paint while going down
the stairs.

I hurried back around to my apartment. I took a
few minutes to shower off the sweat from my ride,
change into shorts and a T-shirt, and grab a granola
bar, before sitting at my laptop at the small desk in
the corner of my living room. Birdy followed me in,
coiled himself, and leapt to the top of the couch next
to me. He perched there in his best Sphinx pose, eyes
closed but alert.

I searched for that time period, starting at five
forty. My heart beat fast with the anticipation. I
peered at the black-and-white video. That side of the
building faced east and was in shadow all afternoon
but still had enough natural light to see by. A dark
truck pulled into the side lot. A tall person climbed
out, holding a can by its handle, a can the size of a
gallon paint container.

I paused the video, staring at the screen, munching
the granola bar. The person was wearing a baseball cap, but so far, I couldn't identify him or her.
Except . . . the profile wasn't big enough to be
Lonnie. Yolene drove a truck, as did Mike, both in
dark colors. Both were tall, although Yolene carried
more weight than Mike. Somehow the figure didn't
seem like Fiona. She was taller than me, but nowhere
near the five-ten, five-eleven range that I thought
both Yolene and Mike were. I hit play again.

The person flicked something away, set down
the can, and pried the lid off. She stalked toward the
camera, but the hat's brim hid her face, and the quality wasn't high enough to distinguish if it was Yolene

or Mike. I swore. And yet . . . I paused and moved back a few frames until she flicked the thing again. That was the gesture of a smoker discarding a butt. This had to be Yolene. Or was it? I examined the truck again. It was dark, but didn't look black, like Mike's truck. Yolene's dark green?

And here was the act of vandalism. One hand on the handle, the other on the bottom of the can. Arms moving back for momentum. Can swinging up and paint flying through the air, splashing the steps. I paused and backed up one frame at a time searching for the exact moment when she looked up toward the camera. I came to it and pressed my eyes closed for a few seconds. The soaring paint blocked a good view of the face. I swore again and tapped the Play button. The figure repeated one more paint launch and turned away. I studied her walk, but I still couldn't prove the person's identity. Was she moving gracefully like Yolene or with a more businesslike stride the way Mike moved? The door closed, and the truck backed up and out of the camera's range. I peered but couldn't make out the license plate numbers.

I sat back in frustration. Either way, I had to notify Buck. I pressed his speed dial. I tapped the desk while it rang. And rang. And rang, finally going to voice mail. I swore a third time, but this time not out loud.

"Buck, someone vandalized the side stairs of my building with red paint. I have the security cam footage. I am pretty sure it was Yolene Wiley, but it might have been Mike Stiverton. Call me." I jabbed the End icon. What to do now? Call the regular police line? 911? Let Oscar know?

I paced the length of my living room and back, phone in hand. It wasn't a very big room, so it wasn't particularly useful as a thinking activity. I glanced at my phone. A new message? When had that come in? I brought it up. It had also arrived when I'd been riding. At least I had one thing to smile about. Turner said he'd be home tonight and would be in to work on Danna's schedule. Good. I cringed, realizing I hadn't checked in on Danna today. I'd do that tonight.

Since Turner was going to be in, I could open tomorrow, so I had to get going on breakfast prep. But first I needed to decide whether to wait for Buck to call back or call someone else. *Wait.* I bet I could e-mail the footage to Buck, or better yet, to Oscar. I slid into my seat again and checked the app's Help menu for instructions on how to extract a section of video.

Two minutes later, I had cut and pasted that portion of the footage into a file and opened a new mail to Oscar, copying Buck. I wrote,

> My back stairs were vandalized while I was out today. I believe this footage shows Yolene Wiley doing it. I can't read the license plate number.

I took a minute to grab a flashlight, run outside, and around to the lot, scanning the gravel. There it was. I snapped a photo of the butt up close using the camera's flash. If I wasn't mistaken, that was the same brand of smokes I'd seen at the building site. So, Yolene was definitely my vandal. I knew Mike hated cigarettes.

I fished a tissue out of my pocket and picked it up. My B&B guests might arrive tonight before the police could come and gather evidence. They could easily drive right over the butt and destroy it. I straightened when I heard sirens approach. More than one, and the rumbling sound of a fire truck, too. Had Buck sent out the cavalry to check my red paint? But no, they sped past in the direction of Beanblossom.

I went back in and laid the tissue on my kitchen counter. I typed, **I found the cigarette butt and have it in a tissue.** I attached the picture of the butt, too, and sent the e-mail. The question was, where was Yolene now? I wasn't even part of the opposition, and she'd attacked my property. What if she went after Adele?

Chapter 47

I called Adele's land line but didn't get an answer. I tried her cell with the same results. I searched my contacts to see if I had Vera's number but came up empty. I couldn't stand still, and my stomach was uneasy. I had to go check on her. I had a strong feeling those sirens had been headed her way. A strong bad feeling.

Ten minutes later, I urged my rattling van to hurry up the last hill before Adele's farm. No matter how hard I depressed the accelerator, the vehicle was incapable of going any faster. I crested the hill and rounded the bend. I gasped and slowed at the sight fifty yards ahead.

Blue and red lights strobed on Adele's cottage and on the barn that sat to the left and behind. I counted two cruisers, a sheriff's SUV, and a fire engine. A strong light mounted on the top of one of the cruisers flooded the front of the cottage and the driveway with illumination. A green pickup truck was parked in the drive. *Yolene's.* My heart strobed in my chest in synchrony with the lights. Adele or Vera must have called the police. Had they arrived in time?

A siren grew louder from behind me, so I pulled to

the side of the road and pressed the emergency blinkers button on the dashboard. An ambulance sped past. It pulled up behind the cruisers. I sank my face into my shaking hands. Adele had to be all right. She had to be. And Vera, too.

I sat erect, took a deep breath, and pulled the van up until I was about twenty feet from the driveway on the other side of the road. I jammed the shifter into Park and switched off the engine, leaving the emergency blinkers on. I knew I shouldn't get out. I would face a severe chastisement from Buck or Oscar—or even Wanda—if I did. But it was nearly impossible not to rush out and try to help.

My gaze roved from one side of Adele's house to the other. What was going on in there? Had the police stormed the house? Was Yolene holding my aunt and her friend hostage? Were the police inside or not? If they were, maybe they'd arrived in time and had apprehended whoever had threatened Adele and Vera. I pounded the dashboard. This had to turn out the right way. It simply had to.

I caught sight of movement at the edge of the road beyond the house, right beyond the lit-up area. The sun had been below the horizon for forty minutes now, but a glimmer of ambient light still hung about. A dark figure dashed across the road. I stared. It was Fiona. All of the other three suspects were taller. I grabbed my phone and pressed 911.

"This is Robbie Jordan. Fiona Closs is sneaking away from Adele Jordan's house to the right as you face the house. She crossed the road." I peered into the twilight. "And is running away from the farm in the direction away from town. Let the team know." I disconnected to the sound of the dispatcher's protest and shoved my phone into my back pocket. I had to find someone and tell them. The figure was disappearing down the road. But if that was Fiona, why was Yolene's truck here?

I slid out and ran across the road to the house. I didn't normally run, but I was in possession of a good set of lungs from biking up hills. I was certainly dressed for a jog and was dying to follow Fiona, but that would make me too stupid to live. Instead, I looked for someone to tell in case dispatch didn't get through. George Mattheos stood guarding the side door. I hurried up to him.

His eyes went wide when he saw me. I spoke quickly. "Officer Mattheos, I just saw Fiona Closs escape the house and head out on the road." I pointed toward Beanblossom.

"What are you doing here, Ms. Jordan? This is an active scene. It could be dangerous."

Did he not have ears? "Did you hear what I said? Fiona Closs slipped out. Somebody has to go after her!"

Wanda hurried around the corner of the house. "Robbie, I heard you were here. I'll figure out why later." She spoke to George. "We need to apprehend Ms. Closs. I'll take over the door. You grab the guy at the road and go find her."

"Yes, ma'am." He took off at a jog.

Wanda looked at me again. "Thank you for alerting dispatch. But you can't be here. We have a suspect at large, and I need you to go home. The situation inside is under control."

"I came out to see if Adele was all right. Is she? And Vera?" It had never occurred to me that two people could be behind Gregory's murder. Fiona was obviously stronger than me, and Mike was both stronger and taller. Or maybe it was only one person, and nobody was in the house. I knew that was Yolene's truck. How had Fiona or Mike been able to steal it? Yolene could be inside the house, and Fiona had been working with her. But had now deserted her partner in crime?

"They are both fine. Please go get in your van and drive home. They can call you when we're finished here."

All I wanted to do was push past her and see for myself. I didn't want to complicate her job, so I trudged back to my van. I slid behind the wheel, inserted the key, and reached for the door to close it. I sniffed. What smelled different? Was that sandalwood?

Two strong hands clasped my neck from behind. *Fiona's scent.* I grabbed at her wrists but couldn't break her hold. She must have circled around and climbed into the back of my van.

"Forget it, Robbie," she snarled. She squeezed harder.

"What are you doing? Let go of me," I demanded, my voice already hoarse. I would have screamed if I could. I clawed at her hands.

She didn't let go. "Stop fighting and do what I say. Start the van and turn around. Drive me to my car and you can go home."

As if. I could see her in the rearview mirror. My feet felt numb and my heart pounded.

"Yolene and I came out here together. Thought we'd talk some sense into that stubborn aunt of yours." She shook my neck and head.

"Planning board. Done deal."

"Nothing's a done deal. Don't you know that by

now?" Her laugh was harsh, incredulous. "Palms can be greased. Decisions reversed."

"Gregory," I croaked out. His death was a done deal. I pulled at her arms with all my strength. She didn't loosen her grip.

"Gregory shouldn't have died." She stared back into the mirror. "But some people are idiots. Can't follow directions."

I scratched at her arms and hands. My vision dimmed. I had only seconds left before I passed out. I pried one of her fingers back until she cried out. The pressure on my neck lightened.

I slammed my other hand on the horn. Fiona reared back. I jerked myself to the side and got loose. I rolled out the door, which I'd never latched. I hit the pavement on all fours.

"Help!" I screamed, scrambling up.

Wanda, blessedly still at the door, started toward me, talking into her shoulder as she came.

"Fiona's in my van." I sprinted across the street and behind the fire engine. "Catch her before she escapes. Get her!"

Chapter 48

They got her. I watched as Wanda and another officer marched a cuffed Fiona to the back seat of a cruiser. Fiona spat when she saw me watching and landed a few last obscenities before the officer closed the door with a *clunk* and a satisfying *click*.

I whirled as the door to the house opened. Two EMTs wheeled Yolene out with both her wrists handcuffed to the stretcher. Her face looked drained of blood, but she still struggled against her restraints. A bulky bandage covered her right shoulder. Oscar accompanied the stretcher reading Yolene her rights, including the right to remain silent. She did not remain silent.

"Everybody's against me," Yolene muttered. "Even that rat Fiona, she didn't pay up like she said she would. You don't got no right to tie me down like some hog waiting for slaughter." She caught sight of me. "And you, Robbie! You're a good-for-nothing snoop, that's what you are."

The EMTs loaded her into the back of the ambulance, one climbing in after the stretcher while the other closed the doors. Oscar conferred with the latter, then walked toward the house. Adele stood watching with arms folded in the backlit doorway. She waved me over.

"Come on in and join the party, Robbie," she said in a grim tone.

I checked with Wanda.

"I guess I can't get rid of you." Her smile was genuine. "Good job escaping the suspect. You might as well go in."

I glanced at Oscar to make sure it was okay with him, too. He nodded, so I hurried over and followed my aunt into the house, Oscar at my heels. Inside, I found quite the tableau in the comfort of Adele's farm kitchen. Vera sat at the table, her chin high but wobbly, and her hand on her chest as if it was hard to breathe. Buck sprawled in a chair next to her, his notebook and pencil on the table. I knew by now the man could look relaxed and still be on high alert. I suspected this was one of those times. A handgun lay abandoned on the floor and a rifle leaned against the stove.

Adele took a seat at the head of the table, so I sat across from Buck and Vera. The cat didn't seem at all spooked by the night's goings on and studiously bathed herself in front of the stove. Oscar remained standing near the door.

"Take a load off, would you, Oscar?" Adele sounded annoyed as she pointed to the chair next to mine. "Don't just stand there and make us all crane our necks."

He complied, but perched on the edge of the chair

as if ready to take off at any moment. "Ms. Jordan," he began, looking at me rather than at Adele.

"For corn sake, Oscar, call her Robbie," Adele demanded. "There's two Ms. Jordans at this table, and it's going to be more confusing than a goat on Astroturf if you keep calling us both that."

Buck smiled to himself and crossed his arms.

Oscar winced. "Robbie, please relate, if you will, what transpired in your van."

What I really wanted to know was what had happened in here, but I would learn that soon enough. "Yolene vandalized my outside stairs this afternoon. I saw her on my security video and found one of her cigarette butts in the parking area. When I wasn't able to reach Adele, I couldn't stand to stay home, especially after I heard the sirens heading away from the police station toward Beanblossom."

"You might shoulda stayed put, Robbie," Buck said. "Coulda gone down a lot worse here tonight."

"I know. All I was going to do was sit in my car across the street. But then I saw somebody running away from the house in the dark. I called it in, and I went across to tell George Mattheos, too."

"Yes, and we thank you," Oscar said. He cleared his throat and rolled his hand as if to say I was being long winded. "About the van, please?"

"Wanda told me to go home, that Adele and Vera were fine. When I got into the driver's seat, Fiona was in the back and put her hands around my neck." A shudder rippled through me. "She was choking me. I couldn't get free."

"You poor thing," Adele said. "Fiona must have thought she could use the van as a getaway car."

"Except I had the keys. She told me Gregory's death wasn't supposed to happen. I think she convinced or paid Yolene to try to scare him and instead she killed him. Fiona called Yolene an idiot. She told me to drive her to her car, and then I could leave. I didn't trust her for a minute. I hadn't latched my door, so I bent her finger back and hit the horn. That startled her enough to loosen her hold. I got out and alerted Wanda. That's it."

"You done good, Robbie," Buck said.

"Thank you." I looked from face to face. "Is anybody going to tell me what happened in here?"

"I think I need a spot of something to drink, first," Adele said, standing. "Vera, Robbie? Officers?" She grabbed the bottle of Four Roses from the cupboard where it always stood at the ready.

"Thanks, but we're still on the clock, ain't we, Detective?" Buck said.

"That would be correct," Oscar said, casting a longing glance at the bottle.

Vera nodded without speaking. I held up my hand. "Yes, please."

Adele poured three little glasses of bourbon and handed them around. She sipped before speaking. "Yolene and Fiona had the gall to drive on out here and offer me money to retract my protest and agree to their appeal. I told them to go shove it where the sun don't shine. But they pushed their way in. Yolene had her rifle, and, you know, you don't argue with a rifle."

"That's when I called the police." Vera's voice was soft but not shaking. "I was in the back room, and I heard what they were saying. That Fiona didn't use much of a conciliatory voice, either. I crept to where I could watch but not be seen."

"I'm glad you called," I said. "Then what happened?"

Adele tossed her head. "Why, Yolene made to aim that rifle of hers at me. When the sirens started getting close, Fiona looked as nervous as a long-tailed cat in a room full of rocking chairs."

"Very nervous." Vera nodded.

"I happen to know that Yolene is a lousy shot," Adele continued. "And there's a reason I been keeping this denim jacket on despite the heat. Wear my holster underneath, I do." She snorted. "Everything kinda blew up at once. The police pulled in. That coward Fiona split out the back door. She probably knew Yolene would rat on her to the police. Vera came around behind Yolene and cracked her on the head with the skillet." She pointed to a cast iron frying pan on the floor near the stove. Vera blushed.

"You did?" I asked in admiration.

"The opportunity presented itself." She shrugged as if she banged skillets onto heads on a regular basis.

"Yolene, though, she's got herself a hard head. She kept coming after me, so I up and shot her in the shoulder so she couldn't do no more damage." Adele slapped the table. "We was all squared away by time Buck and company waltzed in on their own sweet schedule."

"Sure sounds like it." I sipped my bourbon, trying to comprehend it all. I glanced over at Oscar. "What about Gregory's murder? Did Yolene kill him?"

Oscar gave one short nod and measured a half inch between his thumb and index finger. "We were that short of closing in on her. We happened to have her prints on file for a prior infraction, and they appeared to match those lifted from the victim's neck. Then tonight? I hadn't read her her rights yet, but your aunt asked Ms. Wiley point blank if she strangled Mr. DeGraaf. Ms. Wiley said he had it coming to him."

Adele nodded. "That Yolene won't never be a threat to the public again."

"I wonder if Fiona actually paid her to scare Gregory," I mused. "Or if it was just a verbal agreement."

"We'll get the story out of her," Oscar said. "One way or the other."

Chapter 49

Turner showed up at six thirty the next morning, as promised, while I was cutting out biscuits. Last night I'd arrived home in time to meet the new B&B guests, and to apologize for the state of the outside stairs. But I'd talked to Abe on the phone instead of doing breakfast prep. I'd gotten up extra early today to get a head start on the morning meal, made easier by my insides tingling when I thought of Abe coming home tonight.

"My grandmother is still receiving hospice care, but she seems to have rallied for the time being," Turner said as he donned an apron. "I'll keep my work schedule as long as I can."

"I appreciate that, especially with Danna recovering from her accident," I said. I slid the biscuits into the oven and set the timer. "I'm sorry your grandmother is on her way out, though."

He smiled sadly. "She's had a long and happy life, and a virtuous one, and she knows she'll come back in a new body."

I cocked my head. "Reincarnation?"

"Yes. It's part of the Hindu faith. The soul completes

its cycle many times, learning new things, working through its karma. We call it *samsara*."

"Sounds like you believe in it, too." I mixed eggs, oil, and milk into the dry pancake mix and switched on the mixer.

"I don't buy all of my father's religion, but that part seems right to me. Why should we have only one chance?" He headed into the cooler and came out with the tray of condiment caddies.

Why, indeed? "You have a point." As he distributed the caddies to the tables, I took a minute to fill him in on what had transpired last night. "So it looks like they have the murderer and vandal behind bars, and possibly the mastermind, too."

"That must be a big relief to you."

"I'll say. And to Adele. Plus, she can stop all that protest business. The resort isn't going to be built and that's that."

Turner laughed and shook his head. "The image of Vera whacking Yolene on the head is a good one. It's like straight out of an old cartoon."

I laughed with him. "I know. Good for her. She's got spunk and a half. So does Adele."

The restaurant was abuzz by eight o'clock and fragrant with the usual delectable scents of grilled meats, rich coffee, and freshly flipped pancakes. Everybody and their sisters were talking about what had gone down at Adele's. Thanks to Turner on the grill, we were on top of the rush, but I kept being stopped by curious diners.

"I heared your aunt caught herself a murderer last night," one man said after I set his two over easy in front of him. He gazed up at me with eager expectation writ large on his weathered face.

"It's true," I said. "She and her friend did."

"That Adele," the man's wife said. "No flies on her. No sirree, Bob."

"I have to agree with you there." I smiled at them and moved on to take orders and deliver breakfasts, as well as confirm the news to everyone asking.

Buck pushed through the door half an hour later.

I waved from the grill, having switched jobs with Turner. I turned a half dozen sausages and flipped three pancakes. "Morning, Buck," I called. I gazed around the restaurant. "There's a table open back there." I pointed.

He ambled over and laid his hat on the table to reserve it, but he headed toward me instead of sitting. "Morning, Robbie."

I grabbed a mug and poured coffee for him. "Did Fiona admit to anything last night?"

"Nope. Kept her mouth sealed tighter than a fresh oyster. That Yolene, on the other hand, is singing louder than a flock of canaries. We got us plenty of intel on Fiona Closs's aiding and abetting."

"Excellent." I thought back over the week. "I'm glad Mike and Lonnie weren't involved. They're good people. They simply need steady jobs."

"I did learn something interesting about Dinnsen during the course of our discussions earlier in the week," Buck said. "Turns out DeGraaf's ex-wife had contacted him, wanted to hire him to off her former husband. Appears she knew him from when he was working security somewhere in Indy. A place she worked at, too."

My eyes flew wide. "She wanted Lonnie to murder Gregory?"

"Yup. Good for him he refused her."

So that was why Lonnie had recognized Gregory's name in the restaurant that day, but not his face. Wouldn't the ex have shown him a picture? Maybe Gregory's appearance had changed, or maybe the negotiations with Gregory's ex-wife hadn't gotten that far. I checked the next-up order. I poured a disk of eggs for an omelet and laid three sausages on the grill.

"Welp," Buck went on, "now that Fiona is behind bars, Madam Mayor said she's going to hire Mike to do the leveling and seeding up at the building site. She'll have a little more employment, even though it's not long-term." He stuck his chin out and sniffed the grill. "Whoee, I'm so hungry I could eat a roast ox between two bread trucks. Can I get—"

"One of everything?" I smiled at my favorite lieutenant.

"Something like that."

"Go sit down. I'll bring it over when it's ready." I slid a helping of grated potatoes onto the grill and carefully cracked two eggs onto the hot surface, too. Three rashers of bacon went next to them.

The cow bell jangled again as Buck reached his table, this time announcing Martin followed by a limping Phil. He wore plaid Bermuda shorts and a big white bandage around his dark calf. Buck gave them a wave and pointed to the empty chairs at his table. They both joined him. Turner set a load of dirty dishes in the sink.

"Trade?" I asked, pointing to the grill.

"Sure."

I pointed. "Those eggs, rashers, and hash browns are for Buck, and he wants biscuits and gravy, too.

Plus two chocolate chip muffins." Buck would make short work of them.

Turner only smiled and nodded. Buck's appetite was the stuff of legends. I carried the coffee pot over to the newcomers.

"Morning," I said. "Hear the news?"

"Of course," Phil said. "Pretty amazing."

"It's quite the relief," Martin said. "To have the criminals behind bars, and also to know the resort won't be built."

I checked the door when the bell jangled again. My eyebrows went up to see Corrine usher in Danna, sling and all. I hurried toward them. The injured side of Danna's face was still scraped, puffy from the bruising, and starting to turn some interesting colors.

"Great to see you out and about, Danna," I said. "How are you feeling?"

"Kind of like I was in a car crash." She raised one eyebrow. Never without style, even two scant days after a serious accident, she wore a hot-pink, sleeveless, long jersey dress and had wrapped the medicinal-blue sling in a bright yellow scarf.

Corrine snorted. "Pretty much sums it up. Robbie, can you feed this girl? She insisted on coming in, and I have to get over to a meeting. I'll pick her up in a hour."

"I have a doctor's appointment after that, but I wanted to say hi and stuff," Danna said.

"Of course." I pointed to Buck's table. "There's one empty seat in the place, and it's got your name on it. Come on." I led the way to Buck and friends. I still had the coffee pot in hand, so I poured for Danna.

"Hey, kid," Phil said. "Feeling any better?"

"Yeah. That brownie you dropped off yesterday had amazing healing powers." Danna smiled at him.

"Are you now baking brownies with an extra ingredient?" I mock-frowned and put my hands on my hips.

"Not for here, I'm not," Phil replied, glancing at Buck, who pretended not to hear.

I believed him.

"But how about you?" Danna pointed to Phil's leg. "That looks like it hurts."

"I'll be fine." He batted away her concern. "Just took one for the team."

Danna eyed Buck. "I wanted to tell you that Mom had our mechanic check my car yesterday. He found something loose in the steering mechanism but not anything somebody could have done on purpose. It's an old car, so it looks like my going off the road wasn't from tampering, after all."

"I think we was all getting kinda paranoid, what with a homicidal maniac running around," Buck said. "Glad you wasn't a victim, and now your car'll get fixed up, too."

One mystery solved. But there was at least one more. "Buck, did you ever find out who wrote that threat on the slip of paper I found in Gregory's room?" I asked.

"I expect we'll learn it was either Yolene or Fiona," Buck said. "You were right to up and bring it to our attention."

I thought for a moment. "The day before Gregory was killed, he got into an argument with Lonnie and Mike about the resort. One of them could have told Fiona about it. And somewhere she got that note to him."

"Stranger things have happened," Danna said.

"That's for darn sure." Buck pointed a pistol finger at her. "I'll go ahead and follow up on the note."

Martin, who had been following the conversation in silence, smiled. "And sometimes they are expected."

That would have sounded cryptic if I weren't familiar with the words inscribed on the front of his church: STRANGERS EXPECTED. I'd asked Martin about it, and he'd said it referred to Jesus being welcomed as a stranger.

"And how about the vandalism at Adele's farm and to her car. Did Yolene do that?" Phil asked Buck.

"She claims Fiona did it, to try and scare Adele off of her protesting," Buck replied. "I wouldn't be surprised if it was Fiona who put Yolene up to it. Not sure we'll ever know for a fact."

"Good luck with scaring Adele off anything," Phil said with a laugh. "That kind of thing only strengthens her resolve, far as I can tell."

"I'd have to agree with you on that," I said. "Hey, Phil, are you going to press charges against Lonnie for shooting you in the leg?"

"I'm not sure. My parents want me to. I guess I'm still deciding."

A woman across the room caught my eye and gestured to her coffee mug, and two men stood to go.

"Danna, guys, what do you want to eat?" I scribbled down their orders and hurried back to my job. And to my life and my adopted community, where all was well once again.

Recipes

heat; cook one and a half minutes or until seeds begin to pop. Reduce heat to medium-low. Add ginger and garlic to pan; cook one minute, stirring constantly. Stir in salt, turmeric, and garam masala; cook one minute, stirring constantly. Add spice mixture to potatoes, tossing to coat. Arrange potato mixture in a single layer on the baking sheet.

Roast for thirty minutes, stirring every ten minutes, or until potatoes are browned and tender. Stir in cilantro, mint, and juice before serving. Serve the cilantro separately if some of your diners don't like it.

Cucumber-Dill Soup

The weather is too hot for hot soup, so Robbie serves this creamy cold soup at lunch.

<u>Ingredients</u>

For soup
   2 English cucumbers, peeled, seeded,
      and chopped
   ½ cup roughly chopped fresh dill
   2 cups buttermilk
   ½ teaspoon kosher salt, more if needed
   dash habanero sauce
   ¼ teaspoon freshly ground black pepper,
      more if needed

For garnish
   1 large ripe tomato (seeded and diced)
   1 tablespoon fresh minced dill
   1 pint sour cream

<u>Directions</u>

Combine all soup ingredients in a blender and process until smooth. Refrigerate in a covered container for at least two hours. The soup can be refrigerated for longer than two hours, but be sure to give it a shake before serving as it tends to settle the longer it sits. Adjust seasonings after it is chilled.

Pell's Yogurt-Honey Fruit Salad Dressing

This is almost too easy to include here, but I will. Robbie serves it as a refreshing addition to fruit salad in the heat of August.

Ingredients

- 1 pint whole-milk, plain regular yogurt (Greek yogurt is too thick)
- 1 tablespoon local honey
- 1 teaspoon vanilla
- 1 teaspoon cinnamon

Directions

In a quart bowl, stir honey and vanilla into the yogurt. Beat hard to mix. Sprinkle cinnamon over the dressing and stir in.

Serve over cut fruit. Also good with granola or plain with a spoon.